THORNTON BROTHERS

BOOK TWO

Tempted

SABRE ROSE

ISBN: 1718653891
ISBN: 978-1718653894

1

GABE

Facing Lauren's family was terrifying. They looked at me with hatred, as though it were my fault, not theirs, that Lauren's face was stained with tears. I clasped her hand and drew her close to me, trying to protect her from the daggers shooting from the eyes of her mother. Her ex-fiancé, Derek, thankfully, had left when we came out of her room. Morgan started towards us, arms held open, ready to embrace her sister, but Lauren stepped closer to me, her fingers digging into my flesh viciously like she was afraid of what would happen if she let go. Lauren's mother was seated at the kitchen table, pancakes burning on the stove. Her eyes flicked up when we entered the room, but she didn't move to comfort her daughter.

I wanted to wrap Lauren in my arms and take her away.

Thankfully, Lauren's niece, Madison, was nowhere to be seen. Her father, Alistair, must have removed her from the house. Part of me felt sorry for the girl having to spend Christmas this way.

"Lauren." Mr Greer stepped towards his daughter and Lauren's grip on my hand loosened just a little. "Why didn't you tell us?" He walked over and tipped Lauren's chin so she looked him in the eye.

Lauren drew in a ragged breath. "I—I didn't know how. I knew that you wanted children for me and I didn't want to disappoint you."

Tears welled in Mr Greer's eyes and he reached out to take Lauren's hand from mine, his eyes searching for permission. I let go and Lauren stepped into her father's arms, a fresh wave of tears running down her cheeks.

"Listen to me," her father said, holding her close and stroking the hair which fell in waves down her back. "You could never ever disappoint me. Ever," he said with certainty, although his voice was choked with tears. "Your mother and I love you no matter what. You must always remember that. And if this man," he paused and looked over to me. "If this is the man who makes you happy then I will welcome him with open arms. I will do whatever it takes to see you happy, Lauren. That's all I want. That's all I've ever wanted."

A choked sob escaped from Lauren and she wrapped her arms around her father, squeezing tightly. Morgan walked over and joined them, all three with tears glistening in their eyes. Lauren's mother got up from the table and walked out of the room. Mr Greer stepped away from his girls and smiled as widely as his tears would allow. "Never mind your mother," he said. "She's always been slow to adjust to change. Let me talk to her." He released Lauren and Morgan and followed his wife out of the room.

Morgan immediately walked over and embraced me. "Thank you," she said solemnly.

I laughed a little, unsure what she was referring to, unsure of anything to do with the situation.

"Thank you for loving my sister." She stepped back and wiped the tears from her eyes.

"It's not hard," I said, my eyes drifting over to Lauren whose actions mimicked her sisters.

Even with tears in her eyes and mascara staining the skin of her cheekbones, she was breathtakingly beautiful. It astounded me that she couldn't see it. I'm not sure what she saw when she looked into the mirror, but I knew it wasn't what I saw. Sometimes I wished I could let her look at herself through my eyes. Then, she wouldn't see someone who was broken. She wouldn't see the age gap between us. She wouldn't see the scar on her stomach or the stretch marks that finely brushed her breasts. She would see perfection. She would see someone who had lived. Someone who had grown from life. Someone who had been through hell but was still standing strong.

She would see someone beautiful.

For the rest of the day, her mother moved like a ghost around us, never looking at her daughter and throwing daggers at me. She never addressed the fact that Lauren, her youngest daughter, was in pain.

I hated her for it.

We opened presents under the tree and Madison squealed with delight at some and pouted over others. The gift I had bought Lauren was a gold bracelet, nothing fancy, nothing flashy, just plain and simple, and the smile she gave me was worth every penny. Lauren's hand was stuck in mine, holding onto me for strength throughout the day.

After lunch, I saw her smile. And that evening as her mother sat at the piano and the notes of Silent Night broke the quiet of the room, Lauren got up from her seat and stood behind her mother, her voice rising from a place of pain. I had never heard such a sweetly broken thing.

When it came time for bed, her mother walked over and handed me a sleeping bag. "There's a stretcher in the basement," was all she said and pointed to a door. She was about to walk out of the room when she turned back to me. "There will be no sinning under my roof." She said it so solemnly, I didn't know whether to laugh or salute.

It was three in the morning when I heard the stairs creak and Lauren's bare feet padded across the concrete floor. I unzipped my sleeping bag and Lauren crawled in with me, her body half beside mine, half on top. It was a tight fit and I immediately went hard as I felt the soft flesh of her breasts crush against my chest through the thin fabric of her t-shirt. I willed myself not to concentrate on the feeling. Not to think of the way her full breasts felt against my skin. Not to imagine taking her nipple, hard from the coolness of the air, into my mouth. Not to imagine the warmth of her, the softness of her. I thought she would just need comfort, but when her hand slid down my bare chest and wrapped around my hard cock, I knew she had other plans.

"Someone's pleased to see me." She smirked seductively in the dim light.

I found it hard to concentrate as her hand rhythmically stroked up and down. I wiggled as much as I could in the tight fit. "We don't have to do this. You've had a big day and—"

Lauren silenced me by crushing her mouth against mine. "Shut up," she said between kisses. "I want you."

A moan involuntarily escaped at her words. "What about your mother?"

"What about her?" she mumbled as her mouth moved to trail kisses down my neck. She nipped the flesh on my shoulder and my cock swelled in her hand.

"What if…" I panted as her mouth moved onto my chest and her grip around my cock increased. "What if she comes down?"

"She won't," Lauren said against my skin.

"What if she hears?"

Lauren pushed against me, her mouth at my ear, her hand leaving my hardness and being replaced by the dampness of her underwear. "She won't."

She sucked on my earlobe and I drew in air sharply, holding it in before letting it out slowly as I regained control of myself. I found her mouth in the darkness and kissed her urgently and desperately, allowing myself to act on the sensations rippling through every inch of me.

I wanted to be inside her.

I needed to be inside her.

Lauren responded eagerly, opening herself fully and sliding herself further so my cock rubbed her clit, the slight friction of her damp underwear driving me insane. She kept rubbing herself against me while sucking my flesh as I was trapped beneath her, caught in the restriction of the sleeping bag.

"Lauren," I panted.

She twisted around and slowly undid the zipper of the sleeping bag, removing the constriction around us, and slipping down my body hungrily, tugging at my boxers until my cock sprung free. I sucked in another sharp breath as she took me in her mouth.

I almost came there and then, the pressure, the wetness from her mouth just about undoing me. Staring down at her hand snaking up over my stomach, I counted the freckles that dotted her arm in an effort to resist the welling need to come. Ever since she had left for her parents, I had been dreaming of having her again. Our last tryst at the café had only served to awaken me and no amount of masturbation could eliminate the need for her.

There were thirty-seven faint freckles on her arm.

There were precisely fifty-seven visible nails in the ceiling.

Soon I could concentrate on the rhythmic motion of her soft lips as they wrapped around me. I reached down and wrapped my hands through her hair, lightly tugging as it entwined around my fingers. My eyes rolled back as she took more of me. I applied the slightest pressure, pushing her head down, forcing more of me into her mouth. She gagged and I fell out, only for her to take me again, hungrily sucking, pushing down so the tip of my cock hit the back of her throat.

"Lauren," I hissed as the familiar urge built within me. No amount of counting was going to stop me this time. "Careful." I moaned as she ignored my pleading and took more. I released her hair and gripped onto the rails of the stretcher. Just before I was about to explode in her sweet mouth, she lifted her head and clambered up my body, tugging off her underwear and tossing it aside. Without hesitation she mounted me, removing her t-shirt and exposing her large breasts. Her head rolled back as she rocked on my cock. She was completely wet and even though I didn't think it possible, I hardened even more.

I loved her most like this. Unabashed and completely given over to me. Her hair hung over her shoulders and danced over her breast as she rode me. Her hips rocked back and forth, grinding my cock further inside her. Reaching out, she grabbed my hands, bringing them to her breasts, and I moaned again as I toyed with the soft flesh. Her breasts were heavy and heaving and, with a sudden urgency, I rolled her over—not an easy task on a stretcher—and drove myself back inside. Her breasts rippled with the movement. She reached behind and took hold of the frail edge of the stretcher as I pushed into her slowly but forcefully, fixated on her glorious breasts as they shuddered with each thrust.

It was only then that it occurred to me that we weren't using protection. It was the first time I had been inside her without the slightly numbing coverage of a condom.

"Lauren," I said. "I haven't got any protection." I was clean, she was clean, but now, knowing that protection wasn't needed for birth control, my excitement quickened at the thought of releasing completely inside her.

She began to moan and I felt her tighten around me. "It's okay," she said. Biting her lip, she stifled a groan as every inch of her quivered. And then, as though she could no longer contain it, she let out a loud cry and I placed my hand over her lips, muffling the sound as she shuddered and came. Her eyes fluttered open and she took one of my fingers in her mouth, sucking up and down until the sensation of her mouth, her wetness and tightness of her around my cock, the swaying of her breasts and the look of adoration on her face was too much and I thrust hard, the stretcher lurching across the ground.

Then I came, filling her with everything I had as I released inside her. And it felt like heaven.

2

LAUREN

I thought if I crept back upstairs before the sun rose, I would avoid meeting anyone in the hallway. I was wrong. Morgan sat on the floor, a fresh cup of coffee in her hand, another sitting on the ground beside her.

She lifted the spare cup and held it out to me. "You okay?"

I walked over and sat beside her, taking the steaming cup and inhaling the bitter-sweet scent. "Yeah," I said, taking a sip.

"You want to talk about it?"

The familiar tightness in the back of my throat returned and I shook my head.

Morgan reached over and squeezed my shoulder. "So…" she said, letting the word hang between us.

"So…" I mimicked.

Morgan's eyebrow twitched and one side of her mouth curved. "Gabe, huh?"

I smiled and took another mouthful of coffee.

"You're not going to say anything?" Morgan's eyebrow still twitched oddly.

I shrugged. "What do you want me to say?"

"I want details," she said. "I want the dirty, scandalous details. I'm so jealous of you right now. That boy is insanely gorgeous. The things I have imagined doing to him." She shook her head, a slow smile creeping over her face as she lifted her cup.

"That's my man you're talking about."

She sighed. "I know. But I didn't know that before, you know, when I was doing the imagining. We married women need our imaginations sometimes to get us through another boring ordeal when our husbands do the same thing over and over."

"I'm sure Alistair would love hearing that."

"Alistair can go take a flying leap."

I lifted my eyebrows and looked down at the cup in my hands.

"Do you know he wanted to have sex last night? Last night," she repeated as though the idea were scandalous. "We're at my parents' house. Who wants to have sex when their parents are only a few rooms away?"

I lowered my head further and took a noisy slurp of coffee.

"Oh my goodness. That's why you snuck up from the basement, isn't it? You were down there screwing his brains out." Morgan groaned and rested her head against the wall. "Why do you get to have all the fun?"

"I believe you literally just finished saying that Alistair wanted the same last night."

"That's different."

"How?"

"Because Alistair is Alistair and Gabe is Gabe." She snapped her head back and looked at me. "Details now."

Since Morgan and I were six years apart, we had never really been ones to discuss our partners. Sure, Morgan had talked about Alistair over the years, and I had talked about Derek, but our conversations had never ventured into the bedroom.

"Don't be a holdout," she complained when I remained silent. "I need to live through you. I need excitement in my life, and right now, you're it. Well, your boy-toy is it."

"Don't call him that."

She snorted. "That's what he is, isn't he? You're not serious about him."

"I introduced him to the family, didn't I?"

Morgan fell silent and we sat side by side, sipping on our coffees. Out the window, the sun rose above the neighbour's house causing a patch of light to move across the carpet.

"So you met at work?" she asked finally.

I nodded.

"Who made the first move?"

I let a smile creep over my face. "Oh, he made all the moves," I said, teasingly.

"And?" she prompted.

"Okay, fine," I said, admitting defeat and resigning myself to the fact that she was not going to give up. "We met at work. Gabe pursued me until he won. I was hesitant at first because of the age gap, but I've realised I just need to get over that."

"You were together when we all came down for your birthday? That was why he was there, wasn't it?"

I nodded and watched the patch of light spread a little further across the carpet. "This is the first time we've been together in public, so to speak. I guess I was a little worried about what people would think."

"Who cares what people think," Morgan said. "You've got a smoking hot man in your bed and he seems to adore you. What woman wouldn't want that? Is he as good as I imagine he would be?"

"I'm really not comfortable with you imagining how my boyfriend is in bed."

"Well tell me so I don't have to imagine then," she exclaimed. "Is his—" She cleared her throat and wiggled her brows suggestively. "Is it big? I bet it's big. I bet it's glorious." She shuddered and I moved away a fraction. "Oh, come on. You've got to give me something, anything? I'm a bored woman here. I need this."

"Need what?" Madison's door opened and my niece stood in the doorway dressed in short pyjamas which barely covered the cheeks of her butt. I remembered the day she was born. The screams of my sister giving birth haunted me for months. My mother insisted I be in the birthing room with them. I think that may have been part of the reason I was scared when I first fell pregnant.

"Hey you," I said, smiling up at her, pleased for the distraction.

"Hey Aunty L." Madison sat beside me, legs crossed, and reached over to take the cup from her mother's hand. "I'm so sorry about yesterday. I had no idea you can't have children anymore. It sucks. You would have been a great mother." She took a sip of the coffee and handed the cup back to her mother, shuddering at the bitter taste. "Have you ever heard of sugar?" she said to Morgan.

Once again the tightness at the back of my throat loomed and I gently squeezed. "Yep," I agreed, trying not to let the emotion overtake my voice. "It sucks."

The door to my parents' bedroom opened and Mother walked out, fully dressed and ready for the day. "Morning," she said, reaching out to pat Madison's head. She strode past Morgan and me with barely a nod.

"I think we're in trouble," Morgan said once she had entered the kitchen.

"Why would you be in trouble?" I asked.

"Because I never told her what happened to you. I never told her the real reason Derek left. She feels betrayed."

"She told you that?"

Morgan just winced and shrugged.

Another door creaked open and Morgan's eyebrow started twitching again.

"Gabe," I said, getting to my feet and planting a kiss on his lips. "Morning." He looked his usual glorious self with his hair tied back into a messy ponytail, jeans and a t-shirt which clung sexily to his chest.

Gabe wrapped me in his arms, lifting me a little as he squeezed tightly. "You okay?" he whispered into my hair.

I pulled away and smiled. "Absolutely," I said, though the word came out a little torn.

His eyes flicked over to where Morgan and Madison had risen from the ground and were both eyeing him hungrily. "Are you sure?"

I clasped his hand and started walking towards the kitchen where I knew Mother would be cooking up her usual staple for breakfast. Pancakes were only a Christmas morning thing.

"I'm sure," I said.

Madison moved to follow but Morgan held her back. "Put some pants on," she told her daughter.

Madison looked down at her legs. "I have pants on."

"Well, go put some on that will cover your arse cheeks then."

To say breakfast was awkward would be an understatement. Gabe's eyes just about popped out of his head when Mother sat a bowl of porridge down before him, but he smiled politely, thanked her and proceeded to spoon the glue into his mouth. Dad kept his nose buried in the paper. Mother looked anywhere but at Gabe or me. Madison never made an appearance and Morgan and Alistair talked more than I had ever heard before.

After breakfast we headed into town to catch the Boxing Day sales, leaving Mother and Dad behind. We wandered aimlessly, bumping into the hundreds of shoppers that I didn't even know existed in the small town. Morgan smirked every time I caught her eye, and her gaze slipped over Gabe's body every chance she got. When we decided to stop for a coffee, Alistair, Gabe and Madison walked into the sports store while Morgan and I sorted the drinks. After ordering, we took a seat at one of the tables. Morgan's eyes followed Gabe into the store.

"Would you please stop looking at him like that?" I asked, frustrated.

"Like what?" she said, attempting to smile innocently. It came off as anything but.

"Like you want to eat him."

"A girl can dream." She sighed.

"Not about my boyfriend she can't."

Morgan shimmied her shoulders. "So protective. I love it." The waitress brought over our coffees and sat them on the table. "I'm just so bored," she said. "Everything about Alistair is bland, bland, bland. I want some excitement. I want what you've got."

"I thought things were better now that he had sold that app. You've got a new car, a new wardrobe." I nodded to her stylish clothing. "And you've put an offer in on a new house."

"That's only money."

"Money is what you used to complain about."

"Well, we're currently getting sued so that might put a stop to all that."

I took a sip of coffee, holding the cup up to my mouth a little longer than necessary as if it could somehow shield me from the anger I knew my next comment would evoke. "Maybe if you stopped telling him he was useless all the time, things might improve between you."

Morgan's eyes snapped to mine. "And what would you know about marriage? You haven't actually managed to get anyone to marry you yet."

I was surprised at the vehemence in her tone. "Sorry," I mumbled. "You just don't seem to be very nice to him. It's got to be hard on the guy."

"Says the thirty-year-old woman dating a teenager."

"Wow," I said. "Great Clementine impression."

Morgan narrowed her eyes but didn't reply as the others joined the table.

Gabe's hand rested on my thigh as he reached for his coffee. He took a sip and slammed the cup on the table. "Argh," he said, lifting the cup again and examining the contents. "What is this?"

"Coffee," Morgan replied harshly.

Gabe looked at me with a questioning expression on his face, his thumb rubbing circles on my leg.

"Morgan forgot to take her happy pill this morning," I explained.

Gabe gave a half-hearted laugh and then reached into his pocket when his phone rang. He looked at the screen and then excused himself from the table, telling me he'd be back in a minute.

The four of us sipped on coffee and Madison played on her phone until he returned.

"That was my father," he said, sitting back down. "Jake's coming home."

"Who's Jake?" I asked, noting the wide grin that had spread across Gabe's face.

He looked at me, his expression showing confusion, then said, "I forgot I hadn't told you much about them. Jake's the youngest of my half-brothers. He joined the army and was sent overseas nearly six years ago. He's only been home once since, for Clark's funeral." A brief wave of sadness crossed Gabe's features. "But he's coming home tomorrow. My other brother, Tyler, is picking him up from the airport tonight and they are driving to the family holiday home tomorrow. Dad wants me there to see him." Gabe directed his attention to me. "Now that I've met your family, will you meet mine?"

"Well," I said placing my coffee cup on the table, suddenly feeling a little flustered. Introducing Gabe to my family was one thing. Being introduced to his was another. "After the delightful encounter you've had with my family, how could I say no?"

Gabe laughed. "It hasn't been all that bad."

"Oh, really? Remind me of the good parts?"

Reaching across the table, Gabe took my hand in his, brushing his lips across my knuckles. "Well, I did have a rather nice wake-up call this morning."

Madison's eyebrows shot skywards and Alistair cleared his throat. "Perhaps we should head home. You guys will want to get on the road if you're to be there to meet your brother tomorrow."

3

LAUREN

We decided to leave my car at my parents' house, and instead, we travelled in Gabe's old jeep for the three and a half hour drive it would take to reach his father's holiday house. As we reached the outskirts of the pristine town littered with fancy houses, quaint cafés and people with too much money, Gabe's fingers drummed against the steering wheel.

"You okay?" I asked, noting that he suddenly couldn't keep still.

Gabe flashed a smile. "I just haven't been home in a while. I guess I'm a little nervous. Not really sure why."

I lifted an eyebrow and Gabe laughed. "Okay, so maybe I know why. Dad and I haven't always exactly seen eye to eye on things, and Tyler and I have never seen eye to eye."

"Tell me about them," I said, reaching over to still his jiggling knee. "You've barely said a word about your other brothers. What are they like?"

"Tyler is an arsehole."

"Really?" I asked, a faint smile crossing my lips.

"Really," Gabe confirmed seriously. "He thinks he's perfect and he struts around as though he owns the world. And of course, he thinks I'm useless. They all think I'm useless." His head tilted to one side. "Well, not Jake. I guess it's just Tyler and Dad. They are too much alike. Rich men who think they own everything and everyone."

I shook my head. "I'm getting confused. Tyler is the eldest, right?"

"Right," Gabe confirmed. "He and Jake are from Dad's first marriage. They are a lot older than me and I didn't really have too much to do with them growing up because Dad sent them away to some fancy boarding school that breeds rich young upstarts."

"You're not a fan, I take it?"

Gabe snorted. "You could say that."

"How much older?" I asked.

Gabe lifted his shoulders as he turned the jeep down a side street. "Tyler's thirty-two, I think, and Jake's like twenty-six or twenty-seven." He frowned. "Maybe older."

"So they're around my age then?"

Gabe grinned. "Yeah, I guess so."

"And Jake?"

"He's alright. I mean, out of the two of them, Jake's the one I actually like. That's the reason I'm going home, just to see him."

"Okay," I said, bringing my hand up and beginning to count on my fingers. "Tyler is an arsehole, your dad is like Tyler, and Jake is alright. Am I forgetting anyone?"

"Billie."

"Billie? You've got another brother?"

"Billie is Dad's latest wife. They've been married about five years, I guess."

"And?"

"And what?"

"What's she like?"

"Billie?" Gabe chewed on his bottom lip. "She's Billie. You'll see. In fact, you'll see a lot."

"What do you mean by that?" I asked as Gabe pulled into a steep driveway.

Gabe just grinned. "We're here."

I'm not sure what I was expecting but a garage at the end of a short but steep driveway was not it. The remainder of the house stretched beyond the garage, hidden from view. Of the parts that were visible, a corner there, a strip here, they showed nothing but panels of glass and exterior walls covered in schist rock.

Hamish Thornton was one of the wealthiest people I knew. Not that I really knew him, but I knew of him. Everyone knew of him. He owned so many properties both here, at home, in the city, and possibly all over the country. For all I knew, he had holdings overseas as well. The latest property being developed under his company was the city's first casino. Protests over its construction had been featured on the news, my mother joining the march.

Although my first impression of the house was underwhelming, it didn't last long. Gabe opened the door and stepped out of the jeep, jerking his head for me to follow. "We'll grab our bags later. I want to give you the grand tour before they arrive home."

"They aren't here to greet you?"

Gabe shook his head and reached for my hand, dragging me through the garage into the house. We were greeted by a long white hallway with framed photographs along the wall. Each of them was a family portrait, the first showing Mr Thornton, his first wife who stood regally beside him, and two smiling boys with mops of dark hair. One of the boys was smiling politely, and the other appeared to have just finished saying the word 'cheese,' his mouth open and an over exaggerated grin plastered on his face. As we walked down the hallway, the pictures changed as the two boys got older, until, about half way down, the mother in the first picture disappeared, and was replaced by a smiling blonde woman in flowing skirts and a baby in her arms. This picture was less formal than the previous ones, having been shot at a beach, the light shining in from the side, and the lady's head resting on the shoulder of Hamish Thornton lovingly.

"Is that your mum?" I asked, thinking of the woman I had briefly met at the hospital.

Gabe reached out and traced the lines of his mother's face. "She looks so happy here, don't you think?" He squeezed my hand tightly. "It's hard to even think of them together. They are so different."

Gabe tugged me further along the wall, stopping at the next photograph which was taken in a studio with perfect lighting, a staged background and formally posed stances. The two dark haired boys were older and sported serious smiles, hinting at their resistance of being made to pose for the family portrait. The baby was now a young boy and there was a toddler in the mix. A beautiful, blond haired, smiling angel of a boy with his hands on his hips and a wide smile that scrunched the rest of his face so you almost couldn't see his eyes.

"And then came Gabe," Gabe said proudly, looking at the photo and mimicking the exact same grin.

"You were so cute!" I let go of his hand and stepped to examine it closer.

"Were?" Gabe asked, wrapping his arms around my waist from behind and resting his chin on my shoulder.

I turned in his arms, squeezed his cheeks together and planted a firm kiss on his puckered lips. "You're still alright, I guess."

Gabe talked with his cheeks still mushed between my hands, his words coming out mumbled and distorted. "Dad was so pissed about this photo. I remember him telling me in no uncertain terms how I had to stand, how I had to smile, but each time the photographer counted down, I pulled this expression. In the end, they just gave up and took the picture."

We continued down the never-ending hall as the boys grew. The smiling face of Gabe's mother faded until she disappeared altogether. After that, I noticed Gabe's smile faded too.

Gabe stopped at the second to last photo. "This one was taken three years ago. It's the only one of all of us, the only one that will ever exist of all of us."

I studied the photo, barely noticing the new woman draped by Mr Thornton's side. It was the four boys which struck me. The dark and the light of them. Gabe looked so much like his older brother, Clark. He had his arm slung over his shoulder even though the style of the photo demanded formality, and he had this sort of half grin, one side of his mouth sloping upwards, the other laying still. Clark had the same expression as though it were a mirrored reflection.

The lack of the two smiling blond boys in the final image stood out starkly. Tyler and Jake stood tall and straight, their dark hair and handsome faces unsmiling and dressed in dark suits standing beside Hamish and his wife. The photo was taken outside, a casual snap of a shutter rather than a poised stage.

Gabe cleared his throat. "It was taken at Clark's funeral. I refused to be in it. I was so pissed Dad insisted on taking a family photo. It was outside the fucking church for god's sake."

We stood in silence looking at everything the photo didn't say. Something seemed familiar about Billie, Gabe's step-mother, but her face was slightly shielded by the shadow caused by her large brimmed hat, and I couldn't make out why I felt like I knew her.

Gabe tugged on my hand. "Come on," he said. "I want to show you the house."

Gabe led me through every room, and I stared in wonder at the detailed decoration. I felt like I was walking through a showroom rather than a holiday home. The walls were covered in massive paintings that stretched from floor to ceiling, some of them captivating, others making you wonder what the artist had been on while creating them. Gabe narrated the tour with mock reverence.

"And here we have yet another room with stark white walls, accented with off-white tones, and an overly big white table with plush white chairs, just to mix it up a little." We moved through the dining area and stood at the base of a large staircase that led to the upper level. "And if you would be ever so kind as to raise your eyes upwards, you will notice the masterpiece that is Billie."

At the top of the stairs the wall was dominated by a portrait of a naked woman lying on her stomach on a white bed, deep pink silk draped in just the right places, breasts slightly exposed, toned and tanned legs bent at the knees and held in the air, ankles crossed, staring seductively into the lens of the camera. Recognition rippled through me.

"Holy shit."

Gabe crossed his arms and grinned up at the portrait. "I know, right? I told you you'd see a lot of her."

"No," I said, walking up the first steps of the staircase. "Holy shit, I know her. We went to school together." I turned back to him, looking him directly in the eye. "You are dating someone the same age as your step-mother."

Gabe threw his head back and laughed.

"It's not funny, Gabe!" I exclaimed. I was already regretting coming here. Willa, short for Wilhelmina as she was known back then, was someone I was never close to in school, but that didn't negate the fact that we were in the same year, and shared the same classes. I never knew what happened to her after we finished school, to be honest, I never cared. Willa had always been so sure of herself, so embedded with self-confidence she had been someone I couldn't help but despise. Somewhere along the line, I heard she had got a modelling contract, but I never knew if it were true or not.

"I don't know if I can do this," I wailed, looking back at the oversized portrait of Willa/Billie which seemed to have grown even larger.

"Nonsense," Gabe said. "Think of it as my father married someone the same age as his son's girlfriend, rather than the other way around. The girl is nearly thirty years younger than him. They're the ones who should be embarrassed, not us." He started walking up the stairs. "Would it help if we had sex in their bed?"

My eyes flew wide. "No! That would not help one little bit."

Gabe's eyes twinkled as he walked back down the few steps and stood alarmingly close. "What about the stairs then?"

"Gabe," I warned as he moved closer and began to nuzzle my neck. Despite my abhorrence at his suggestion, the familiar warmth began to tug between my legs. I took a step back, tearing myself away from his lips which felt so good, so soft and so seductive on my skin. "Gabe, no," I said firmly to his smirking face.

"They won't be home for a while yet. Please?" He pouted playfully and I slapped away the hand which had reached out to stroke my breast.

Crossing my arms over my chest, I frowned at him. "I don't want the first meeting with your father and step-mother to be one when I'm naked."

"Oh, go on," he teased. "Then you and Billie will be on even ground."

"Haha," I said dryly.

"But what am I going to do about this?" Gabe looked down at the bulge in his pants.

"You can sort that yourself."

Gabe sucked in a breath and whistled, his mouth somehow still showing the hint of a smirk. "Harsh. I seem to remember someone being rather horny at her parents' house."

"That was completely different."

Gabe lifted a single eyebrow, something I was momentarily distracted by as it came off sexual.

"It was three in the morning, everyone was asleep and it was private."

"Right," Gabe said, drawing the word out and turning to walk back down the stairs.

"Hey," I said, stepping after him. "Where are you going?"

Gabe, having reached the bottom of the stairs, turned around but continued walking backwards. "You said to sort it myself." He shrugged and blew me a kiss as he disappeared into the next room.

4

LAUREN

"That was quick," I said when Gabe returned only seconds later, staring at his phone.

He threw me a withering look. "Dad just texted and he wants us to meet him in town for dinner. You cool with that?"

"Yeah." I nodded, trying to hide my smile. "I'm cool with that," I said, mimicking his choice of words.

"He said I'd need to change."

"But he doesn't even know what you are wearing."

Gabe's choice of clothes was a little more formal than his usual attire. He had on nicely fitting jeans which clung to his backside delightfully instead of sagging like his others, and a cobalt blue dress shirt.

"It doesn't matter," Gabe replied. "It's still not good enough. He's given us half an hour. You know which bedroom we're staying in, right? I'll go grab the bags and you start changing. If we're lucky we might be able to slip in a quickie first. I seriously need to fuck you." He slapped me on the backside and left in the direction of the portrait hallway.

Our bedroom was decorated in the same colours as the rest of the house. White walls, white ceilings, white accents. It was only the furniture, painted a faded light blue that broke the stark whiteness. An ensuite, also stark white, hid behind a white door. Glancing at my watch, I figured I'd have enough time to quickly rush through the shower. I wanted to look presentable in order to officially meet Gabe's father. I was also worried about Willa/Billie. I hadn't seen her in years and, judging from the portrait hanging above the stairs, she had aged a little better than I had. In fact, she barely looked as though she had aged at all.

I had my head under the water, letting the powerful stream wash away the shampoo when I felt arms snake around my waist and a warm mouth attach itself to my shoulder.

"My god, you look good," Gabe said as the water poured over us both.

He turned me around and pushed me against the cold tiles which hadn't had the chance to be warmed by the water. I sucked in a breath as the coldness made my skin prickle and my nipples harden. Gabe looked down and groaned. Ignoring the water which fell over his face, he bent down and gently took my left nipple between his teeth. Another hiss of air escaped and, despite my resistance to his previous advances, my body responded to his, arching and offering more of myself as he rolled my nipple between his teeth, applying just the smallest amount of pain. Gabe, encouraged by my reaction, took more of my breast into his mouth, suckling on the flesh while still stroking my nipple with laps of his tongue, toying and teasing me.

"We've got to get ready," I murmured, my head tilted against the hard tiles, my hands tangling themselves in his hair, belying the words I had just spoken.

"I've got to have you," he said, his voice dark and ragged. His mouth moved down my body, skimming over my stomach until he knelt before me, applying pressure on my thighs with his hands, begging for me to open. Running a single finger down my clit, his eyes darkened in appreciation at the silky wetness he found. His finger trailed lower until he pushed inside me, pulling in and out, one finger, then two, his bottom lip caught between his teeth as he concentrated on the task. He withdrew his fingers and pushed my legs further apart, leaning forward until his mouth covered my sex and he started to suck. A lightning bolt of arousal coursed through me and I gripped his hair tighter, pushing his head further into me. Gabe sucked again, milking me with his mouth. The consistency of the single motion almost had me coming right there with his face mashed against me, his hands reaching behind and massaging the flesh of my backside. Suddenly he stopped and I cried out, protesting at his departure so close to release.

Gabe stood and turned me roughly so my front was plastered against the wall, my head turned to the side, my breasts splayed against the now warm tiles. "Don't be impatient," he said. "I'm not done with you yet."

I felt him against my backside, his hardness trailing down the space between my cheeks. I lifted onto my tip toes, arching my back, begging for him to enter me. Then I felt nothing but the warmth of the water, and I turned my head, suddenly annoyed by the spaciousness of the shower, wanting him pressed against me, pressed into me. Gabe leaned against the glass wall, his hand gently stroking the length of his cock as he stared at me hungrily.

"Fuck me," I whimpered.

Gabe's cock twitched in his hand and he began stroking himself more urgently. Over the noise of the shower, Gabe's cell phone began ringing. Ignoring it, he stepped forward, grabbed my hips and pressed himself against my backside. The phone call faded to voicemail. Gabe ran his cock down my crease until he found me wanting and ready and pushed just the tip of himself inside. The phone started ringing again. Gabe slumped and removed himself so he could look through the glass wall to read the display on the phone.

"Fuck," he cursed.

"Please," I begged.

"It's Dad." Gabe twisted the nozzle on the shower head and held his head under the water. "We've got to go."

"Seriously?" I asked, panting heavily and needing release. My fingers slipped down to myself but Gabe caught my hand before reaching its destination.

"Don't you even think about it."

"But I can't go to dinner like this," I said, my wrist caught between his fingers.

Gabe stepped forward, his naked and wet body plastered against mine. "Yes, you can. And you'll think of me the entire time, wondering what I'm going to do to you when we get back."

A shiver ran through me and I nodded, content to obey his command.

"And remember, I will be right beside you, thinking exactly the same thoughts. Mind you, it's kind of nice to leave you wanting for a change. Maybe now you'll understand how I felt that day in the coffee shop."

"So all this is to punish me?" I teased.

Gabe kissed me. "Just think of it as a promise of what's yet to come."

We got out of the shower and changed quickly. Fortunately, I had packed a couple of nice dresses, and I pulled out a black one that clung to my body, but not too tightly, and had a single silver zipper which ran up the back from hem to neckline.

Gabe looked over me appreciatively and walked closer. "Somehow it makes that dress even better knowing what's under it."

I had teased Gabe while getting dressed, seductively pulling on black lace underwear. "Enough," I said, pushing him away. I needed things to cool off a bit before dinner.

Gabe's hand ran up my thigh, slipping under the material of the dress until his thumb stroked the lace of my underwear. "That might be a little hard while you're still wet." He removed his hand and brought his thumb to his mouth, sucking and biting it.

"Ready?" he asked.

"Very much so," I replied, smirking at his innuendo.

* * *

The restaurant that Gabe's father had requested we join him at was elegantly decorated and dimly lit by sparsely glowing chandeliers hovering above each table.

Hamish stood as we approached, dominating the room even from a distance. He stretched out his hand and smiled confidently. "You must be Lauren." He shook my hand firmly, surprise overcoming me at how similar he was to Gabe. It didn't show in the photos that lined the walls of his home, but in the flesh, there was no denying it. It was in the smile. "It's a pleasure to meet you." He reached over and shook Gabe's hand. "Son," he said, nodding in acknowledgment, and then turned to the woman sitting beside him. "And this is my beautiful wife, Billie."

Billie, who had been absently tapping on her phone, looked up, smiled brightly and extended her hand, not a flitter of recognition passing over her features.

"It's a pleasure to meet you," she gushed.

I looked over at Gabe and widened my eyes wryly. Billie sat back down and leaned over the table. "You look a little familiar. Have we met?"

I cleared my throat as Gabe pulled out my chair and I sat opposite the woman, trying not to notice her flawless skin or perfectly straightened hair.

"Actually," I said, picking up the glass of water before me, and trying to block the images of her lying seductively on the bed from flashing through my mind. "We went to school together."

Billie's eyes widened. "Oh my goodness! Lauren? You're that Lauren?" she exclaimed.

"The one and only," I replied, trying not to mock her tone.

"Hamish!" Billie tapped her husband's shoulder. "Hamish, Lauren and I went to school together, can you believe it?"

Hamish looked over at his son but Gabe kept his eyes down. "No," he said tightly. "No, I can't believe it."

"Oh, she was such a goody-goody at school." Billie laughed. "I see you've gotten over that now. Look at you with Gabe." She reached over and shoved Gabe lightly. "Your very own toy-boy."

I smiled wider as though it would somehow relieve my discomfort. "And look at you," I said, allowing myself to mimic her tone, although my sarcasm was lost on her. "Your very own sugar daddy."

Billie tossed her long hair over her shoulder and laughed loudly. "Good to see you're the same old Lauren."

"But you're certainly not the same old Willa," I replied.

"Argh." Billie took a sip of wine. "I let that name go years ago, as soon as I got my modelling contract. Willa just didn't seem right anymore, you know? I wasn't Willa. I wasn't Wilhelmina. I was someone new, someone better, so I became Billie. Wilhelmina is the feminine version of William, in case you didn't know. That's why I called myself Billie. You know, William, Bill, Wilhelmina, Billie." She looked at me expectantly, waiting for a reply.

"Yes, I figured." Gabe's hand found mine under the table.

Hamish clicked his fingers and a waiter appeared. I was surprised when he ordered for the entire table, not even giving us a chance to look at the menu. Gabe's jaw-line hardened.

"So," Billie said, draining the last drops of wine from her glass and waving for a refill to a passing waiter. "Tell me what you've been up to for the last few years. Where has life taken you? I guess you're not with Derek anymore." She laughed loudly again and a few of the people at the tables surrounding us looked over curiously.

I wondered what they saw. I wondered what they assumed our situation was. A father with three children? Or perhaps, three siblings and their nephew. Hamish didn't show his age. I shuddered and turned my attention back to Billie who was yet to draw breath.

"Derek was such a handsome man." She knocked her shoulder into Hamish's. "I was a little jealous back then, if I'm honest." Hamish raised one brow and took a sip of his wine. "I was," she gushed. "Of course, I'm not now. How could I be?" She wrapped her arms around Hamish's and leaned closer, puckering her lips until he reached over and they pecked each other. "Aren't we lucky, Lauren? Look at us sitting here with the two most handsome men in the room. And look at you, Gabe, growing up so quickly."

Gabe smiled tightly and tugged on his shirt as though he suddenly found it stifling. He wore black dress pants and a silver shirt which caught the light of the chandeliers. His hair was loose, but he had gelled it back from his face and it curled at the nape of his neck.

34

"We've got the whole night planned," Billie continued. "Dinner here, dessert if you want, although—" She reached over and patted my arm knowingly. "As always, we must remember a moment on the lips, a lifetime on the hips."

I had to stifle my laugh with a drink of water as the words of my mother fell out of her mouth.

"And then we can go back home to the lounge bar, we'll put a little music on, have a few drinks and oh!" she exclaimed clapping her hands again. "Maybe we can have martinis. Do you like martinis, Lauren? I never used to like them before this man converted me." She smiled at Hamish. "He makes them like no one else on this planet. You'll be amazed, Lauren, simply amazed. You'll be a convert in no time. I just can't believe you're really here. That it's really you. Did you like the house? I hope you found everything okay. I instructed the cleaner to leave fresh towels out for you. I hope she did that. She doesn't always listen. Were there towels in your ensuite? Did you get the chance to check?"

I had forgotten how much Willa, now Billie, liked the sound of her own voice. She talked non-stop through dinner, only pausing when there was food in her mouth, which wasn't often. She toyed with her food a lot, moving it around her plate, slicing it into small mouthfuls but very rarely putting any in her mouth. The wine was a different story.

5

LAUREN

"Well," I said as soon as the jeep's door shut. "Your dad was talkative."

Hamish Thornton had barely said more than two words to either Gabe or me during the entire dinner conversation. Gabe laughed as he pulled onto the road and it warmed me. He had been quiet during dinner too.

"To be fair," he said. "Billie doesn't give him much of a chance. Or anyone else for that matter."

I reached over and covered his hand on the gear stick. "You okay?"

He nodded, keeping his eyes on the road. "Just brings back memories."

"You want to talk about it?"

He shook his head and moved his hand back to the steering wheel, knuckles turning white as he gripped. He swallowed and turned to me, a smile replacing the sadness that was there before. "There's really only one thing I want to do right now and with Billie having planned our entire evening, I'm not sure when I'm going to get the chance."

"Well, I have to admit the dinner kind of changed my urgency for that."

"Damn that Billie," Gabe cursed, then laughed.

"Her fashion show sounds interesting," I said, barely containing my smile. I held my hands up like Billie did, displaying an imaginary billboard. "Winter in Summer by Billie August," I mocked in the same hushed and reverent tone as Billie had.

Billie had informed us over dinner that she was launching her own fashion label called Billie August. Where the August had come from, I had no idea. At school, she had been known as Willa Peterson. She had explained the concept for her first collection as fur, skin and lace and I had no idea what that meant.

Gabe rolled his eyes. "We will have to make sure we leave before then."

I shrugged. "I don't know. It almost sounded alright. Just think of the fun we'd have watching models strut their stuff in a style of clothing I can't even begin to imagine."

Gabe reached across and took my hand, brushing his lips across my knuckles as he often did. "Thank you for tonight. I know it was weird."

I nodded solemnly. "Weird is certainly one word for it," I said, my mouth splitting into a wide grin.

Hamish and Billie were waiting in the kitchen when we arrived. Hamish had removed his jacket and loosened his tie. He held a glass of whiskey in his hand.

"Shall we?" He swept his arm towards the lounge area, the cubes of ice clinking in the glass.

Gabe held up a finger. "Would you just give us a couple of minutes? I desperately need to discuss something with Lauren."

A look of worry passed over Billie's face. "I hope everything is okay?"

Gabe threw her a winning smile as he took my hand and led me up the stairs. "Everything is wonderful. I just need a minute or two. Back soon. Pour me a whiskey, no mixer, just ice."

Gabe pulled me into the bedroom and shut the door. "Is everything okay?"

"Take it off," he said, nodding to my dress as he hopped on one foot, yanking his shoe off the other.

"Now?"

"Seriously," Gabe said, fumbling with the zipper of his pants. "I can't wait any longer." His pants dropped to the floor and he stepped out of them, tugging his shirt over his head and coming to me with nothing but socks adorning his body.

"Gabe!" I exclaimed as he reached behind me and undid the zipper, leaving me standing before him in nothing but lacy underwear and high heeled shoes.

"Perfect," he said, stepping back so his eyes could travel over my body.

I was surprised to see how ready he was. His cock stood tall and eager, even though I hadn't touched him. With desire beginning to warm my insides again, I started to slip one of my shoes off but Gabe stopped me.

"Leave them on." He walked forward and pressed me to the wall, sliding downwards until he was kneeling. "Now, let's see if we can't get you as wet as you were before." He leaned forward and licked the fabric that shielded me from him. The smoothness of his tongue combined with the roughness of the lace created a friction that sent shivers of anticipation through me. Gabe paid careful attention to what he was doing, deliberately teasing me with long slow licks and gently sucking me. I opened my legs wider as he pulled the underwear aside and inserted a finger, gently massaging until I began to groan and my legs felt weak.

"I need to lie down before I fall down," I panted.

Gabe reached up and held me firmly against the wall, my words only intensifying his attention. When he grew frustrated with the material between us, he pulled my underwear to the floor and sat back on his heels, stroking himself with one hand while finger fucking me, his bottom lip caught between his teeth, his eyes stuck on his fingers as they slowly moved in and out. I watched him as he pleasured himself, surprised by how much it turned me on. Gabe's breath started to hitch as his hands moved faster. The further they plunged into me the harder he worked himself. After minutes of torture when all I wanted was to have his throbbing hardness inside me, he brought his mouth back to my wetness and used one hand to once again pin me against the wall, while the other still stroked his cock. My legs turned to jelly as his tongue moved faster and faster, bring me closer to the edge. I threaded my fingers through his hair as he tilted his head, gaining more access and inserting his tongue deep inside. I gasped when I came and Gabe latched on, sucking my clit as the pulses of pleasure rippled through me. And then, without any warning, he stood, let go of himself, his cock hard and strong and upright, and turned me so I faced the wall.

"My turn," he whispered.

He held the cheeks of my backside apart, groaned with desire and then plunged into me hard, slamming me against the wall. Reaching around my body, he took my hands and stretched my arms high and wide on the wall, pulling back so only the tip of him stayed inside me. He held me like that, thrusting in and out as he pleased, my breasts squashed against the wall each time he drove into me. The urgency and forcefulness of his desire ignited another wave of pleasure and we came together, my front pressed against the wall, my rear covered by Gabe's hot and sticky body. He came so hard I felt the force of each spurt. It seemed forever before his hardness finally softened and he pulled himself from me.

Turning me back around, he gently held his lips to mine. "Thank you," he murmured. "I needed that. Now I might be able to relax and enjoy drinks. Then again, my father will be there." He flopped back on the bed and, even though I had just come twice, the image of him lying there excited me. I climbed on top, pressing my wetness against him and pressing my cheek to his chest. With a contented sigh, Gabe ran his fingers lightly over my back. He lay there for a few moments until I felt him twitch beneath me.

"Seriously?" I said, sitting up.

His cock swelled a little more. "Don't do that," he said once I was sitting upright. "That just makes it worse." He lifted his arms and looked at his watch. "Do you think they'd notice if we were a little longer?"

I climbed off him and walked into the bathroom, calling over my shoulder. "You're insatiable."

"Only around you," he called back.

Gabe joined me in the bathroom and we cleaned ourselves before hurriedly slipping back into our clothes.

"Gable?" The faint sound of his father's voice drifted up from below.

Gabe hurried to put on his shoes as I tugged on my zipper.

"Gable?" his father called again, more urgent and demanding this time.

"Be right there," Gabe called back. "You ready?" he asked, placing a quick kiss on my forehead and tucking a stray strand of hair behind my ear.

I was feeling dishevelled and flushed but I had no choice but to nod. Gabe grabbed my hand and we ran down the stairs, laughing quietly between ourselves as we heard Billie asking, "What on earth are they doing up there?"

We rounded the corner of the stairs to find Hamish and Billie joined by two dark haired men. Gabe stopped in his tracks and I bumped into him.

"Jake!" he exclaimed and rushed forward to bear-hug one of the men. "What are you doing here? I thought you weren't arriving until tomorrow?"

Jake and Gabe clapped each other on the back, a wide smile spread across Gabe's face. Jake had changed from the last family photo. His hair had grown and he sported a full beard. He looked nothing like I imagined. For some reason, when I heard he was returning from his post with the army, I had automatically expected him to have razor cut hair and be dressed in a camouflaged uniform. Jake's frame engulfed Gabe's. He was a large man and reminded me of a cross between a Dothraki warrior and Tarzan. Rugged, wild and untamed.

My eyes shifted to the man standing beside them. Tyler looked just like he did in the portrait only, it somehow didn't do him justice. I had never seen such a classically handsome man. He wore jeans and a t-shirt, though somehow, it still gave the impression of a fitness magazine cover. Unlike the unruly hair of his brother, Tyler's dark hair was perfectly styled, too perfectly styled. His jaw was set in a hard line and dark eyes met mine from above perfectly chiselled cheekbones. He appeared as though he was amused as his eyes ran over me and I took a step back.

If Gabe was an angel, then Tyler was the devil.

His mouth curved slightly as he noticed my discomfort. "Jake decided we should travel down tonight, rather than spend the night at my apartment in the city," he said, still looking at me with an amused smirk.

41

"Well, I'm pleased you did," Hamish replied.

Gabe, having untangled himself from the brotherly embrace stepped back to my side. "Tyler." He nodded at his eldest brother.

"Gabe." Tyler nodded back.

"I'd like you both to meet my girlfriend, Lauren. Lauren, these idiots are my brothers, Jake and Tyler."

Tyler shook my hand politely while Jake stepped forward and engulfed me in another bear-like hug. I felt so small.

"Well, you're a surprise," Tyler said. "I didn't know my kid brother had a girlfriend."

"There are a lot of things you don't know about me," Gabe bit back.

Hamish stood between his sons and once again swept his hand towards the lounge. "Shall we start with a drink?"

"Perfect," Gabe muttered. Jake clapped him on the back again and they walked together into the lounge.

As I stepped to follow, Tyler's fingers on my wrist stopped me. Just the slight touch of his skin against mine sent shivers down my spine. I tried to shake it off, blaming Gabe and my recent encounter in the bedroom as the reason I was so sensitive to his touch.

"Lauren, is it?" he asked, his voice low and quiet.

I nodded, my body frozen and all my awareness focused on where his fingers burned against my flesh.

He waited until the others had moved into the lounge and then let my wrist fall, stepping behind me. His hand swept my hair across my back and over my shoulder. "I'm not certain what the custom is in your household," his hand trailed down my back and tugged at my zip, "but here, in the Thornton household," he pulled my zipper up to the neckline, "it is customary that we finished getting dressed before we come down the stairs."

Heat flared up my cheeks as Tyler walked past and joined the others in the lounge, not even glancing back to see if I followed.

6

LAUREN

The rest of the evening was spent sipping on wine and listening to Billie talk about her fashion show. Tyler and his father talked over in one corner while Gabe and Jake chatted in the other. Billie occasionally pestered Jake, asking about his duties in the army, but every time it was mentioned, he ducked his head and said he couldn't really talk about it. No one knew what he did, where he was stationed, but judging from the pain that flickered across his hooded eyes each time it was mentioned, we all knew it was something he hadn't recovered from.

I fell into bed exhausted and was a little relieved to hear Gabe's gentle snores, brought on by the quantity of alcohol he had consumed.

My mind raced back to the sensations that had travelled through me at Tyler's touch, and I felt guilty that another man had distracted me. But I reasoned with myself that it was okay to notice another handsome man, and if the Thornton men were anything, they were handsome. Jake was wild and untamed, Gabe was gorgeous and had a smile like no other and Tyler was dark and dangerous. Each had their appeal. It would have been almost strange if I hadn't been slightly attracted to them. Besides, it was Gabe who lay beside me. Gabe who I loved. My beautiful, sweet, Adonis of a man. I inched across the bed and Gabe sleepily snuggled into me, draping his arm over my shoulder and pulling me close.

Billie insisted we stay for the New Year's Eve party, and I spent the next few days exploring the tourist-driven town with Gabe. My original attraction to Tyler faded, and I began to wonder if it was merely a wave of hormones that somehow flooded my system at the surprise of being surrounded by such beautiful humans. He had barely spoken to me since that night, and even Jake, although polite and respectful, kept his distance. It was as though there was an unspoken rule between the brothers. I was Gabe's and Gabe's alone. Nothing more than a considered and courteous friendship was required.

Billie, on the other hand, never shut up. She dragged me shopping and took me to her studio to show me the strips of fur and frills of lace she called clothes.

The New Year's party was filled with well-dressed strangers. Since I had only brought a couple of dresses with me, and one was only a little cotton thing, I felt a little underdressed wearing the zipped up black number again, but it was my only option. Everything else was too casual. Music tinkered in the background, Billie floated around the house, slipping from room to room, exclaiming over this woman's dress and laughing over that man's jokes. She was the perfect hostess as I cowered in the corner with Gabe who sat on the couch, leg jiggling. It reminded me a lot of the cocktail parties I used to attend with Derek, only there was far more money represented at this one. I hid in the corner during those too.

"I hate parties like these," Gabe said, scowling at the peals of fake laughter pouring from Billie. Jake leaned against the wall behind him, beer bottle in hand instead of the long-stemmed wine glasses and crystal whiskey glasses in the hands of the other guests. He looked out of place among the well-groomed guest list.

"It's almost worse than war," he said. He meant it as a joke, but the tightness in his throat betrayed him.

Earlier, I had walked in on Jake and his father arguing over his long hair. It was longer, and if I was being honest, more beautiful than mine. His father hated it.

"Real men don't have long hair," he had told his son.

Jake hadn't said anything and continued to stare at the newspaper.

"What is it with you and Gabe and your insistence on embarrassing me?"

Jake, who had been eating a slice of toast, merely lifted it to his mouth again and crunched loudly.

"I'm going to book you into my barber," Hamish had announced.

"No," Jake said, his mouth filled with toast.

"No?" his father replied.

Jake looked up. "No," he repeated.

It was only then that Hamish Thornton noticed me and excused himself gruffly.

"Sorry about him," Jake had said to me. "Sometimes he forgets he doesn't rule the world."

Jake's compromise had been to tie his hair back into a ponytail.

"Got a pretty good grip on that bottle there, Jake." Gabe nodded to where Jake's fingers were white against the green bottle.

"Can't say this is exactly my scene anymore." His eyes were fixed where Tyler was seamlessly integrating himself into the party.

Tyler smiled easily. He flirted with the women and joked with the men. He was a perfect replica of his father and nothing like his younger brothers.

"Doesn't his perfection just make you want to retch?" Gabe asked Jake as he took a sip of whiskey. "Look at them fawning over him. I think some of the men even have boners."

Jake smiled. "Tyler's alright."

"Whatever," Gabe muttered. "Hey," he said looking up at Jake. "Want to get out of here and escape down to the basement like old times?"

"Like old times?" Jake repeated. "You were fifteen when I left, little brother. There were no old times."

Gabe rolled his eyes. "Fine. Like last time then?"

Jake looked over to where Tyler and Hamish were cornered by a group of men who were nodding seriously, and then over to where Billie was busy playing barmaid, pretending to spin bottles in the air. He winced as one smashed to the ground and a squeal of laughter poured from Billie.

"She coming?" Jake nodded to me.

"She?" I repeated. "I have a name."

"Sorry," Jake apologised. "Is Lauren coming?"

"Oh, Lauren's definitely coming. I'm not leaving her here alone with these vultures. We'll get back and find her overly tanned or something, Billie's orange having rubbed off on her."

Jake snorted. "Alright then. Why not?"

Gabe got to his feet. "I'll go grab something out of the jeep and meet you two down there. Try not to make it obvious we're leaving or Dad will have a fit."

I tried to imagine the poised and controlled Mr Thornton having a fit. It wasn't possible.

"What's he talking about?" I asked Jake as we made our way through the crowd of people. Every now and again someone would stop and exclaim over him, claiming they hardly recognised him under all that hair. Jake would nod awkwardly and take a step closer to me as if I could protect him from their over-exuberant onslaught. One man in particular gripped Jake's arm, his fingers digging into the flesh of his forearm. He leaned in close, and whatever it was he asked Jake, it caused a storm to cross over his eyes. Jake peeled the man's fingers off his arm and I saw the man wince.

"Excuse me," I said to the man, looping my arm through Jake's, "but I've promised to introduce him to someone I know. Perhaps he can catch up with you later."

"Thanks," Jake whispered when we walked away, swiping a bottle of whiskey from the table. He took me back out to the garage and opened a trap door I hadn't noticed before.

"What did he ask you?" I asked.

Jake's eyes clouded over again. "I don't want to talk about it." He held the trap door open expectantly. "Are you going down?"

"Down there?" I asked, peering into the darkness.

"It's the basement."

"I'll follow you."

That brought a smile to Jake's lips and he began to walk down the steep steps. After a few seconds, a light switched on. "It's okay now," Jake called out, his voice coloured with amusement.

I walked down the stairs cautiously. The room below was plain and simple, decorated only with a few couches and beanbags, a TV on the wall and an expensive looking sound system attached to it. The only windows were where the walls met the ceiling, just narrow strips illuminated by the street lights.

Gabe pounded down the steps behind me, waving a plastic bag of tightly wound green leaves. "Found it," he said to Jake.

"Is that weed?" I asked, pulling Gabe aside.

"Have you seen the guy?" Gabe said, nodding to his brother. "He's like a caged animal. He is in serious need of relaxation."

"What about your dad? What about all the people upstairs?"

Gabe grinned. "I haven't got enough for them all."

"Gabe," I scolded.

"Lauren," he mimicked and kissed my forehead. "It's fine. Jake and I have done this before. It's our brother bonding time, right Jake?"

"Whatever you say," Jake replied.

I looked over to where Jake was pacing the floor, his eyes glancing at the small windows. Gabe was right. He was in need of relaxation. The party Billie had planned was meant as somewhat of a welcome home bash for Jake, but anyone could have told from his posture that he would have preferred to be anywhere but trapped in a house with all those people.

Gabe turned on the TV and flicked through the channels until he landed on a music station. 'Hits of the sixties and seventies' was splashed across the bottom of the screen. Gabe started moving his shoulder seductively in time to the music as he rolled the joint, licking along the strip of paper to seal it. The song changed and Gabe sang along with the lyrics. He handed the cigarette to his brother.

"How on earth do you know this song?" Jake said. "It's years before your time."

"It's years before yours too," Gabe replied, still crooning along to the lyrics.

Jake took a drag on the smoke, coughing as he exhaled. "Shit," he said pounding his chest. "It's been a while." He held it out to me but I shook my head.

"Not with a house full of people upstairs, not to mention your father and your tightly wound brother." I shook my head again. "I don't think so."

Gabe wrapped his arms around my waist and swayed in time to the music, singing in my ear. "Come on, Lauren. You know you want to."

Gabe took the outstretched cigarette to his lips and inhaled, blowing smoke over my face, and then wiggled it before me. "No one will come down here, I promise," he said, nuzzling into my neck.

I took the offering from Gabe, and he released the hand wrapped around my waist to walk over and crack open the windows.

"You can blame my mother for my tastes in music," Gabe said to Jake, as Jake flopped his large frame down on a bean bag, a slow smile crossing his face.

Jake's eyes moved over to where I relented and sucked enough to send me into a coughing fit.

"That'a girl." Jake's grin widened. "Fuck," he said as he put his hands behind his head and sunk further into the bean bag. "I forgot how good this feels." He closed his eyes, though his head moved to the beat of the music.

Still not having recovered from my coughing fit, I pounded my fist against my chest as Gabe returned and pulled me onto the couch beside him. "This lot's a little different from the last stuff you tried." He took the cigarette out of my hand and sucked on the base. "Best to go a little easy."

Gabe stretched back on the couch and I lay down, resting my head in his lap and staring at the hair framing his beautiful face. Absently, he reached down and stroked away the strands of hair that were covering my face. I reached up and pulled him down to me, kissing his lips hungrily.

The music played in the background as we lay in silence, passing the cigarette from person to person. It was nice to see Jake smile.

"What was it like over there?" Gabe asked.

Jake kept his eyes closed. "I can't really talk about it."

"Nothing?" Gabe asked. "Not even where you were?"

Jake sucked at the last of the cigarette and blew the smoke into the air in a steady stream. "Nothing."

"So there's this whole chunk of your life that you can't share with us?"

Jake nodded. "It was hell. Let's just leave it at that."

Silence fell over us again until the next song came on. Gabe pulled me to my feet and started dancing and singing. "Why don't they still make music like this?" he yelled as Jake turned up the volume.

"You sound like such an old man," Jake said, joining us and forming a circle. I was surprised at how well he could move. Throwing my head back, I laughed at the both of them as they danced towards me.

"Man," Jake exclaimed. "I need my guitar."

"You play?" I asked.

"Does he play?" Gabe snorted and shook his head. "He can play the fuck out of the guitar."

"Go get it for me. It's in my room," Jake said.

Gabe shook his head vehemently. "I'm wasted. There is no way I'm leaving this room. How do you feel about sleeping on the couch?" he asked, raising an eyebrow.

"I'll go get the guitar," I piped up.

They both looked at me stunned.

"What?" I said. "I should be able to sneak up to your room without anyone noticing, shouldn't I?"

"Have you met Billie?" Gabe asked.

"TV music it is," I replied.

We were so intent on enjoying the music, swaying to the songs that came on that we didn't hear the trapdoor open, and we didn't notice Tyler was in the room until he turned down the volume of the music. We froze, Gabe's arms wrapped around my waist from behind, his mouth at my neck.

"What the fuck do you think you are doing?" he asked angrily.

I straightened, shrugging Gabe off, and looked at Tyler's stern expression, eyebrows furrowed and arms crossed.

I burst out with laughter. "My god, you're so serious!"

"We're just chilling for a while," Jake drawled, grinning at his older brother. "It's no major."

"No major? Dad is upstairs with some of the men interested in investing in the casino and you idiots are down here stoned off your faces."

"Oops." Gabe held his hand over his mouth, feigning regret.

"Oops?" Tyler stepped towards Gabe. "That's all you have to say? Oops? Grow up, Gabe. The whole lot of you are acting childish. Jake, I can understand because he's just returned from a nightmare we can't even imagine and I don't blame him for needing to let off a little steam, and Gabe, well... no surprises there, but you, Lauren—"

"Me?" I said, pointing to my chest.

"Yes, you," he growled angrily. "I actually thought you might be good for my little brother, but here you are, wasting your life away by hanging around with teenagers. That stuff kills your brain cells."

"I'm not a teenager," Jake replied.

Tyler turned on his heels and walked back up the steps, slamming the trap door behind him.

Gabe twisted around. "See?" he said to me. "Absolute arrogant arsehole."

Jake rolled his head to the side. "Mum," he said.

Gabe dropped his head. "Yeah." He sighed. "I forgot about that. He's still an arrogant arsehole though."

"Mum?" I asked Gabe.

He pulled me close, lowering his voice, but I could tell from the way Jake watched us, he could still hear every word said. "Ty and Jake's mum had a bit of a problem with pills, and Tyler didn't like it. Still doesn't change the fact that he's an arsehole though."

Jake stretched out on the bean bag, resting his hands behind his head and yawning as he spoke. "He doesn't seem to remember that it's still her." He closed his eyes. "Her demons just speak a little louder than his."

"I hope she's okay," I said awkwardly, not sure how to respond.

Jake shrugged, eyes still closed. "She's been off them for years now, not that he would know that."

* * *

At some stage during the night, I woke, my back uncomfortable on the couch, my head resting on Gabe's lap, and ravenously hungry. I tried shaking Gabe awake, but he merely adjusted his sleeping position and continued to breathe deeply, the odd snore escaping from his lips.

I crept up the stairs, marvelled at the length of the hallway, and snuck into the kitchen, surprised when I turned on the light to find Tyler standing at the window, staring out at the lights that dotted the edge of the lake, whiskey glass in hand.

His eyes roamed over me, stained with what I could only assume was repulsion. I felt compelled to apologise under his glare.

"Look, about earlier," I started, but Tyler interrupted me.

"Tell me something," he said, his words slightly slurred. He was drunk. "Why are you with him?"

"What do you mean?" I stammered out.

"He's a lot younger than you," he said bluntly. "It's noticeable. You're a woman and he is a boy. And he works in a coffee shop with, as far as I can tell, no ambition to improve himself."

I crossed my arms over my chest. "I also work in that coffee shop. Does that also mean I have no ambition?"

"That depends." Tyler walked over to the table and pulled out a chair, sitting down and resting his feet on the spotless white surface. He was so handsome, so flawless. Too handsome, too flawless, even if in his current state he was a little less put together than earlier. His hair was slightly tousled and his shirt was unbuttoned, revealing his tanned and muscled chest. "Do you plan on always working at the coffee shop?"

"So what if I do?"

"But do you?"

I hung my head a little, annoyed to admit defeat. "No. I would like to get back into photography."

"Right," Tyler said, swirling the contents of his glass. "Well then, it's different."

"What have you got against coffee shops? I know it can't be the coffee itself, I've seen you drinking it."

Tyler took a sip of whiskey. "Nothing."

"Then what's wrong with working at a coffee shop? You've got a rather elitist viewpoint."

Tyler placed his glass on the table, looking up at me with an irritated expression. "Enough about the coffee shop. It's got nothing to do with the shop. It's the fact that Gable has no plans."

"Yes he does," I replied.

Tyler just lifted a single eyebrow. It reminded me of Gabe.

I lifted my chin a little higher. "Architecture."

Tyler smiled, though it wasn't a warm one. It was one meant to placate me as though I were a child. "And for how long has my little brother wanted to be an architect?"

"As long as I've known him."

"Which is how long, exactly?"

I swallowed uncomfortably. "Three months." It sounded like such a small amount of time when spoken aloud.

"And Gable told you he wants to be an architect?"

"Yes, Gabe did."

"And what exactly is he doing to ensure that happens? Is he studying? Enrolled in classes?"

"No. But he's taking a course next year." I thought for a moment and corrected myself. "This year." Midnight had passed without any celebration.

"Right." Tyler said it in such a way that made me want to slap him. "Because he hasn't said that before." He looked up, the amusement gone from his expression. "So Gabe is twenty-one, works in a coffee shop with no desire to change or improve himself, and that's who you choose to be with?"

I didn't know why Tyler was firing all these questions at me. Maybe he really did think I would be good for Gabe and was disappointed to find the state I was in down in the basement.

Maybe he really did care for his brother. I struggled to think of an answer. "He makes me feel good," I said finally.

Tyler stood up from his chair and walked over. He leaned in close and my heart started beating erratically. "He makes you feel good? Is it his smile that makes you feel good?" An exact replica of Gabe's carefree smile passed over Tyler's lips before he let it fall and leaned in closer, his breath brushing against my ear. "Is it his smooth skin?" Tyler drew his thumb over the stubble dusting his chin. A cold smirk covered his face. "Or is it the way he fucks?" Tyler laughed at my look of horror. "What? No come back? Well, at least Gabe's doing the family name proud in one area of his life. If we Thornton men are good at anything, it's how to fuck."

I took a step back, trying to make my escape.

"Oh, I'm sorry," he said. "Have I shocked your innocent small town sensibilities? Was my language too elitist?" He straightened and I couldn't help but notice his bare and chiselled chest that showed through the exposed strip of his unbuttoned shirt. "Look, I'm sorry," he said, moving away from me. "No doubt I've had one too many of these." He swirled his almost empty glass in the air. "I will behave tomorrow. I just don't understand how the little upstart did it."

"Did what?" I asked, even though I should have just turned and left.

"You," Tyler replied, his dark eyes burning into mine. He emptied the last drops of whiskey from the glass.

"Be careful," I warned as he walked past. "That stuff kills your brain cells."

Tyler didn't turn back, only threw over his shoulder, "The leftovers are in the fridge. No doubt you are hungry. Goodnight."

And then he was gone.

7

LAUREN

I decided to leave Gabe sleeping in the basement and crept up the stairs to the bedroom. But when I woke the next morning, Gabe's hand was under the material of my nightshirt and gently cupping my breast. He didn't do anything further, he didn't move, just rested his hand on my breast, holding it protectively as the rest of his body warmed the side of mine. I was still tired from the night before, unsure what time it was when I had finally fallen asleep. After a few minutes of stillness, Gabe's thumb moved across my nipple and my breath caught as it hardened in response. Gabe toyed with my nipple, gently caressing it with his thumb until he moved down in the bed and lifted the sheet so he could bring his mouth to my breast. His tongue took the place of his thumb as he teased and tugged, gently biting when I responded by arching my chest closer to his mouth. He moved over me, his face still shielded by the sheet and urged my legs apart with his knee, his mouth still fixed on my breast. He lay over me, the hardness of him pressing into my stomach as he took more of my sensitive flesh into his mouth, sucking and pulling. A moan escaped as he moved to my other breast and, after that sign of encouragement, he reached down and his fingers sought out the wetness that seeped between my legs.

Lifting his head, Gabe brought his fingers to his mouth. "I love how wet you get," he said, putting one finger to his mouth and sucking it from end to tip. "I want to taste you." He started to trail down my body with his mouth, but I stopped him, knowing that I would only last seconds once he reached his destination.

"No," I panted, squirming with the intensity of the feelings that had risen. I pulled him back up and whispered in his ear. "I need you inside me."

Gabe didn't need any further invitation and guided himself to sink into me gratefully. He kissed the tip of my nose as he rested, his cock hard and warm inside me. I felt full and content and stopped him when he started to move.

"No," I said. "Just let me feel you."

Gabe stilled and brought his mouth to mine, hungrily devouring me as we lay still and connected. The more we kissed the harder he got.

"I'm not sure how much longer I can do this," he moaned as I gripped onto his backside, stilling the small grinding movements he had begun. I moved my hips slowly in a circle and Gabe sunk to my mouth again, letting groans of frustration and pleasure pepper his kisses. Gabe rocked, moving his length up my body, the base of him pressing hard against my sensitive flesh. He rocked gently at first, encouraged that I didn't restrict his movements, but the more he rocked the more I responded until he withdrew from me and thrust back down forcefully, my head getting shoved into the pillow.

"Lauren," he panted. "Lauren, I'm not going to last much longer. I need you to come. Let me taste you." He began to withdraw so he could move down my body but I gripped onto his shoulders, holding him in place and digging my nails into his skin. Unable to control himself any longer, Gabe pounded into me. My head hit the headboard, but he didn't stop. He couldn't stop. His body was covered in a fine sheen of sweat, his hair was slicked to the side of his face, and his lip was caught between his teeth. I reached behind and grabbed the headboard, holding it tight, as my head rammed against it time and time again until I saw the familiar tension creep into Gabe's expression, and I let myself surrender at the same time he did.

Gabe rolled off and lay beside me, arms resting under his head and his chest rising and falling with exertion. "And good morning to you too, Mrs Robinson."

I took the pillow from under my head and whacked him across the face. Gabe laughed and tugged it from me, throwing it aside before twisting to grab my wrists. "Care to play again?" he asked, a twinkle in his eye as he climbed over me, pinning my arms above my head and kneeling with a leg either side of me. His cock lay on my stomach. It swelled a little as his eyes fell to my breasts.

I shook my head. "No way, Gabe Thornton. You seriously cannot recover that quickly."

Gabe let go of my hands and moved to touch himself. His eyes roamed my body. "Give me a minute."

I bucked my hips. "Get off," I teased.

He closed his eyes as I bucked under him. "That's really not helping you," he said. I looked down and saw him hardening, though his hands were now pressed over each of my breasts. Gabe moved up my body, straddling my sides with his legs until his cock rested between my breasts. He pushed them together until they engulfed his hardness, and then he began moving back and forth, rocking gently as he slid between them.

A loud knock sounded on the door and I laughed as Gabe scrambled from me, pulling the sheet back up to cover us both. The knock sounded again.

"Get up. Billie's cooked breakfast." Jake's voice wasn't tainted with tiredness like I had thought it would be.

"Give us a minute?" Gabe called back to him.

"Is that all it will take?" Jake joked.

"Is he gone?" I whispered a few seconds later when there were no other words exchanged.

Gabe threw the blanket off, his cock standing loud and proud. "Now," he said scrambling back over me. "Where were we?"

I pushed him off playfully. "This can be resumed later," I said rising from the bed. "I believe breakfast is ready."

Gabe watched as I walked into the bathroom. "I don't believe they will be serving what I want to eat."

I turned on the shower, ignoring his comments. Leaving the door open slightly, I knew he had the perfect view when I lifted my nightshirt and walked naked into the glass covered shower.

Gabe flopped back onto the bed. "You're killing me over here," he yelled out.

It wasn't until my hair was covered in shampoo and I was rinsing it under the water that I felt Gabe's arms slip around my waist.

"Gabe," I said, laughing.

"I just need you once more," he said, pressing me against the tiled wall. His hands roamed over me. His mouth pressed against my neck. "Just once more, okay?" He lifted his head. "Please?" He batted his eyelashes. "I'll be quick."

For an answer, I threaded my hands around the back of his neck and widened my stance. Gabe reached behind, cupping the cheeks of my backside and lifted me to gain better access. He entered me, his thrusts plastering my back to the wall, his fingers gripping into my backside as he fucked me until he shuddered and came, his head falling to my shoulder and nuzzling my neck once he was done.

When we walked to the dining table, I didn't meet anyone's eyes. To be honest, our little meeting in the shower although satisfying Gabe, had only served to wake me again, and I was afraid my cheeks were flushed with desire.

"About time you joined us," Hamish Thornton greeted his son. The plate in front of him was empty, as was Billie's and Tyler's.

Gabe's eyes flicked to mine. "I was busy," he said with a smirk.

Tyler cleared his throat and Jake muffled a laugh around the mouthful of food he was chewing.

"In this house, we prefer to serve breakfast before ten o'clock," Hamish said sternly, tossing back the remainder of his coffee.

Gabe ignored him and reached over the table to select a couple of pieces of French toast to put on his plate.

"Did you sleep well?" Billie asked as she brought over a tray of bacon and sat next to me.

"Quite, thank you," I replied. The table was laden with every sort of breakfast food available. There were cereals, and fresh fruit, a rack of toast with every spread imaginable, bacon and even a little jug of maple syrup. "This looks delicious," I said to Billie. "You must have been up super early to prepare all this."

Billie laughed, waving her hand as if to dismiss my comment. "The bakery opens very early," she said. "But there is a motive for all of this." She looked hopefully over at Gabe who was shovelling food into his mouth at a rate that rivalled Jake.

"What?" he asked, mouth full of French toast and a slight frown between his eyes.

"Don't speak with your mouth full," Hamish said.

Tyler sat opposite his father, nothing but a long black sitting in front of him. "How's the coffee?" I asked, eluding to our conversation the night before.

Tyler looked up at me, no amusement or acknowledgement crossing his face. "It is adequate, thank you," he replied.

"You do know that Lauren and I are leaving today," Gabe said to Billie.

"Well…" Billie took the napkin from her lap and draped it across her plate. "The thing is, I've got the fashion show tonight and—"

"We really can't stay," Gabe said, biting down on the toast again. "We've got to go back to Lauren's parents' to pick up her car before driving home. We've got around seven hours of travel ahead of us."

"Oh, I'm not asking you to stay simply to watch and I wouldn't ask unless I absolutely had to."

Gabe braced himself, his expression holding a pained wince.

"You don't need to pull that face while your step-mother is talking to you, Gable," Hamish said, clearly annoyed.

Gabe's shoulders slumped. "How can I help?" he asked Billie.

Billie clapped her hands together. "One of the models has come down with this terrible stomach bug or something. It really is quite terrible."

"And?" Gabe asked.

"And I need you to fill in."

"Me?"

"Yes, you," Billie said. "You'd be simply perfect."

Gabe held up his hand. "No fucking way," he stated. "I'm not dressing up in some stupid costume and strutting my stuff in front of people."

A small flutter of annoyance crossed over Billie's expression. "My clothing line does not feature any 'stupid costumes'," she said.

"That's not what I meant," Gabe replied, trying to backtrack.

"Why can't Jake or Tyler do it?"

Jake just about choked on his food. "I don't think I have the look she's going for."

Hamish pushed his chair back from the table and stood. "So you're happy to pour other people's coffee, but you're too proud to help out your family by strutting down a runway? You will do this, Gable. You will help out your step-mother."

Gabe tensed and I reached out and place my hand on his thigh under the table. Gabe turned to me. "Lauren, would you mind if we stayed another night?"

Tyler's phone rang and he excused himself from the table.

I smiled tightly, unsure of how Gabe wished me to respond. Hamish Thornton looked at me expectantly, Billie looked at me hopefully and Jake kept shovelling food into his mouth. "Of course not," I said finally, hoping that Gabe hadn't been looking to me to protest on his behalf.

"It's decided then," Hamish said, looking at his watch. "I will see you all later. I've got to meet someone at the show home." He walked around the table to plant a kiss on Billie's head. She looked up at him adoringly.

"Wait," Tyler said, walking back into the room. "That was the photographer. It looks as though he's come back with the same illness your model has, Billie. They both attended the same party last night and a few of the guests are reporting the same symptoms today. It looks as though it's a bout of food poisoning."

"Well, instead of raining it is pouring," Billie exclaimed.

Jake stopped chewing. "I'm pretty sure that's not how the saying goes."

Billie just did the flapping thing with her hand again, dismissing his comment.

"Fuck," Hamish Thornton said forcefully. It was strange having that word come out of his mouth. Everything about Hamish Thornton spoke of control and calm and the way he said the word defied that image. "Fuck," he said again, sitting back down at the table. "Those images must be sent by tomorrow afternoon. Tyler, do you know of someone who could fill in?"

Tyler looked across the table at me and tilted his head. "Lauren," he said.

"Lauren?" Hamish echoed, looking over at me with a confused expression. "You're a photographer?"

"She's a great photographer," Gabe said proudly.

"Forgive me if this comes across as rude, but do you have any experience? These days everyone claims to be a photographer and there's a lot more to it than simply cropping and shoving a filter on."

I swallowed the nervous knot at the back of my throat. Every person at the table looked at me expectantly. "Some," I offered weakly. "I used to shoot weddings and I did all the photography for the real estate company I used to work for."

Hamish's head snapped up. "You worked in real estate?"

"Yes, I was Derek Lee's personal assistant."

"I know Derek," Hamish said, a small wave of relief passing over his face. "Good man. How come you don't work there anymore? What made you give up being a personal assistant for working in a coffee shop?"

Billie reached over and patted her husband's hand, whispering loudly, "He was her high school sweetheart."

My eyes dropped to my lap, but not before I caught Tyler's burning glare. "Working relationships aren't always the best with ex-boyfriends."

"No," Hamish said. "I suppose they are not. Will you do it?"

"I haven't got any of my equipment with me."

"You have a camera though, correct?" Tyler more stated, than asked.

I nodded.

"Right," he said, getting to his feet. "I can take Lauren to the showroom if you like?" He looked to his father.

"Perfect. I had double booked myself anyway and would have had to spend the entire shoot on a conference call. If you could oversee Lauren that would be wonderful."

"I can take her," Gabe interjected.

Billie shook her head. "You're with me. We've got to get you ready for the show and I'll need to let you know what's expected. There's a dress rehearsal on later today so the rest of the morning will be spent getting you ready."

"Ready?" Gabe replied. "Whatever for? Aren't I already perfect?"

Tyler moved behind me and rested his hand on my shoulder. I tried not to let his touch affect me, but my skin burned. It was like the parts of me that he wasn't touching didn't exist. There was nothing but him and his hand resting on my shoulder. I drew in a shaky breath.

"Are you ready, Lauren?" Tyler asked.

"I guess so," I replied, pleased that the shakiness hadn't extended to my voice. I stood, brushing off Tyler's hand and leaving the rest of my breakfast uneaten.

Hurriedly, Gabe got to his feet. He pressed his lips to me at the same time Tyler's hand brushed against mine. I could have sworn his fingers danced with mine for a fraction, but then he walked out the door, instructing me to gather my camera even as Gabe's mouth kissed mine urgently.

"I'm sorry," he mouthed against my ear, drawing me in for an embrace. "We'll be home tomorrow and it will just be the two of us."

I smiled and moved to follow Tyler up the stairs to collect my camera.

8

LAUREN

Tyler's car was flashy and sleek and the complete opposite of Gabe's. He drove through the narrow streets, barely looking at me or engaging in conversation.

"A little information of what is expected would be good," I said as the GPS announced we were getting close to our destination.

"It is a show home for a retirement village. The photographs are expected to entice occupants."

"Expected?" I said, growing more and more nervous. I hadn't done any professional photography in years and the thought of what I was about to do was weighing on me heavily.

Tyler didn't respond, just manually shifted the car down a gear and turned into a wide driveway. "This is just one of the houses planned for replication over the entire village. Hamish would like a sense of home and personality installed within the photos."

"Is it at least furnished?"

Tyler's brows furrowed. "Of course it is."

The car slid to a smooth stop and Tyler got out of the car to open my door while I fumbled with my camera.

"Thank you," I mumbled as he shut the door firmly behind me.

"This way," he instructed.

Tyler said very little as he wandered around the house. The words 'sense of home and personality' echoed in my ears and I was afraid, due to the rigid placement of the furnishings, I was going to fail miserably. Tyler disappeared while I strolled through the recently planted and obviously staged garden, pressing my finger to the shutter without feeling like I was capturing what I was supposed to. Tyler returned, coffee in hand.

"I hope you told the person behind the counter that they were capable of more with their lives," I said, taking the cup from him. It was a latte and made just the way I liked it.

Tyler didn't acknowledge my little dig because his phone rang and he excused himself. When I walked into the kitchen an idea popped into my head. I thought back to how I used to stage the houses I photographed for market, the way I let the mess of everyday living creep into my shots. I searched the cupboards and found a row of pristine white cups. Placing one on the white bench, I poured my coffee into it, letting some splash onto the counter top. I took a picture with the sun streaming in through the window, almost illuminating the spill. Then I went back into the bedroom and took off my top, opening a dresser drawer and dumping the blue material into the open crack, letting the sleeve spill out and fall down the dresser. After messing up the sheets on the bed, I pressed the shutter, the exposed garment of clothing crisp, clear and vibrant against the blurred background of the bed which looked like someone had just climbed out of it. I was so intent, so focussed, that I got a fright when Tyler cleared his throat.

"I'm not sure if 'mess' is the personality my father was after," he said, leaning against the doorway.

"Don't worry," I said, holding my eye to the camera. "I took lots before I messed it up. I was just trying to make it more lived in."

"With a top draped over a dresser that clearly does not belong to an older woman?"

I looked at the thin material. It was one of those tops that was for looks only, not offering any warmth or perfection with its loosely woven gaps.

"It was all I had," I replied, letting a little bit of annoyance creep into my tone. "There isn't a lot else to work with."

"You don't like this home?"

"It's very…" I paused taking a few more photos, before spinning around and taking a shot of Tyler leaning against the doorway, arms across his chest and not even a shadow of a smile on his expression. "It's very clinical," I finished.

"Clinical sells," he said.

"Personality sells," I replied, quoting Derek, though even he mocked the way I took photos, well, at least, he did until he saw the spike in interest they brought.

"Why did you suggest me?" I asked.

"Because you said you were a photographer."

"You remembered that?"

Tyler moved from the doorway to stand next to the window and looked out over the snow-capped mountain ridge that framed the horizon. "Of course, I remembered. It was only last night."

"You were very drunk."

"And you were stoned." Tyler lifted one brow, again reminding me of a dark-haired, less smiley, more intimidating Gabe. "Besides, you're the only one I've ever come across that is comfortable completing a job in a singlet top."

I grabbed my top back from the dresser, tugging it over my head and trying not to look at Tyler who I knew was smirking at my discomfort.

"What do you see in him?"

"Who?" I asked, feigning ignorance.

"My kid brother."

Absently, I pressed the shutter, barely aware of the shots I was taking, and unwillingly concentrating on the way Tyler was following me around the room, head tilted to one side, thumbs hooked in the belt loops of his jeans.

"I know what you're trying to do," I said.

"Really? Enlighten me. What am I trying to do?"

"Always calling Gabe your kid brother, trying to put him down."

"He is my kid brother," Tyler replied.

"I get that you two don't like each other very much, but you don't need to drag me into the middle of it."

"Is that what you think I'm doing?"

"Well, it is, isn't it?"

Tyler shook his head and sat on one of the black leather couches in the lounge. "You've got me all wrong. I'm not asking how he is because I'm trying to put down my little brother. Why would I do that? I'm asking because I'm genuinely interested. What do you two do together?" His eyes twinkled mischievously. "Do you go dancing at the club? Do you sit at home and watch TV?"

I took a deep breath and blurted out the first thing that came to mind. It wasn't the best choice I could have made, but by the time that dawned on me, it was too late. "We play pool."

Tyler looked up, a slow smirk spreading across his face. "Pool? You play pool?"

"I like playing pool," I said stubbornly.

Tyler nodded. "As do I," he said. "But it's certainly not how I would choose to spend my time with you."

I pressed down on the shutter forcefully. "I think we're done here."

"We are?" Tyler said. "I was hoping we were just getting started."

I narrowed my eyes.

"What?" Tyler asked. "I enjoy watching you click that button."

I gathered my bag and what little equipment I had brought with me. "Can we just go now?"

Tyler stepped closer. "Am I making you uncomfortable?"

I side stepped around him. "Not at all. It's just that Gabe texted and he and Billie are back from the hairdressers. I can't wait to see how he looks."

"Just the same, but with shorter hair, I imagine," Tyler said grumpily.

"They better not have chopped it short." I opened the car door and climbed in, waiting until Tyler was seated before finishing my statement. "I love running my fingers through his hair."

Tyler didn't speak on the way back, except to tell me that his father would require the photos the following morning.

I walked into the lounge to find Gabe sitting on the couch, staring glumly at the TV, dressed in nothing but boxer shorts. His skin was dark and stained with drip lines. His hair had been shaved short at the sides, but was still long on the top, like a thick mohawk. And it had been coloured darker, with a tint of auburn. His eyes moved to meet mine just as he reached into a bag of chips. A smile twitched at the corners of my mouth.

"Don't," he said.

"Don't what?" I asked, this time smiling fully.

"I had to stand there while some woman sprayed me like a fucking car."

He frowned and I noticed even his eyebrows had been shaped and coloured. I sat down beside him, careful not to touch in case the dark-orange stain rubbed off on me.

"I hate it," he said when my eyes moved to his new hairstyle.

I ran my fingers through the shock of hair. "I don't know," I said. "I think I rather like it." I tugged it tightly against his scalp. "It's still long enough to hold onto."

A light sparked in Gabe's eye. "Do you?" he asked. "You don't hate it? I was afraid you'd hate it."

"I definitely don't hate it." I leaned over and pressed a kiss to his forehead. Gabe grabbed for me, but I caught his hand. "Not when you're covered in this stuff."

He strained against my grip playfully. "You can help me wash it off, if you like."

"Don't!" Billie screeched behind us and Gabe repelled from me like someone had slapped him.

"Don't do that!" he yelled back. "You gave me a hell of a fright."

Tyler and Jake stood behind Billie, Jake grinning stupidly and Tyler glaring as though someone had just run over his puppy.

"You will ruin everything if you smudge it now." Billie stormed over and physically removed me from Gabe's side and deposited me next to Tyler. "You stay away from him," she warned, wagging her finger in my face. Beside me, Tyler tensed and took a step away.

"Why am I the only one who has to do this?" Gabe wailed from his place on the couch. Already some of the stain from his skin had smudged against the white material.

Billie's eyes flew to the intruding colour. "You were supposed to only sit on the towel," she complained angrily.

"But it's so small," he said.

Jake laughed. "Didn't I hear you say something similar this morning, Lauren?"

I elbowed his side.

"Why don't Jake and Tyler have to walk in this stupid show?" Billie put her hands on her hips and glared at him.

"Sorry, it's not stupid," he amended.

"Look, honey." Billie sat beside him and attempted to adjust the towel beneath him. "They're simply not pretty enough."

Jake scoffed. "Says you."

Billie shot him a glare. "They are not pretty like you are pretty." She patted his cheek. "You are beautiful."

Gabe crossed his arms. "And they are not?"

Billie uncrossed his arms and placed them at his sides. "Not in the same way that you are. I have a winter in wonderland theme, going on. I want all things light and heavenly and beautiful. I want angels. Not demons." Billie checked the time on her watch. "Right," she announced. "You may now go and shower."

"Thank goodness," Gabe said, getting up from the couch. He reached for my hand but Billie slapped it away.

"Alone," she said. "You shower alone."

9

LAUREN

Since I had already worn the only nice dress I brought with me twice, I borrowed one of Billie's for the fashion show. She and Gabe had left hours before everyone else and I had spent the free time flicking through the photos I had taken earlier on a borrowed laptop. I made a note of each of my favourite shots, choosing a selection of both staged and formal, as well as my 'messy' personality ones. I would need to do a little touching up later before supplying Hamish with a copy, but I was pleased with what I had seen so far.

It was arranged that I would meet Jake and Tyler downstairs at exactly seven o'clock and we would travel to the show together. Tyler had arranged for a date to meet him here, leaving Jake to be my escort for the night.

Although Billie and I were close enough in height, my body filled the dress in ways hers didn't. It was a slim fitting dress that on Billie, no doubt, looked stunning, but on me, it looked as though someone had attempted to wrap a present without enough paper. My breasts spilled over the neckline of the dress and jiggled as I walked down the stairs. The shoes on my feet were too tight and too tall, and I struggled to walk gracefully, scared that one wrong placement of my foot would send me sprawling down the stairs to land in a glorious pile of emerald green material, black heels and wobbling boobs at Tyler's feet.

I didn't though. I managed to walk down without one misstep and loop my arm through Jake's.

"You look stunning," he said.

"I look like an over-filled sushi roll," I said under my breath.

A small smile flickered across Jake's face, but it vanished as Tyler and his date joined us at the bottom of the stairs. Tyler's eyes moved over me and I felt embarrassment burn up my cheeks. Next to his date, I looked like the frumpy cousin that everyone wished they could leave off the invitation list. Her dress was styled the same as mine, but instead of spilling out in all the wrong places, it draped over her body beautifully, fitting like it was made for her. Which it probably was. No wardrobe selection from her boyfriend's step-mother for her.

"Lauren, I'd like you to meet Amanda."

The creature called Amanda smiled and nodded gracefully, inclining her head just slightly in my direction.

"Shall we?" Tyler moved down the hall, Amanda draped on his arm, without even waiting for Jake's reply.

"Guess that's our cue," Jake whispered in my ear.

I groaned, watching the way Amanda's lack of hips swayed under her dress. Already, I felt so out of place and we hadn't even arrived.

Jake patted my hand resting in the crook of his arm. "Don't worry," he said, noting my discomfort. "If you ever feel out of place, just look next to you." He laughed loudly and tossed his long hair over his shoulder.

I gave him a feeble smile and didn't bother telling him that somehow, dressed in a suit with a wild beard, and long tangled hair, he still managed to look as though he belonged on a runway.

The room was dark when we entered, the only light coming from the spotlights that ran down either side of the empty runway. I was grateful for the dim light and felt myself relax, ever so slightly, though it didn't last long as I felt my stomach fold into the tight material of the dress. The curtain behind the stage fluttered and Billie waved me backstage and over to a nervous Gabe. His eyes bulged when he saw me, and then they fell to my chest.

"Wow," was all he said.

"Don't." I covered my chest with my arms. "I'm self-conscious enough as it is."

"Why on earth are you self-conscious? You look divine. In fact," Gabe tugged me towards him, "if we weren't surrounded by all these people right now…" He kissed my forehead.

"Distance!" Billie pushed Gabe away from me. "You cannot let this stuff rub off. Lights please!" The lights came on and for a moment I was blinded by their intensity. Billie cursed. "I'm going to need makeup here," she yelled.

With my eyes adjusted to the brightness, I was able to see Gabe in all his glory. His skin shimmered under the light, having been dusted with some sort of gold glitter. His hair had been teased and stood high above his head and he wore nothing but a cropped white fur vest and black leather shorts. Very short shorts. Shorts that barely covered the cheeks of his backside. Strips of the same white fur as his vest, wrapped around his wrists like handcuffs. I swallowed the urge to laugh.

"I cannot believe I am going out there looking like this." Gabe dropped his head between his hands just as Billie walked over and yanked them away.

"How many times do I have to tell you, Gabe? Watch the makeup." A makeup artist followed in Billie's wake and began dusting more gold sparkles on Gabe's chest, carefully avoiding getting any on the fur.

"Please," Gabe begged playfully. "Just kill me now. I am never going to hear the end of this from Tyler and Jake."

"You look good," I said, trying not to smile too much.

Gabe looked up at me. "Sure," he said, staring at the smirk that spread across my face.

I leaned close so I could whisper in his ear. "I'll help you forget later on. We'll see just how much of that gold dust I can—"

"Gabe?" a surprised voice interrupted. "Gabe, is that really you?"

I turned around to find a girl with a shock of blonde curls staring at Gabe, her mouth slightly ajar.

Gabe stared back at her a moment before splitting into a grin. "Isabel?" he said, walking over and wrapping his arms around her.

"Gabe!" Billie yelled from across the room.

Gabe stood back and held her at arm's length. "Sorry. I think that might be my final warning. She'll get the whip out soon. What are you doing here? I thought you were over in the UK?"

Isabel laughed. "Home for the holidays."

"What are you doing here? Are you in the show?"

"It's Kaitlyn's first show. I just came back to wish her well. I can't believe I ran into you. I thought you were off travelling the world?"

"I was. I'm home now," he replied without offering a reason why. And then, as if it suddenly dawned on him that I was standing silently by his side, Gabe turned to introduce me.

"Isabel, this is…" He paused, searching for the right word and I was taken back to when I had to introduce him to my parents for the second time and struggled to know how to label us. "This is Lauren," he finished lamely.

Isabel stuck out her hand and I shook it awkwardly. "It's a pleasure to meet you, Lauren," she said confidently. "Are you a friend of Billie's?"

I looked over to Gabe but his eyes had drifted to the floor. "Sort of," I replied.

A buzzer sounded and Gabe took a step away. "That's my signal," he said. "We'll catch up later." And then he was gone.

I walked back through the curtains and found where Jake had reserved a seat for me between him and Tyler's date. I sunk into the chair just as the announcer welcomed the audience to the show.

"You okay?" Jake nudged me as my eyes glazed over the next model wearing nothing but lace, fur, and leather.

I mustered a smile. "Sure."

"Are you sure you're sure? Because you don't look sure."

"I'm fine, honestly," I replied.

The fashion show took a small break and Tyler's date excused herself, walking down the aisle in front of me. I spotted the girl Gabe had been so thrilled to see sitting further down the row. "Who is that?" I asked Jake.

Jake scanned the crowd until he locked on the girl. His eyes clouded over and he shook his head.

Tyler leaned across the now empty seat beside me. "That, is Isabel Flintoff, the reason Clark is no longer with us."

"Tyler," Jake growled a warning.

"She asked," Tyler said, resting back in his seat.

"Wasn't it a car accident?" I asked, confused. Gabe had told me that his brother fell asleep at the wheel while driving back to the city later one night after getting into a horrible argument with his father.

"It was," Jake quickly assured me, but I couldn't help the twist in my gut at the way he glared at Tyler. He was clearly warning him to stop speaking.

Tyler scoffed.

"Are you referring to the argument Clark had with your father before he took off?" I asked.

Tyler lifted his brows at Jake as though challenging him. "Is that what my kid brother told you?"

"Yes," I replied through gritted teeth. "That's what your kid brother told me."

Tyler's date moved back down the aisle, excusing herself to the people who had to move their legs in order to make way for her.

"Interesting," Tyler mused.

"Are you saying that's not what happened?"

"That's not what he's saying at all," Jake said.

"I suggest you talk to your boyfriend again if you want to know exactly who Isabel is," Tyler said just as the curtains were pulled open to reveal a golden Gabe in all his fur-covered glory. Down the aisle from me, Isabel raised her fingers to her lips and whistled loudly. Gabe smiled at her and walked down the runway, oozing confidence with each step, grinning and waving to the crowd in a purely un-model-like way. He posed at the end, hand running through his hair, the muscles in his arms, chest and stomach rippling with a golden glow. I looked back at Isabel who was looking on adoringly, hands clasped under her chin, eyelashes batting and I was hit with a wave of jealousy like I had never experienced before. It wasn't in the way she looked at him. I had seen many girls look at Gabe in a similar way. It was because of the way his eyes slid to her and not to me as he walked off the stage.

With the show over, nibbles appeared on trays floating through the crowd, resting in the hands of invisible waiters.

Tyler's date complained each time a tray floated past. "How can this possibly be considered finger food?" she asked, looking down her nose at the small savoury pancakes topped with cream cheese and salmon. "The only way these could be defined as bite-sized were if you were a horse."

The tray was just about out of my reach, but I stretched out and grabbed one of the pancakes, shoving the entire thing into my mouth. Tyler watched me with an amused grin as I struggled to chew without it escaping.

Jake grabbed another pancake and followed suit, easily devouring it. "Just call me Phar Lap."

"Who's Phar Lap?" Tyler's date asked. I'm sure I had been told her name at some stage, but I couldn't be bothered recalling it.

"You ready?" Gabe appeared at my side, scrubbed clean of gold powder and dressed in normal clothes again.

I swallowed the rest of my mouthful and planted a kiss on his cheek. I could have sworn he tensed a little. "You were great out there."

"Yep." Gabe laughed, though it was a little forced. "Such talent displayed in walking."

"Hey," Tyler's date protested, confirming her career choice. "There is more to it than simply walking."

Gabe shook his head. "I know, sorry. I've just got a wicked headache." He looked over at Jake. "Would we be able to just go back now?"

Jake nodded at Tyler. "Tyler drove."

"Hamish and Billie are staying for the after party, but I don't see why we have to. Sure, let's go home," Tyler said. "I'm sure you have a lot on your mind right now."

"What's that supposed to mean?" Gabe snapped.

Tyler looked over to me, and then let his eyes drift to where Isabel was talking with a group of girls. She looked over and waved to Gabe.

"Nothing," Tyler said. "Nothing at all."

I sat squished between Jake and Gabe in the backseat of the car. Gabe's head rested against the window, staring blankly out at the street lights as they flashed by, their reflection caught by the odd drop of rain that plastered itself against the glass.

"You okay?" I asked quietly. He had barely said a word since we left the venue.

Gabe smiled sadly. "Headache," was all he said.

I was surprised when Tyler walked his date to her car without inviting her in. Gabe stalked inside, heading straight for the liquor cabinet and grabbed an unopened bottle of whiskey. He slumped onto the couch, the dark stain from his spray tan gone. Unscrewing the cap, he lifted the bottle to his mouth.

"Help yourself," he said, motioning to the bar.

"Allow me." Tyler moved gracefully behind the bar and poured a drink. I wasn't sure what it was, but it tasted great and I swallowed hungrily. I needed something to dull the twisting in my gut. Isabel meant something to Gabe. Meant enough to plummet him into this dark mood that had overtaken him. I watched as he brought the bottle to his mouth time and time again, barely swallowing as he poured the liquid down his throat.

"Easy there," Tyler walked over and attempted to ease the bottle out of his hand.

"Fuck off," Gabe growled.

"I just think you need to slow down a little," Tyler said.

Gabe pulled himself off the couch and walked over to the sliding door. "I need some air."

I moved to follow but Jake pulled me back. "I'll go," he said, flashing a warning look Tyler's way.

The two brothers sat outside on the balcony, Jake sipping on his beer, and Gabe hungrily chugging on the bottle of whiskey as though it were nothing more than juice. I envisioned the rest of his night spent bent over the toilet bowl. Already, over a quarter of the bottle was gone.

"You need to tell me what happened," I said, looking over at Tyler who had loosened his tie and removed his jacket. He sat on the couch, arms spread out over the back and one ankle resting on the knee of his other leg.

"I'm under very specific instructions from Jake that I must wait and let you talk to Gabe."

"Gabe isn't exactly in the mood for talking at the moment."

Tyler leaned forward. "What has he told you?"

I sighed, recalling the brief conversation we had not all that long ago. "He said that Clark had travelled back from the city and that your father started on at him about what he wanted to do with his life. They had this huge argument and Clark decided to travel back, upset and tired."

Tyler nodded. He leaned back against the couch again and ran his hand through his hair. I was momentarily distracted, imagining that it was my hand running through his dark hair, before scolding myself and returning to reality.

"That's a version of the truth."

"But not the full version?"

Tyler shook his head. "Gabe should really be the one to tell you."

I looked out the window, my eyes focusing past my own reflection and falling to where Gabe leaned over the railing, pouring a thin dribble of dark liquid onto the ground. It hurt a little knowing that I had opened up to Gabe, yet he was still holding secrets from me. "I need to know," I said firmly.

"Very well," Tyler said. "But you've got to tell him that you were the one who asked."

"I will," I promised.

"When Clark returned from the city, he did have an argument with Dad. There was a lot of yelling. There was a lot of slamming doors. What Clark didn't count on was walking up to Gabe's room and finding his girlfriend in bed with him."

"Isabel," I said under my breath.

"Isabel," Tyler confirmed.

"It's not like Gabe did it just to get to Clark. They were close. I think Isabel and Gabe really felt something for each other. Gabe just kind of fell to pieces after that. He blamed himself for Clark's death, though he took it out on Dad. I think tonight was the first time he and Isabel have spoken since Clark's funeral."

I didn't know what to say. My heart ached for Gabe at the same time as being annoyed by his behaviour. No wonder it had thrown him. I remember Drew telling me of the darkness that had descended over Gabe after his brother's death. Darkness that haunted him still.

"Should we stop him drinking so much?" I asked.

"Sometimes it's just best to stand aside and let him drown his misery." Tyler looked out the window. "Jake will look after him. I'll look after him. You should just go to bed. Things will be better in the morning."

No sooner were the words out of Tyler's mouth when the door opened and Gabe stumbled back in. Behind him, Jake looked to Tyler and jerked his head in my direction questioningly.

"She knows," Tyler confirmed.

"Who knows what?" Gabe asked, his voice too loud, his movements too clumsy. Holding his bottle in the air and stumbling across the carpet, Gabe yelled, "Who knows how to party?" He tipped the bottle so the liquid spilled from the opening and poured into his mouth, most of it hitting its target, the rest splattering onto his face or falling to the floor. "Lauren," he slurred, walking over and flopping onto the couch as Jake excused himself. "Lauren," he said again, shakily putting the bottle on the floor and moving closer to me. He held his mouth close to my face and the scent of alcohol repelled me. "I'm drunk, Lauren," he attempted to whisper.

"That you are," I said, pushing him away.

Gabe frowned and pouted. "Hey, I want a kiss." He moved across the couch, smacking his lips together.

"You're drunk." I pushed myself into the corner of the couch, trying to get away from the smell. Tyler watched our interaction.

"That I am." Gabe mimicked my previous words. He moved so he was leaning over me, pushing his mouth into my neck and groping my breast through the tight material of Billie's dress. Over his back, my eyes met Tyler's. They were burning and his jaw tightened.

"Come on, Lauren," Gabe urged. "I want to fuck you."

"Gabe!" I exclaimed, attempting to push him off, but his body lay heavily on me, dulled from alcohol. "Gabe, get off me. This isn't the place."

Gabe mashed his lips against mine and slipped the strap of the dress off my shoulder, his mouth diving to the over spilling flesh of my breast. I pushed harder against him and Gabe lifted his head. "What? Is it because Tyler is here? You don't mind watching, do you, Ty? In fact, I bet you like it." Gabe's tongue dipped between the crease of my breasts and he moaned with lazy desire.

"Not now," I said, pushing forcefully. "Leave me alone."

Suddenly, Tyler leapt from his seat and grabbed Gabe, shoving him against the wall and pressing his forearm over Gabe's throat. "She said to leave her alone," Tyler growled.

"Are we turning you on, brother?" Gabe laughed.

Tyler applied more pressure to his throat and Gabe's laughter turned to a choking splutter. "She asked you to leave her alone. I suggest you leave her alone, little brother." Tyler released the pressure to Gabe's throat but still held him against the wall, pushing against his shoulder to hold him in place.

Gabe coughed, drawing in deep breaths once Tyler released him. He leaned over, heaving in gasps of air before straightening himself and throwing a punch at Tyler. But because Gabe was so drunk, Tyler was able to avoid the blow by simply moving his head to the side. Gabe swung again and Tyler moved out of the way.

"Gabe," I pleaded walking over to him. I hated seeing him like this. Hated that seeing Isabel again had brought out this darkness.

Tyler held his arm out, shielding me from getting any closer.

"You are protecting her from me?" Gabe spluttered. "You? You arrogant piece of shit. Let me tell you exactly what this piece of shit is like, Lauren."

"Lauren, go to bed," Tyler instructed.

"He keeps women on a rotation schedule, just so none of them get too attached. He takes them to various functions, eye-candy on his arm, then takes them back to his apartment to fuck them senseless before sending them on their merry way. That's right, isn't it, brother dearest? That's what you do. Use and abuse. All because they don't tick all the boxes on your stupid lists. I am nothing like you. Nothing."

Tyler was fuming. "At least I've never slept with a girl who was going out with my brother."

Gabe's eyes snapped to Tyler, all drunkenness draining away with that one movement. And then he lunged at Tyler, wrapping his arms around his waist and knocking him to the ground. Gabe rose over his brother, one hand clenched in a fist, but he never got to bring it down as Tyler's hand enclosed around his. The two brothers glared at each other, both waiting for someone to make the next move.

I was frozen to the spot, unsure what to do. Should I interfere? Should I try to pull Gabe off? Or should I just let them sort it out themselves? Gabe was clearly drunk and not thinking straight, but Tyler was sober and hopefully had the situation under control.

Just as Gabe's fist wavered in Tyler's grasp, Jake ran back into the room and pulled Gabe off. "What the fuck?" Jake pushed Gabe away.

Gabe stumbled over to the wall, hit it and then slid down, holding his head in his hands as giant tears rolled down his cheeks.

"Gabe?" I asked. He clawed across the floor towards me and curled into a heap at my feet.

"I'm sorry," he sobbed. "I'm so sorry."

Jake stretched out his hand to help Tyler to his feet, but Tyler jerked away from the offered help. "This is who you're dating," he said to me as he glared down at Gabe. "This is who he is."

10

LAUREN

After Tyler and Jake had assured me that they would look after Gabe, I left him drunk and crying on the floor with his brothers watching from their protective perch on the couch and went to bed. I was exhausted, but sleep evaded me. I stared at the ceiling and moved my hand across the sheets to feel the coldness of the empty space beside me. Gabe's behaviour scared me. When something upset him, he turned to drink and not me. I wanted to help. I wanted to comfort him, but he turned away every time.

Around three o'clock, I gave up my attempt at rest and walked down the stairs in search of the laptop Tyler had let me borrow in order to edit the photos. If I couldn't sleep, I may as well spend the time productively. The lounge was empty and I hoped Gabe was sleeping it off somewhere. There was a lot of talking we needed to do.

Armed with the laptop, I sat down and opened the photo files. The glow of the screen burned blue over the whiteness of the dining table. Selecting the favourites I had identified earlier in the day, I set to work adjusting the colours and applying a few finishing touches to the images. I was pleased with them but was unsure if they were what Hamish required. Going over the images one final time before heading back to bed, I jumped when Tyler spoke behind me.

"You're good," he said, arms crossed and leaning against the wall, wearing only loose fitting grey pants and nothing else. I couldn't help but notice the way his biceps curved, pressed against his chest, or the fine dark hair that trailed under the waistband of his pants. Simply put, he was gorgeous. Taller, and slightly bigger, his muscles had lost some of the leanness of youth that Gabe's had. They dipped and swelled seductively and his stomach was lined with smooth ridges. His pants hung low over his hips and I felt myself swallow unconsciously as I followed the valley of his muscles down to his waistband. There was something undeniably sexy about Tyler Thornton. Something I needed to avoid.

Tyler pulled out the seat next to me and planted himself down, leaning forward to get a closer look at the photos that glowed on the screen. The bare skin of his arm brushed against mine and goose bumps erupted at the touch.

"I get the whole 'mess' thing now," he said as I studied the layer of stubble that dusted his chin. "It gives the images more personality, makes people believe they could be the ones living there."

"Thanks," I said, flicking through the files one last time and trying not to notice how fast my heart was beating.

"You're talented." He reached over and closed the laptop lid even though I wasn't done flicking through the images. The room fell into darkness, the only light coming from the moon shining through the window. "I'm sorry," he said finally.

I looked up at him quickly, not trusting myself to meet his eye. "What do you have to be sorry for?"

Tyler ran his hand through his dark hair. "I shouldn't have told you the way I did. I should have left it between you and Gabe."

"I asked you," I reminded him.

"Yes, but I made it so you had no choice in the matter. I wanted you to know."

The coldness of the night brushed against me and I wrapped my arms around myself, willing warmth back into my body.

Tyler sat back against the chair and crossed one ankle over his knee.

"So why did you tell me then?"

"About Isabel?"

I nodded.

Tyler's steel-grey eyes burned cold when he met my gaze. "Because you adore him." Reaching out, he tucked a stray strand of hair behind my ear. My heart pounded as his finger grazed my cheek. "I don't want you to adore him." He said it so quietly, his voice barely more than a growl, I wondered if I had imagined it.

Sitting next to me, leaning so his arms rested on his knees, there was nothing to break the silence between us but the sound of our own breaths.

"We've met before, do you remember?"

"We've met? You and me?"

"Yes, you and me."

"I think I'd remember."

"It was at the boxing match that Derek and Gabe fought in. You literally ran into me on your way out."

"I did? I would think I'd remember if I ran into you."

"Why?"

"Why what?"

"Why do you think you'd remember?"

Unbidden, the colour fled to my cheeks. "Because…" I cleared my throat. Because you're gorgeous, I wanted to say. "Because you look like Gabe."

"I wish I'd met you first." Tyler's eyes locked with mine.

"Tyler," I said.

He looked away, his eyes moving to scan the blackness of the lake. "I know. You're with Gabe." He stood and moved behind me, his hands resting lightly on my shoulders. The heat of his breath warmed my scalp as he spoke, bending down close. "I just wanted you to know." And then, his lips pressed briefly against my hair and he was gone and the coldness of the night enveloped me again.

Once back in bed, I couldn't get the image of Tyler out of my head. I replayed the moment he reached across and tucked my hair aside over and over, my heart pounding with both excitement and guilt. But I knew who Tyler was. I knew what sort of a man he was. The fact that he had brought Gabe's past to me during a time when Gabe was hurting the most spoke to that. I wondered where Gabe was, if he and Jake were spread out on the couches in the basement, or if he had crawled into one of the beds in a spare room, drunkenly snoring the night away.

At some stage during the night, sleep won me over and I woke the next morning to a gentle knock on my bedroom door. I croaked out a greeting and the door opened to Gabe, hair mussed and dark smudges under his eyes from the mascara he had been made to wear for the fashion show. He wore loose-fitting grey pants just like Tyler had the night before, but Gabe had a black t-shirt pulled over his chest. He walked over and I scooted up on the bed as he sat at the end, staring at the floor, his newly cut hair falling over his eyes.

"I can't tell you how sorry I am about last night."

"It's okay," I said, thinking of all the thoughts that must have crashed over him after seeing Isabel again. "I under—"

Gabe shook his head. "No, it's not okay. Jake told me how I behaved and I keep having these flashbacks. I treated you badly. I embarrassed you."

"You were upset." I patted the space beside me, but Gabe remained perched at the bottom of the bed.

"So, you know?" His voice broke and tears welled in his eyes.

I nodded. "Tyler told me." At Gabe's expression, I added, "I asked him to."

Gabe chewed on his bottom lip. "He shouldn't have. I should have been the one to tell you and he should have known that. It's not like he doesn't have things from his past he's ashamed of. Just ask him about a girl called Claudia. He almost threw his life away for that girl, and he wasn't even the father."

"What?" I asked, confused by his mumbled words.

Gabe let out a breath of air and looked up at me hesitantly. "Never mind, it's just a story Jake told me." Another sigh. "I'm so sorry. It just all came rushing back. At first, I was so thrilled to see her. All I saw was the first girl who ever made me smile. The first girl who ever saw me as me and not just as an extension of my family. She was the only girl who ever saw me like that, until you." His eyes met mine briefly. "But then, after the show, when everything was quiet and I had time to think, it just brought back all these memories of her and me and Clark, memories which I've tried to block out. I just…" Gabe's voice fell away to nothing.

"Why did you do it?"

He lifted his eyes to mine, not needing to ask what I was referring to. "I thought I loved her."

"Did you?" I asked hesitantly.

"I didn't know what love was."

"But you do now?" I asked.

"I love you, Lauren. I know I love you," Gabe stated plainly. "I need you to forgive me."

"There's nothing to forgive," I said, but in my heart, I knew it wasn't true. I hated the way he treated me the night before. I hated the way he groped me when he was drunk, no thought of how it would make me feel, no thought of his brother watching on. I hated that he turned to violence and drink and not to me.

Gabe lifted himself off the bed and walked closer to me, depositing himself at my feet as I gripped my knees to my chest. "Yes, there is. I hated who I was last night. I was a pig. I was disgusting. I should have never treated you like that. You know it and I know it. Please don't hate me."

"Gabe, I could never hate you," I said, finally meeting his eyes which were still swimming in unshed tears.

Gabe inched closer. "I couldn't stand it if I hurt you."

"You didn't hurt me." I reached over and cupped his cheek with my hand. He nuzzled against it and kissed the palm, pleading with his lips instead of his words. Kissing his way up my arm, he tugged me closer.

"I need you," he said hoarsely when I withdrew a fraction. "I need to know you have forgiven me."

"Of course I have," I replied.

"I need to feel it," he said, pulling the covers aside and climbing over me as he pushed me back on the bed. "I love you, Lauren Greer. I need you to know that."

Gabe brought his mouth down, kissing me tenderly yet passionately, moving his lips against mine, dipping his tongue into my mouth. He groaned and crushed his body to mine so I could feel his hardness pressing on my pelvis through the thin material of his pants. His mouth was glued to my skin, kissing my lips, my jaw, my neck. His hands roamed, taking my breast and applying the slightest amount of pressure.

"I need you," he said again. "I need you to want me."

Gabe tugged at the hemline of my nightshirt and I sat up a little as he peeled it from my body. Sitting back so he was resting on my thighs, Gabe stared down at me, naked and exposed, trapped under him, and sighed.

"I want you," he said, bringing his mouth down to cover my belly button. "I need you."

He toyed with me, kissing the flesh of my stomach, my thighs, but carefully avoiding the one place on my body that was now screaming for him. Reaching down, he ran a single finger down the slit of my sex, his eyes darkening when he found me wet and ready. "Do you want me?" he asked and began to rub in slow, soft circles.

I nodded, my head pressed into the pillow, eyes closed. Gabe reared over me, his fingers moving more urgently. "Look at me," he instructed, as he inserted a finger deep inside. I gasped and opened my eyes obediently.

"Do you want me?" he asked again as another finger slipped in. And again, I nodded. Gabe shook his head, removing his fingers and tearing off his shirt and pants. He pressed the tip of his hard cock against my trembling entrance. "I need to hear you say it," he grunted. I moaned as he rubbed his tip back and forth over my wetness. "Say it," he begged. "Say you want me. Say you need me."

My breath came out in short sharp gasps. "I want you," I said, my mind blocking out everything but the blond haired man-god above me and the way he made me feel. Gabe pushed inside, but not all the way, and I ground against him, my body begging for him to fill me.

"I need you," I said and he thrust deeply, entering me fully. My eyes locked on his as he rocked in and out, his gaze piercing and demanding, yet at the same time tender with need. Reaching down, he grabbed the back of my thighs and lifted my legs for better access, pulling me further down the bed and closer to him. His eyes fell to where our bodies joined, watching himself slide in and out. Pushing my thighs closer to my chest, he pushed in deeper and I whimpered, unsure whether the sensation was pleasure or pain. Holding himself in place, he started massaging my clit and I squirmed, enjoying the sensation of him hard and full as he pleasured me, urging me into submission with his fingers. He watched me as I came, writhing on his cock as the waves of pleasure washed over me. When I finally collapsed and lay limp beneath him, he withdrew and lay beside me, pulling me close and laying tender kisses on my neck.

"What about you?" I asked, feeling his hardness pressing into my back.

"Not this time," he said.

I rolled over to face him, taking his face between my hands. "Gabe, I want you."

He shook his head, pressing a kiss to the tip of my nose. "I don't deserve it. Not after last night."

I sat up and pushed him onto his back. His cock lay over his stomach, hard and heavy and ready.

"Lauren," he said as I started to move my way down his body. "I didn't want—" His breath came out in a low whistle as I wrapped my mouth around him. "Lauren," he panted. "I—"

I wasted no time, sucking hard and bobbing my head up and down, my body tingling with the knowledge of how easy it was to pleasure him.

"Lauren, careful," he warned. "This wasn't supposed to—"

He groaned and came in my mouth, the warmness of him hitting the back of my throat.

"I needed you too," I said, after swallowing and wiping my mouth with the back of my hand. I pressed a kiss to his lips and wondered if he could smell himself on my breath.

After showering, we packed our clothes into our bags and headed down the stairs, ready to grab some breakfast before hitting the road. Hamish, Jake, and Billie were already at the table, a box of sweet croissants and a tray of takeaway coffees ready and waiting. Jake glanced between Gabe and me, his eyes holding a question. I nodded ever so slightly and gave him a reassuring smile. His brother was fine. The events of the night before had worn themselves out of his system. I just wondered when they would return again.

Billie sat slumped at the table with her head in her hands. She looked up and half smiled when I sat beside her. "Why do you look so refreshed when I feel like shit?" she asked. "Last night was way too late and involved entirely too much alcohol."

Hamish, looking groomed, ready for the day and nothing like his wife, reached across and brought her hand to his lips. "You deserved to let your hair down a little. It was a wonderful show."

She brightened a little at that, a smile replacing her frown. "It was good, wasn't it?"

I scanned the room searching for any sign of Tyler before sitting down and reaching for one of the coffees.

"And in no small way, it was thanks to you, Gabe. I'm not sure how I'll ever repay you for filling in."

"Nonsense," Hamish said gruffly. "You don't need to thank the boy. He was happy to do it."

Gabe rolled his eyes in my direction. "Yes," he drawled. "Happy to do it."

Tyler still hadn't appeared by the time I had eaten a croissant and finished my coffee. "Where's Tyler?" I asked even as a little guilt ate at my gut for caring.

"He left to go back to the city first thing this morning. He said to say goodbye," Hamish said.

My heart dropped a little. He had left without saying goodbye.

"But," Hamish continued. "He did forward on your photos and I must tell you how impressed I am. You have a real eye for the market. In fact," Hamish said, reaching down and grabbing some paperwork from a briefcase resting on the floor. "I would love it if you would consider taking on a project for me. I already had a photographer lined up, but after seeing your work, I think you'd be a far better option."

Somewhat surprised, I took the offered paperwork, my eyes growing wide when I saw the contract and the offer. "The casino?" I asked, looking over the proposal.

"A lot of people have money tied up in this project and in order to keep them happy, I need to provide regular updates on the progress. Tyler has arranged a website, and I would like for photos on the progress to be uploaded weekly. Do you think you could handle that? I believe the remuneration is adequate and, of course, all travel expenses to and from the city would be covered. You would be required to be there every week or two, sometimes more often if the development dictates it."

"She already has a job, Dad," Gabe said, his voice holding bitterness.

"And this wouldn't interfere with it," Hamish replied sternly.

"I'm not sure if—" I stammered, but Gabe's father interrupted me.

"Tyler spoke very highly of your work and I have to say I agree with him. I would appreciate it if you seriously considered the proposal." He drained the last of his coffee.

Gabe covered my hand with his under the table. "You don't have to do this," he whispered quietly.

"Of course she doesn't," Hamish said, annoyed. "But I don't see why she would refuse. As I said before, the remuneration is generous, more than I was offering the previous contractor. Of course, you wouldn't be an employee of the company, it is contracted work. You will do it, won't you?"

"Give the poor girl at least enough time to look over the proposal, Hamish," Billie said.

"Once a week?" I asked, staring down at the numbers which were swimming in my vision. It was a very generous offer. I would make more in a single day's work than I would from an entire week's worth of shifts at the café.

"More when the work dictated," Hamish answered. "I don't imagine that would occur on too many occasions though."

A thrill of excitement washed through me. Here was my chance to get back into photography and earn a living doing something I loved. Of course, I would keep my job at the café as well. I would easily be able to juggle my shifts to accommodate the new work. "Yes," I said before I could think my way out of it. "Yes, I would love to take the contract."

"It's settled then." Hamish pushed back his chair and stood up. Taking his jacket from where it was hanging over the back of his chair, he flung it over his shoulder. "I will get Tyler to call you with the details."

"Tyler?" Gabe asked.

"He is managing the project for me. Lauren will be reporting directly to him."

"Tyler?" Gabe said again, this time with a little more anger in his voice.

"Is that a problem?" Hamish asked. "She could have reported to you or Jake, had you chosen to work in the family business, but you didn't."

Gabe didn't answer and instead gripped my hand tighter and bit off a piece of croissant.

Billie cried when I hugged her goodbye. I didn't know whether it was because she was hungover and tired, or whether it was simply because she didn't appear to have many friends. All the people I had seen over the past few days were acquaintances and business contacts, none of them appeared to be friends of the couple or, at least, not friends of Billie. I wondered how many of them knew Hamish's previous wives and my heart went out to her a little.

Soon we were on the road and Gabe gripped the steering wheel tightly, his knuckles white and jaw clenched.

"It was nice to meet your family," I said, watching him carefully.

Gabe looked at me out of the corner of his eye, his jaw clenching and unclenching. "All of my family?"

I laughed. "They're not so bad, are they? Well, compared to mine, at least."

We reached the open road so Gabe opened the engine up a gear and sped up to the limit. "You didn't have to say yes to my father."

"I wanted to. I'm actually a little excited about it."

"Even working with Tyler?"

I shrugged. "The money makes it worth it."

Gabe simply nodded and kept his eyes trained on the road.

"Did you want me to say no?" I asked finally when it was clear Gabe wasn't going to say anything else.

"It's not my choice."

"And yet you seem annoyed at the choice I made. Is it because of Tyler?"

Gabe's eyes flicked to mine quickly and then back to the road. "Partly. He is one of the most demanding, exacting people I have ever come across. I'm almost certain he came out of the womb with a fully planned list of what he was going to do with his life. He has lists for everything. He even has a list of all the requirements a woman must meet in order for him to marry her."

"You're kidding."

Gabe shook his head. "Nope. The guy's a freak."

"You don't mind me working with him though?" I asked, sensing something hovering under the surface of his words.

"And if I did?"

I looked at him apologetically and smiled. "Sorry?"

"That's what I thought."

"So you're okay with it?"

Gabe chewed his bottom lip. "Clark's death changed things for me. Afterwards, I saw my family for who they really were. I've worked hard to separate myself from them and in one visit you've managed to weave me back into their lives."

I swallowed the knot of guilt forming at the back of my throat. "I'm sorry," I said reaching across and placing my hand over his knee. "I didn't know."

Gabe smiled tightly. "Of course you didn't. I never really told you and that was my fault, not yours. I just want you to be happy and if that means taking the job, then I'm all for it, even if it does involve Tyler. He just better respect the fact that you're mine."

"Yours?" I asked.

"Mine," he said. And then at my incredulous look, he added with a teasing smirk, "If that's alright with you."

11

GABE

I hated the fact that Lauren said yes to Dad's job offer. I wanted to tell her to say no, but who was I to tell her what to do? Was it my place to tell her to turn down a job, her dream job? And the fact that she would be reporting to Tyler sat uneasily with me. I had seen the way he looked at her. It was the same way he looked at most of the things he wanted. Like he already owned her.

The car trip back to her parents' house was quiet. She tried engaging me in pointless conversation about my family, about her family, but I didn't want to talk. All I could think of were the steps I had put in place to separate myself from them. And the fact that they were now destroyed.

I had told Lauren that I hadn't known what love was. It was true to a certain point, but it was also true that I had loved Isabel Flintoff. I never meant to fall in love with her, she was Clark's girl, not mine. But as Clark became more and more obsessed with becoming a better person, a person who wanted to change the world, he had left his girlfriend alone, and she and I started to spend more time with each other. His absence had left a hole in both our lives, and though I wasn't making excuses for what we did, we loved each other. She was the first girl to look at me and see only me. I never meant to end up in bed with her. She was the only one I ever loved until Lauren came along, and seeing her again messed with my head. It brought back the love I felt for her. It brought back the guilt I felt when Clark barged into my room, wanting to vent about the argument he and Dad had just had, and instead, found me on top of his girlfriend. I wished I could have spared him that pain. I wished I had made him stay. I wished I had never fallen for her.

But I did. And afterwards, the guilt of it all was too much.

So after spending weeks in a drunken stupor, I took some of my father's money and fled the country. I thought I would be able to flee my guilt but it followed me around the world. And the only time it would quiet was when I drowned it with alcohol.

When I finally returned home I cut up my father's credit card, moved to a quiet town away from him and the rest of my family, and started a life of my own. One that had nothing to do with Hamish or Tyler Thornton. My life. My terms. My money. It was only Jake's return that tempted me back into the fold. And, if I was being honest, I wanted to show off Lauren. She was everything they would want me to find in a partner. She was beautiful and smart and talented, and to be honest, there was a little part of me that wanted to parade her in front of my father and Tyler and Jake. A part that wanted to show her off as mine. But look where it had got me. Right back where I didn't want to be. Part of the Thornton family once again.

I was almost pleased when we picked up Lauren's car and she travelled separately back home. Not that I didn't want to spend time with her. I did. It was just that I knew she didn't understand why I needed to be separate from my family. Even though she had hidden parts of her life from her family, she didn't realise how much I needed to be apart from mine. She didn't know how much the Thorntons could overtake your life. Let them in just an inch, and before you knew it, there was very little left of the person you were.

And all that remained was very clearly branded Thornton.

When we picked up her car, her mother wouldn't meet my eye. It reminded me that no matter how proud I had been to introduce her to my family, her family might never accept me as worthy of her. In their eyes, I would always be someone too young, someone who wasn't Derek. They couldn't see how much I loved her. They couldn't see that no matter what had happened to her in the past, I was the one person who would never hurt her. I loved Lauren and not simply the thought of Lauren or the promise of what she could bring me in the future. I didn't care if she couldn't have children. I would remain childless my entire life if it meant having her by my side. I just hoped she knew that.

By the time we finally pulled up outside Lauren's house, we had been travelling in darkness for hours. Lauren stepped out of her car and stretched high into the air, her top clinging delightfully to the curves of her breasts. I longed to get out of the car and climb into bed with her. I had an insatiable need to be close to her. It was as though it was only when I was inside her that I felt she looked at me the same way I looked at her, that she needed me the same way I needed her.

I was worried that I had scared her the night before. She assured me I hadn't. She let me fuck away my insecurities that morning and I needed to again, but I wouldn't allow myself to use her like that.

Noticing that I hadn't stepped out of my jeep or turned off the engine, Lauren walked over to my door, and I wound down the window.

"Aren't you coming in?" she asked, looking at me both expectantly and hopefully. She ran her tongue over her bottom lip and for a moment I was transfixed by the movement.

I tore my eyes away and shook my head. "I think maybe it's best if I go home."

"You don't want to spend the night?"

There was a look of disappointment on her face that I longed to wipe away, but again, I shook my head and studied how white my knuckles were wrapped around the steering wheel.

"Is it because I took the job?"

My head jerked up. "No," I said vehemently. "It has nothing to do with that. It's just that with everything that happened last night, the way I behaved, the way I almost forced myself on you this morning just to make me feel better about—"

Lauren leaned through the window and stopped my words with a heated kiss. A surge of desire rippled through me, awakening my already semi-hard cock.

"I wanted you just as much as you wanted me," she said, breaking the kiss. "And I want you now. And tomorrow. And the next day." She leaned through the window again, pressing her mouth to mine and making the thought of denying her again even harder. "Stay," she begged.

"But—"

"But nothing, Gabe Thornton." She opened the car door and tugged my hand. "You don't even have to stay the night if you don't want, but I feel like there is some sort of awkwardness between us and I don't want you to leave while I feel this way. At least just come in to say goodnight." The way she looked at me showed she wanted to do everything but say goodnight.

I couldn't resist her. Why bother even trying? Climbing out of the car, I wrapped my arms around her waist, pushing her against the hood of the jeep. I found her mouth and kissed her passionately, groaning with desire as she pushed herself against me and slipped her hand down to feel my hardness.

"I want you," she mumbled.

I swelled against her.

Lauren fumbled with the buttons of my jeans, ripping them apart and pushing her hand under the waistband of my boxers. Her hand was warm and tender and caressed me with just the perfect amount of gentleness and need. Overcome with desire, I ran my hand up her back and entangled my fingers in her hair, tugging her closer and taking her bottom lip between my teeth. Lauren pushed her hand deeper under my waistband, encircling my hardness and stroking more urgently.

"I want you inside me," she whispered against my ear. I jerked away from her, surprised at how suddenly the need to come in her hand overwhelmed me.

"Careful," I hissed.

"I don't want to be," she panted, stroking me faster. "I want you, and if you don't come inside and take me right now, I am going to drop to my knees right here on the street and suck you until you come."

It was then that I knew Lauren was doing this for me. She knew the only way I could feel forgiveness for how I had behaved was to be inside her. She knew the only way I would be able to forget about everything that had happened, about Clark and Isabel, about Tyler and Dad, was to fuck her senseless. If I didn't, I would go home and drink myself into a stupor. She knew what I needed and she was willing to give it to me. I think I loved her more in that moment than I ever had before.

Gathering her in my arms, I plastered my hands to the cheeks of her backside while her legs wrapped around my waist, and I walked towards the front door, my mouth locked on hers as though I would die if we weren't connected. I dropped my mouth to her neck as she fumbled with the key in the lock until the door finally gave way and we fell onto the floor of her lounge, unable to even make it fully inside, let alone to the bedroom. I tore at her clothes like someone possessed. All I could think about was being inside her. The need for her overwhelmed me. I needed to feel her warmth and wetness surrounding me, needing me.

Soon we were both naked and I rose over her, reaching down and directing myself into her wetness. Her head rolled back when I entered her, and her eyes fluttered. She breathed heavily, her breasts rising and falling under me. I took a nipple in my mouth as I plunged further, rising back only to watch her expression as I filled her.

"Gabe," she breathed. Reaching up, she pulled me close, sinking her teeth into the firm flesh of my shoulder and digging her nails into my back. "Fuck me," she panted.

And fuck her I did.

Drenched in sweat, I thrust in and out, slamming my body against hers, causing her breasts to wobble with the motion. She watched me with hungry eyes, naked and exposed on the floor of her lounge, a cold breeze from the open door floating over our skin.

When she cried out and her walls clamped around me tightly, I came inside her, filling her with spurt after spurt of my seed until there was nothing left of me and everything was inside her. With glazed eyes and a satisfied smile, she trailed her fingers gently over my back as I slumped over her, content, happy and spent.

Then the cat came and started pushing itself against me, rubbing its head on mine.

"Smudge!" Lauren exclaimed, reaching up to pat the black and white cat. The cat ignored her outstretched hand and continued to push against my head. "Traitor," she hissed.

We lay there entwined in each other until Lauren gently nudged me and excused herself. Returning moments later, still completely naked, she lay down, curling herself into the crook of my arm and resting her head on my chest. She pushed the cat away. My heartbeat thudded under her cheek. Kissing the top of her head, I breathed in the scent of her.

"Thank you," I whispered, unsure if she realised how much I had needed her.

She laughed a small laugh. "I'm never sure what you say to that. You're welcome? It was my pleasure? It seems a strange thing to thank a person for, especially since it wasn't exactly one-sided."

I tightened my grip. "I needed to feel close to you."

"I know," she said quietly. Lauren lifted her hand and trailed one finger through the small spattering of blond hair that led to my pelvis, the one strip left untouched by the waxing for the show. I twitched in response, and Lauren slid down my body and wrapped her mouth around my spent cock.

"Lauren, we don't—" I sucked in a breath as her teeth gently grazed me and I grew inside her mouth. Her tongue licked my shaft from base to tip and I surged with awareness. "Lauren we just…"

But she rose to all fours, her mouth still wrapped around me and her ample backside jutting into the air in front of my face. Unable to resist, and not wanting to even if I could, I ran my finger down the line of her butt cheeks, past the small pucker of her arsehole and inserted it into her folds which were still swollen and moist from our last encounter. Lauren pushed herself onto my hand, inserting my finger further. Once again, I was surprised by the intensity of my need to be inside her.

106

I played with her as she sucked me, inserting one finger, then two, and finally adding another, pushing hard into her and forcing her head further down my shaft with each thrust. My fingers were slick with her wetness and I brought them to my mouth, tasting her, inhaling her. Lifting her shoulders, I pulled her away from my cock and positioned myself behind her, the cheeks of her arse, plump and inviting. Her sex was pink and ready, slick and wet, and all I wanted to do was plunge inside her, taking her from behind. But first, I lowered my mouth and licked away some of the wetness, hungry for her. She tasted sweet and ready and I squeezed the tip of my cock, in an effort to quell my rising need. Finally, when she was squirming beneath me, I lifted my head and gripped onto her hips forcefully. She pushed back, open and ready and wanting. I held the tip of my cock at her entrance, waiting, hovering until she arched her back and pushed herself against me. She was as hungry for me as I was for her. Removing my hands from her hips, I simply watched as she pleasured herself, rocking back and forth. Sometimes she would plunge herself forcefully against me, our bodies making a sharp clap as they connected. Other times, she would move slowly, just teasing the tip of me with small movements. I thought I had spent everything inside her earlier, but the need to fill her again came with a vengeance. Placing my hands back at her hips, I gripped onto her and held her in place as I slammed against her.

She was perfect. The roundness of her arse. The gentle curve of her waist. The smoothness of her skin. The noises she made. Everything about her had me wanting to take her but please her at the same time. I leaned forward and reached between her legs until I found her wet slit and began to massage, determined to make her come with me again. She widened her kneeled stance to allow me better access, and she began to pant as I felt her tighten and clench before trembling to a climax that coated my fingers with a fresh wave of moisture. It was all I needed to explode inside her again. Holding her in place against my cock, I filled her, coating her wetness with my own.

I stayed the night and fucked her twice more, slamming into her repeatedly until her pussy was red and swollen and unable to take me again. And then I let her sleep.

I lay awake watching her, happy in the knowledge that she got me. She saw me for who I was. She knew what I needed and was more than willing to give it to me. Finally, I was able to fall into a blissful sleep that wasn't haunted by memories of my dead brother, or stained with the shadow of Isabel's smile. The only thing on my mind was Lauren.

12

LAUREN

"Tell me everything."

Peta sat at her kitchen table, coffee cup at her mouth and waiting expectantly. I took a sip of my own drink and smiled slowly.

"Out with it!" she demanded. "How did your mother take it? What made you want to tell everyone? Spill everything."

I laughed. It was so good to be around her again. Peta was my girl. The one I knew would be there for me no matter what.

"Well," I said, deliberately talking slowly. Peta made a 'move it along' motion with her hands. I had already explained to her how I had decided that I no longer wanted to keep Gabe a secret and invited him to come to my parents' house. "I got up Christmas morning, and there was Derek sitting there like an unwanted present."

"Derek? What the heck was he doing there?"

"Mother."

Peta held up a hand. "No need to say anything more, but what on earth did she think it would accomplish? Did she really think you two might get back together?"

"Not when Gabe knocked on the door."

Peta slapped her thigh. "I wish I could have been there."

I shook my head. "It didn't exactly go as planned."

"You didn't plan on revealing to your family that you were dating a man almost a decade younger than you in front of your ex-fiancé? Why ever not, Ren?"

"Mother had no idea of the real reason that Derek and I broke up. She thought it was solely over the lying-man-stealing-bitch."

"You never told her?"

I shook my head. "It was too painful. I just never knew how to broach the subject. How do you tell your own mother that her daughter will never be able to give her grandchildren?"

Peta patted my hand. "I wish I could have been there for you."

"Gabe was wonderful," I said, thinking of the way he stood up for me. The way he comforted me.

"Did your mother warm to him?"

I shook my head firmly. "Not even slightly. She called him a child. Dad could barely look him in the eye and Morgan kept on doing this thing whenever she was around him, like she wanted to jump him or something. It was rather disturbing."

Peta sighed. "My Christmas was so boring in comparison. The most exciting part was when Shrek announced he had a surprise. For a moment I thought maybe we were going on holiday. You can imagine how annoyed I was to discover it was merely that he was going on a sugar-free diet for January and wanted the whole family to join in. Did you know that sugar-free also means wine-free?"

"Surely not!" I exclaimed with mock indignation.

"Five days in. Only twenty-five to go." Peta sighed dramatically, before perking herself back up. "So, tell me about his family."

"Do you remember Willa from high school?"

"Willa Peterson?"

I nodded. "She's married to Hamish Thornton now."

"You're shitting me."

"Nope," I said, taking another sip of my coffee and smirking behind the ceramic. "Not shitting you."

"She's the same age as us." I nodded again. "And she's married to your boyfriend's father." Again, I just nodded. "That had to be awkward."

"You're telling me. She's also younger than Hamish's oldest son."

"Gabe has a brother?"

"Gabe has two brothers. Had three. Two half-brothers, Tyler and Jake. Clark, his full brother, died a couple of years ago in a car accident." I didn't tell her of the family dramas that went before the accident. To do so would have felt like a betrayal of Gabe. It was his story to tell, not mine.

"My goodness," she said in a hushed voice. "Do they look anything like Gabe?" Her eyebrows hooked into a question.

I pulled out my phone and flicked through a few of the photos I had taken while we were away, until I reached the one of Hamish Thornton flanked by his sons. Billie had begged them to pose for it, and none of them were keen. None of them smiled. Jake had his arm flung around Gabe's shoulder but it was the only affection shown in the photo.

"Here," I said, holding it out to her. "Tyler, Hamish, Jake and Gabe."

Peta studied the photo, her eyes growing wide. "Wow," she said. "Those are some mighty fine genes."

"Jake has just returned from a stint with the army and Tyler works for his father."

Peta pointed to where Tyler stood at the edge of the photo, a frown firmly planted on his expression and glaring at the camera.

"Which one is the tall, dark and dangerous one? He's pretty much sex on a stick."

"That's Tyler," I replied without even checking which one she was pointing to. "The eldest."

Peta whistled and handed my phone back. "Not a bad family to marry into."

"Marry?" I replied. "That's getting ahead of yourself. Gabe and I have only just gone public and now you're marrying me off to him?"

"Speaking of going public…" Peta glanced at me and winced.

"What?" I asked.

"Mark may have let the cat out of the bag a little prematurely. Everyone at work knows."

"Everyone?" I asked, letting a slight hint of panic into my voice.

"Everyone," she confirmed. "Should be a fun shift for you two tomorrow."

"Can't wait," I said, groaning.

For the rest of our visit, I filled Peta in on every detail I could think of concerning my time away. She filled me in about her family Christmas and how the in-laws gave her children too much sugar, bringing on her husband's announcement for a sugar-free January, and all the university students who had covered shifts over the holiday break. Things had not gone as smoothly as she had hoped and she was looking forward to Gabe's and my return. Part of me thought she was just pleased that Gabe and I had finally resolved things and there wouldn't be a need for him to repeatedly miss his shifts.

* * *

Gabe and I were both scheduled to close the café the following day. He had spent the last few days at his own house, catching up with his flatmates, and dodging the repeated harassment they threw at him for abandoning everything to spend Christmas by my side.

Gabe arrived before I did and I flashed him a hesitant smile before heading into the storeroom to pull on my apron.

"Well, well, well," Mark said, leaning against the doorframe. "Mrs Robinson finally returns to face the music."

"Good to see you too, Mark," I replied, giving him a wry smile. "How was your time off?"

"Time off?" he said. "What time off? Unlike you, I was chained to this god-forsaken place for all of the holiday break."

Peta walked in from the back, sweeping past Mark with a steaming tray of muffins. "God has not forsaken this café, thank you very much, Mark Hofstadter. Ren?" she called back over her shoulder. "Can you man the register? It's getting a little hectic out here."

Mark stuck his head around the corner to peer into the café. "Someone's acting as your protector today." He smirked.

I rolled my eyes and walked over to the counter to serve the one person waiting in line. I keyed in their order and repeated it to Gabe who moved to fill the jug with milk, brushing himself against me every time he moved past. Jordan was just finishing her shift and looked at me with daggers. Gabe grinned at her, but she refused to smile, huffing loudly as she removed her apron.

"I don't know why we didn't just let everyone know earlier," Gabe whispered in my ear. "This is going perfectly."

"I think our definitions of perfect are a little different."

Gabe laughed, a carefree happy laugh that made my heart sing as he pecked a kiss to my nose.

"Am I going to have to speak to you about PDA in the workplace, Gabe Thornton?" Peta asked as she walked back from where she was filling a basket with the still warm muffins. "This is an order for the business two doors down. Be a dear and deliver it for me, would you?"

Gabe bowed. "Anything you say, boss lady."

He took the basket off Peta and kissed me again before heading out the door, grinning stupidly at Peta's over-exaggerated frown.

Someone cleared their throat behind me, and Peta glanced up before giving me a warning glare. "Derek," she said tightly. "I didn't expect to see you here."

"I've come to talk to Lauren," he said.

I turned around slowly, unsure of why he was there. "Can I help you with something?" I asked, crossing my arms.

"Your mother told me you were returning to work today."

"How nice that you two are still talking," I said.

Derek cleared his throat and looked uneasily around the café. "I just came to apologise. I had no idea what your mother had planned. I would have never put you through that, if I had known."

"Okay," I said.

"I didn't know that you hadn't told her everything. I thought she knew about..." He left the sentence unfinished.

The door opened and Gabe walked back into the café. He froze when he saw Derek, before his shoulders rose and he walked behind the counter to stand beside me.

"Gabe," Derek said and nodded in his direction.

"Derek," Gabe acknowledged. "Is there something we can help you with? Another soy latte perhaps?"

"I just came to apologise to Lauren. I had no idea what her mother had planned. I had no idea that you two were together and I must admit it took me by surprise."

Gabe slung his arm around my shoulder. "And?" he asked.

"And I just wanted to apologise. I felt awful for the way things went down."

"Well, you've apologised now," I said, jutting my chin out a little. I didn't want Derek here. He wasn't part of my life anymore. He had chosen a different path, and now he needed to let me find my own.

"I have," Derek said.

We all stood in an awkward silence, Derek fumbling with the keys in his hand before finally speaking again. "Do you think I could talk to you for a moment alone?" he asked me, then added, "Please?"

I narrowed my eyes. "What about?"

"Alone?" he said again, jerking his head in Gabe's direction.

I expected Gabe to protest, but he merely kissed the tip of my nose and said he would be in the kitchen if I needed him. As soon as he walked through the doorway, Mark bellowed at him to leave, but Peta quickly hushed him. I was sure they were all standing just out of sight, straining to hear what Derek would say.

"I received a call from a Tyler Thornton," Derek said once we were alone.

"From Tyler?" I asked, confused.

"Yes. He claimed to be checking out your work history but it felt like something more. It felt like he was digging for information on you. He asked how long we were together."

"He did?"

"Yes," Derek said, getting annoyed. "Do you think I'd lie to you?"

"You've done it before." I couldn't help the dig at our past.

Derek chose to ignore the comment. "How well do you know the Thorntons? Are you considering working for them? Are you aware of their reputation?"

"I hardly see how it is any of your business," I said.

"I still care for you, Ren."

"Don't call me that," I warned.

"I'm just looking out for you. The Thorntons are a powerful family. They could destroy your career in a heartbeat, if they wanted. They are ruthless when it comes to business."

"Destroy my career?" I laughed. "You mean the one I gave up for you?"

"It wasn't just for me, Ren. It was for the baby too."

"I told you not to call me that." Tears smarted in my eyes.

"I just don't want to see you hurt."

The tears quickly dissolved, replaced with anger. "See me hurt? How can you even say that with a straight face? You were the one who hurt me, Derek. You hurt me when you walked out, remember? You hurt me when you told me you no longer wanted me because I couldn't give you children. You hurt me when you fucked another woman!" I was yelling, but I didn't care.

The few customers that were in the café looked over at us, but I refused to back down. How dare he come in here and claim to care about me. He had been the person to hurt me the most, and yet, he was worried about a business partnership with the Thorntons.

"Leave," I ordered.

"They are powerful people, Ren. They will—"

"Leave!" I ordered again.

Peta shuffled out of the kitchen and over to Derek, smiling apologetically at the startled customers. "I think it best you leave." She ushered Derek out the door.

"I was just looking out for you, Ren," Derek called over his shoulder.

Peta gave him an extra shove at the door and then turned to apologise to the customers, offering them a free cup of coffee for their inconvenience. I walked out to the storeroom, trying not to cry. Gabe, Mark and Peta all followed.

"I'm so sorry," I said, bursting into tears. "I never meant to do that in front of the customers. It was very unprofessional of me."

Peta hushed me and pulled me in for an embrace. "Hey," she said. "They got coffee and a show. I should be charging them extra."

"I didn't know whether to come out or not." Gabe stood awkwardly beside Mark, looking on as Peta embraced me. "What did he say to upset you? Do you want me to go after him? I'll knock some sense into him if you say the word."

"How brutish and manly of you," Mark drawled.

"It was nothing," I said, pulling myself away from Peta and wiping my eyes. "I don't even know why I'm crying. It's stupid. It was nothing."

Mark and Peta shared a knowing glance and left the storeroom, leaving me and Gabe alone. He pulled me into his arms and I sighed, feeling stupid for letting Derek get under my skin once again.

"I'm sorry," I said, my mouth against the fabric of the t-shirt covering his chest.

"You're not the one who needs to say sorry. I should have stayed. I shouldn't have left him alone with you. What did he say?"

I shook my head. "It was nothing. It was stupid," I repeated. I don't know why I didn't tell him that Tyler had called Derek. It seemed like such a strange thing for Tyler to do, and yet, I guess maybe with the unconventional way I had got the job, he decided he needed some references. Maybe it had nothing to do with the fact that I had been engaged to Derek. Maybe it was simply because I had worked with him.

13

LAUREN

The day February arrived, Gabe announced that he had enrolled in an architecture course at the local polytechnic, starting in a week. It would mean that he would have to cut back on his shifts at the café, and it would be a struggle financially for him, but it would also mean the start of him chasing his dream.

The day February arrived was also the day I heard from Tyler. It was a simple text message that enquired if it would suit me to do the first photoshoot at the casino the following week, the same day Gabe started his course. I quickly checked my scheduled shifts and, discovering his request fell on one of my days off, sent back a reply to say that it suited fine. The next text was simply a confirmation of flights there and back on the same day.

If Gabe was nervous about starting his course, it didn't show. He didn't appear to fuss over every little aspect like I was doing with the casino shoot. In fact, I was impressed at his patience as I attempted to pack the night before. Gabe was staying over and he lay on the bed, hands under his head and smiling at me, amused, while I sorted through lenses and tripods and reflectors and lights.

It had been years since I had used all my equipment, and worry chewed at my gut that it wouldn't be up to scratch.

"Dad and Tyler loved what you did with just a camera, having all this added stuff..." Gabe picked up one of the lenses and rolled it in his hands. "Well, that's just a bonus. Stop worrying. You'll be great."

I sunk onto the bed. "I can't help it. Worry is in my blood."

Gabe grinned. "Want me to take your mind off it?"

Gabe had made love to me every chance he got since we returned. His need was insatiable, and as much as I loved it, there were times I just longed to lay in bed without his hands roaming over my body.

"I need to get this sorted," I said.

Gabe rose to his knees, pouting. "Please?" he said. "It won't take long."

"Gabe." I put my hands on my hips and glared at him.

He laughed and held his hands up. "I suppose you need a break sometimes. But I'm warning you, it won't be for long. I'm not sure how long I can last without you." He lay back on the bed, cupping his hands behind his head and crossing his legs at the ankles. "God, you're sexy."

"I'm packing," I said, getting up and toying with one of the lenses.

"I don't really care what you're doing. You're sexy."

I looked over at where he lay across the bed, a cheeky smirk on his face and a bulge in his pants. "You're not so bad yourself."

"But not enough to tempt you?"

My shoulders fell in feigned frustration. "You are unbelievable. We've already had sex today."

"And?" he prompted.

"And... are you excited about starting your course tomorrow?" I changed the subject.

Gabe shrugged.

"A shrug? That's all I get?"

"I'll admit it's a lot less than I want to give you."

"Gabe," I warned again.

He laughed. "Okay, I'll stop. But I am a little worried about you heading away to spend the day with Tyler."

"I'm not spending the day with Tyler. I'm going up there to do a job. He probably won't even be there."

"Oh, he'll be there," Gabe replied. "No doubt he'll be waiting at the airport to pick you up."

I rolled my eyes. "Are you jealous?"

Gabe lifted an eyebrow. "Honestly? Yes. But I do have a way that you could help me feel a little better about it all." He grinned wickedly.

"Do you ever give up?" I asked.

"On you? Never?" Gabe leapt from the bed and scooped me in his arms, lifting me off the ground and kissing me deeply. When he threw me onto the bed, panic hit as the lenses jostled on the mattress. Climbing on top of me, Gabe caged my body with his thighs. "Just give me a little something to remember you by."

"It's one day," I said, but I couldn't help laughing.

Gabe kissed my nose. "One day too many, if you ask me." He kissed my lips and then my neck. A small wave of heat flushed at the apex of my thighs and I began to rethink my refusal. Still kissing the curve of my neck, Gabe lifted up the hem of my shirt and exposed the soft flesh of my stomach. "You're so beautiful," he said, lowering his mouth. Only, instead of peppering me with kisses, he held me tight and blew a raspberry on my stomach, causing me to close in on myself, paralysed with laughter.

"And here you thought I was only after one thing," Gabe said. He held my protesting arms above my head and brought his mouth to my stomach again, the vibrations sending me into another fit of laughter.

* * *

Instead of my alarm waking me the next morning, it was Gabe's hands gently massaging my breasts. His head dipped under the sheet and his mouth found its way to my nipple, pulling it into his mouth. I rolled my head to the side, the bright red numbers on my clock showing that it was ten in the morning. Panic jolted through me.

"Gabe!" I exclaimed.

His head popped up from under the covers. "Morning, beautiful."

"It's ten o'clock," I all but shouted.

Gabe looked at me, confused. "What time does your plane leave?"

"What time does your course start?" I shot back.

"Shit!" Gabe tossed the covers away and leapt from the bed, his pale backside bringing a smile to my face. He ruffled through the mess of clothes lying on the floor. "Shit, shit, shit," he said before slumping onto the bed. "Is there really any point in going?"

"Gabe!" I scolded. "You can't start out by missing the first day."

"But arriving over an hour late is okay?"

"Better than not arriving at all."

Gabe reached down and pulled a shirt over his head before standing up to face me, his erection proud and strong. "What am I going to do about this?"

"Want me to whack it with a pencil?"

Shock twisted Gabe's expression. "Not exactly what I was thinking. Why would you whack it with a pencil?"

I shrugged. "I heard somewhere it's what the nurses do in the rest homes when the old fellas get a little over excited."

"Well I'm not an old fella, and you're not a nurse. I can think of things I would far rather you do with it. Things that don't involve a pencil."

I shook my head and reached down to the ground where his jeans lay and flung them at him. "Get dressed." I laughed.

Gabe put one foot through the leg of his jeans. "Maybe I should stay and make sure you get to the airport okay." His eyes lit up. "Maybe I should just come to the city with you."

"Or maybe you should go and start the course you enrolled for."

Gabe fought with the other leg of his jeans. "And you don't want a quickie?"

I threw my pillow at his head. He ducked and grinned, leaning over to plant a kiss on my nose. "Catch you later, beautiful. Hope you press the shutter well."

"Hope you listen well," I shouted as he left the room.

Flopping back down, I tucked the blankets under my chin once he was gone. I didn't need to be at the airport for another hour and a half, so I had plenty of time to shower and get ready.

Smudge strolled into the room and appeared to look around for Gabe. The traitorous cat loved Gabe, despite the fact that I was the one who served him. Since arriving back, Gabe had spent most nights at my place. His toothbrush sat on my bathroom counter. His clothes were sprawled across my floor. His scent clung to my pillows.

I drove the short trip to the airport and checked in online, using the link to the app that Tyler had sent me. There had been very little communication about what was expected of the photoshoot and I didn't even know what stage the construction was at. I didn't know whether to expect a large building rising to the skyline or nothing but the foundation. But I was guessing, if Tyler wanted me there, there would be more to photograph than a concrete pad.

I hadn't told any of my family about my new job, mainly because when the consent for the casino was brought to the public's attention, my mother was one of the first in line to travel to the city to protest it. I doubted if finding out that her daughter was involved in some way was going to help our already strained relationship at all.

I had flopped down with my single carry-on into a chair to wait for the signal to board when my phone vibrated in my pocket. It was Billie.

Billie had decided that we were to be best friends and texted me repeatedly. A lot. Many times. She informed me when a large chain-store showed interest in stocking her clothing label. She texted through photos of the fashion show. She texted when she spent the morning vomiting after consuming, yet again, too much alcohol. This text was merely to wish me luck for my first day on the job. It was nice of her, but I wasn't sure if I was as invested in this new-found friendship as she was. While in high school, we knew each other but never really got along. And now, the only thing we shared in common was being with men from the same family. And that in itself was awkward enough without us becoming best friends. Well, on her end at least. No one would, or could, ever replace Peta.

Tyler did not meet me off the plane. In his place was a smiling, pimply-faced boy holding a sign which had my name on it. He grinned awkwardly when I approached and stuck out his hand. "Jimmy," he said.

I shook his hand then pointed to the sign. "Lauren."

"Mr Thornton said to say he was awfully sorry he couldn't meet you himself, but he got tied up on a conference call." He stuck out his hand again. "I'm Jimmy."

I smiled and shook his hand again, once more pointing to the sign. "Lauren."

He laughed nervously. "Yeah, right. We've already been over that, haven't we? Sorry. I'm not usually the one doing this sort of stuff. I'm just the dogsbody around the construction site. This is the first time they've trusted me with something so big."

"I'm not that big, am I?" I teased.

Colour flooded Jimmy's cheeks. "I—I'm—I didn't mean—" he stammered.

I laughed. "It's okay, Jimmy. I was just teasing." Somehow the nervousness of the boy relieved some of mine. "Shall we get going?"

"Have you got more bags or anything?"

I held up the pack hanging from my hand. "I've got everything I need right here."

Jimmy threw the sign into a rubbish bin before running his hands down his pants. "Right then, let's go. I've parked a little far away. I hope you don't mind walking a bit. I wasn't sure where I was supposed to park and there were all these signs everywhere saying taxi lane, and bus lane and big crosses and green ticks. In the end, I just pulled to the side and hoped I wouldn't get towed." Jimmy stopped walking. "You don't think they will have towed the car, do you? The boss would kill me if I got Mr Thornton's car towed." His face paled and he started walking quicker, muttering under his breath, "Please don't let the car have been towed."

"You've got Hamish's car?" I asked.

Jimmy shook his head. "Hamish?"

"Mr Thornton," I clarified.

"Hell, no." He looked at me quickly. "No, ma'am."

"Ma'am?" I repeated. "I'm not that old, am I? Please, call me Lauren."

Jimmy nodded seriously, promising not to call me ma'am again. "I work for the company that has the construction contract. And I believe Mr Thornton's name is Tyler, not Hamish, all due respect, ma'am."

I pursed my lips together at his insistence on calling me ma'am. "You call Tyler Mr Thornton?"

"Everyone calls him Mr Thornton," Jimmy said reverently.

We walked out of the airport building and I followed Jimmy as he walked briskly down the sidewalk. He wasn't exaggerating when he said he had parked a long way away.

When we finally reached the car, the same sleek black one that Tyler had driven during the Christmas holidays, Jimmy popped the boot and then cursed when he realised I had carried my bag the whole way. "I should have carried that for you." He cursed again. "Please don't tell Mr Thornton. He made me promise to treat you with the utmost respect."

I smiled and tapped my nose, winking at Jimmy as he roughly threw my bag into the boot. I winced as it bounced on the hard floor. "It will be our little secret. But there will be no hiding if you break any of my equipment though."

"Shit," Jimmy said, picking my bag back up and placing it more gently in the boot. "Fuck!" he exclaimed. "He also told me not to curse and here I am swearing like a trouper. I'm awfully sorry about that."

"I'm sure I will survive your disgusting language somehow."

"I'm so sorry," he started before seeing my grin. "Oh, okay. You're kidding. I'm really sorry, I'm just so fucking nervous. The boss hasn't trusted me with anything this important before." He looked up at me, grinning, before it dawned on him that he had sworn again. "Fuck, I did it again, didn't I?" He shook his head. "Fudge, I meant, fudge. Sorry, the construction site isn't really the best place for restraining colourful language."

Jimmy held open the passenger door and I climbed into the seat. "You can stop being so nervous, Jimmy. You're doing a fine job."

Jimmy manoeuvred his way out of the airport and soon we were weaving into the traffic that flowed into the centre of the city.

"Mr Thornton told me to take you straight to the site, is that okay? Do you need to stop for food or anything? Are you staying at a motel that you need to check into?"

I shook my head. "It's just a quick trip up and back in one day."

"Mr Thornton said you were a brilliant photographer."

"Well, I can confirm that I do take photos."

Jimmy laughed. "I guess that's a good start."

Fortunately, the traffic wasn't bad and it wasn't long before we pulled up to the construction site. A large sign boasting 'Thornton Industries' sat proudly at the entrance. Two people sat under it, holding signs condemning gamblers to hell.

"That's Dustan and Daisy," Jimmy said, rolling down the window and waving to them as we passed. "They're here every single day."

"Every day?" I repeated.

Jimmy nodded. "Mr Thornton says he admires their commitment to their beliefs and sends them lunch each day. They refuse to eat it though, claiming it was bought with blood money. I'm not sure where they think Mr Thornton made his money, but I'm pretty sure he never killed anyone for it."

At least Jimmy was entertaining.

The casino was more than a concrete pad, but little more than framework. Scaffolding stretched high into the sky and men with harnesses wandered over it with barely a care that they were high above the ground. As we crossed over the tape that signalled the construction site, Jimmy reached into a tub and pulled out a hard hat.

"Here," he said, holding one out to me as he placed another over his head. "It's the rules."

In the far corner of the site, Tyler stood with his back to me, phone placed on his ear. He wore a dark suit that accentuated his broad shoulders and tapered down to his hips. He wasn't wearing a hard hat. When he turned, his eyes flashed, but he didn't smile. He strode over, informing the person on the other end of the line that something important had come up, and held his hand out. "Lauren."

I shook his offered hand and smiled nervously. All the anxiety that had left at Jimmy's appearance returned with a vengeance. "Mr Thornton," I said, mimicking the way Jimmy spoke of him.

Tyler's head tilted to the side and a ghost of a smile crossed his face. "I hope the lad looked after you well?"

"Jimmy performed his duties perfectly," I replied, giving the boy a warm and reassuring smile.

Tyler dismissed him with a jerk of his head and nodded for me to walk with him. "He's a good kid, that one," he said as Jimmy disappeared around a corner.

"He is," I agreed.

"Off to a good start considering he's only twenty-one."

"Twenty-one?" I asked, it suddenly dawning on me why Tyler sent him to collect me. Jimmy, little, nervous, pimply Jimmy was the same age as Gabe.

"Yes," Tyler confirmed. "Maybe I should have sent someone else? I know how tempting men of that age are for you."

Anger flooded my veins but I chose to ignore Tyler's comment. I didn't see what else I could do. "Do you have any instructions?" I asked tersely.

"Instructions?" Tyler mused. He crossed his arms and stared high into the air. "There are many things I could think of to instruct you to do, but in this particular case, I'm going to leave it up to you. Just do what you did at the show home. I like the way you see things, showing the flaws as beauty."

"Is that what you think I did?"

"It was, wasn't it? Well, that's the way I saw them. You are very talented. I haven't come across anyone else who sees through the lens the way you do."

"Thank you," I said, and then added, "I think." Even though he was essentially complimenting me, there was a general hint of amusement in his tone.

Jimmy strolled past pushing a wheelbarrow and waved.

"So, how's my little brother?" Tyler asked.

I gritted my teeth at his smirk. "He's not little."

Tyler lifted a brow. "Good to know. We Thornton men aren't known for being small."

I resisted the urge to roll my eyes. Even though Tyler was extraordinarily handsome, he was also infuriatingly annoying. At least it kept me in check when my eyes got stuck on him.

"Billie informs me he has enrolled in some sort of class?"

"Architecture. It is his first day today," I said.

"And he made it on time?" Tyler asked.

I remembered the panic of the morning. "Of course. He's a lot more responsible than you think."

"Forgive me if I reserve judgement. I've known Gabe a lot longer than you."

Tyler's phone rang and he pulled it out of his pocket, quickly checking the screen before bringing it to his ear. He answered with one word. "Speak." Then he fell silent, listening to the voice on the other end which was nothing more than a faint mumble to my ears. "Okay, okay," he said, as though calming someone. "I'll be there soon. No. Don't go anywhere. Don't move, just wait there." His eyes flicked over to mine. "I know you don't want to put me out, but I told you to call if you needed me. You obviously need me. I'm on my way." The voice continued, low, dark and pained. "Yes. Nothing important." Again Tyler's eyes flicked to mine. "It's fine, Jake. Fine. Yes, I know where it is. Be there soon."

"Sorry," he said, turning his attention back to me. "I'm afraid I'm going to have to leave you to it. Just get what shots you would be interested in seeing if it was your money being invested in the place."

"You're leaving?"

"You can handle this on your own, can't you? I will get Jimmy to show you around and make sure you don't walk anywhere you shouldn't. This is a construction site. You need to be careful." He looked down at the flimsy shoes I was wearing, toes exposed. "Next time bring better footwear."

"Yes, sir," I said with mock severity.

Tyler scowled. "I look forward to seeing what you produce."

"As will I," I mumbled under my breath.

"Sorry, I didn't catch that," Tyler said, raising an eyebrow.

"You weren't supposed to."

Tyler looked around the site and signalled for Jimmy to come over. Jimmy started to run but Tyler shouted at him, telling him not to run on a construction site.

"Is everything okay with Jake?" I asked.

"He's staying with me at the moment. He isn't doing too well."

"I'm sorry," I replied. I couldn't imagine the things Jake had seen while he was overseas. He hadn't told his family anything about his time over there. They knew nothing of what he had seen, where he had been, what he had done. "Has he talked to you about any of it yet?"

Tyler shook his head as Jimmy reached us, grinning from ear to ear. "What's up?"

"I have a matter to attend to and I need you to escort Lauren around the site. Make sure she doesn't get into anything dangerous."

Anything dangerous? He sounded like he was giving instructions to a babysitter. There were signs all over the site, warning of possible dangers, placing restrictions on access. Everything I needed to keep safe was plainly spelled out.

"I can read," I said.

Tyler grunted and started to walk away before turning and walking backwards, grinning at me as he said, "It was good to see you fully dressed this time, Lauren."

Jimmy looked over questioningly.

"Don't ask." I shook my head. "Is he always this pleasant?"

Jimmy threw his head back and laughed, causing his hard hat to wobble on his head. "Mr Thornton isn't one for pleasantries."

We spent the next two hours strolling around the site. As well as the usual photos of the construction, the working men, and the progress of the build, I made sure to include images that caught my eye. Footprints in the dust. A half-eaten sandwich sitting on a beam of wood, the cluttered work site blurred in the background. An orange hard hat hanging on a nail.

It was exactly two hours before my flight left when there was only one image I wanted to capture. It required shooting from above, so I instructed Jimmy to find me an extension ladder, and he held it firmly at the base as I climbed the rungs, my camera banging against my chest with each step. The sun was just beginning to set and there was always something magical about any object when photographed in the golden glow of twilight. Even a construction site. The men's hard hats glinted in the sun, their tanned arms covered in a sheen of sweat, wet patches under their armpits. I was just taking the final images when a gruff voice sounded below.

"Just what do you think you're doing?"

I looked down to find Tyler glaring up at me, arms crossed and mouth in a hard line. "You're back," I said before training my eye back on the camera and pressing the shutter once more.

"Get down from there this instant."

I let the camera fall around my neck. "Why?"

"Why?" Tyler's frown deepened. "You're up a ladder on a construction site."

"There are many people doing more dangerous things than that," I said, looking around at the varying positions some of the workers were in.

"They are employed to be in those positions. You are not employed to be in that position."

I turned my back to Tyler and took a step down the ladder. "I needed to be up here to get the angle I wanted." Reaching the bottom, I stood on firm ground, squinting up at Tyler. "And I'm not employed by you, I am contracted by you. You didn't exactly give me any instructions, and I was merely doing what I thought was best, so which position did you expect me to be in?"

Tyler's mouth twitched. "Not a dangerous one."

"I was up a ladder. It hardly calls for danger money."

"But it does mean that since this is my project, and my father's company running it, anything which happens on this site is my responsibility. If you were to fall and injure yourself, I would be held legally responsible. I am not ordering you to not climb ladders because I am worried about your safety, I am ordering you not to climb ladders because I'm worried about the legalities of it."

My skin prickled. "Ordering me?"

"In this case, yes."

I lifted the camera from around my neck and placed it securely in my pack. "I will be sure to follow orders next time, Mr Thornton."

"That's all I ask." Tyler strode away and talked to the site manager while I packed my gear away.

"I think they'll be the best shots," Jimmy said quietly.

"Thank you, Jimmy. I think so too."

14

LAUREN

Tyler insisted on driving me back to the airport, even though I assured him that Jimmy could complete the task. He barely spoke and the silence weighed heavily on me. I was fine with silence, but this one was too obvious, too strained. I instructed him to simply drop me off, rather than walking me to the terminal, and he seemed more than happy to oblige.

Even though my car was waiting in the airport car park, Gabe was there to greet me. He embraced me, lifting me off the ground and planting a sloppy kiss on my forehead.

"I missed you," he said and I couldn't help but return his brilliant smile. Dressed in his usual jeans and t-shirt, his blond hair was loose and falling to his shoulders, the sides still short from Billie's haircut, though they were beginning to grow.

"I missed you too." I kissed him briefly before throwing my pack over my shoulder. "How was your first day?"

"Boring," Gabe replied. "Extremely boring."

"Many people in the class?"

"A few. How was the big smoke? How was Tyler?"

"He wasn't there for most of it," I said. "Something to do with Jake."

Concern crossed Gabe's face as we exited the terminal and started the short walk to the carpark. "Is he okay?"

"I'm not sure. Tyler doesn't exactly give much away."

Gabe snorted. "You noticed that too, huh? He's a great conversationalist. I sometimes think that if he can't phrase something as a direct order, he simply doesn't bother saying it."

Gabe walked with me to my car, leaning on the passenger door. "The boys have ordered pizza, you good with that?"

"The boys?" I questioned.

"I told them you'd come over tonight. I hope that's okay." Gabe pulled himself off the car and wrapped his arms around my waist, smiling and planting a small kiss on my nose. "I kind of want to show you off a little, you know. We haven't been to my house since we've been officially dating."

I sighed. "I've got a lot of work to do."

"Do it later," he said.

"But I've got to sort through the photos and edit them all before sending them through to Tyler. He's expecting them tomorrow."

Gabe laughed. "See? An order. Just ignore him. Do it tomorrow night. You aren't working tomorrow and he can just wait."

"Tomorrow night we're going out with Peta and Shrek for dinner, remember?"

"Shit," Gabe cursed. "And here I was planning on spending the night in bed with you."

"I thought you said I could edit the photos then?"

"I may have tried to distract you once or twice."

"How about we go to your place, have pizza and then I'll just leave a little early and sort through the photos. You can stay at your place for the night."

Gabe pouted, then tugged me close and bent his head to my neck. "But I want to play with you tonight."

I pushed him away playfully. "You can play with me tomorrow night." Gabe's eyes gleamed. "After we go out for dinner," I added.

We drove our separate cars and arrived at Gabe's house. The music pumped through the open windows and the pizza delivery man pulled up just as we did, so we took the pizzas from him and walked inside.

"Lauren!" Drew said when I walked in. "It's so good to see you. This guy has been talking about you non-stop, so now that you're actually here, maybe I will get a break from his constant whinging about how wonderful you are."

"Well, look at her." Gabe placed the pizza boxes on the coffee table. "How could I not go on?" Flopping onto the couch, he tugged me onto his lap.

Stefan emerged from his room, hair mussed up and sleep in his eyes. "Oh," he said. "You're here."

"Nice to see you too," I replied sarcastically.

We ate pizza and watched some reality show of naked people left alone in the wilderness to fend for themselves. I didn't get it, but Stefan cursed at their choices and Drew yelled at the TV, proclaiming it wasn't real. All I could think about were the images I had shot. I was keen to get to my computer and start sorting through them. When enough time had passed that I felt it polite to leave, I excused myself and walked out the door, Gabe following close behind.

"I wish you didn't have to leave," he said, pulling me close.

"You'll see me tomorrow," I replied, stretching on my tiptoes and placing a chaste kiss on his forehead. He jerked me tighter, my chest pressing against his.

"I'm not letting you away with that."

Lowering his mouth to mine, he kissed me gently, his lips moving over mine seductively. Then his hands moved up my back and knotted into the hair at the base of my neck, forcing our kiss deeper. I surrendered, pushing further into him as though I could lose myself in his skin, running my hands over his shoulders and gripping onto the firmness of the muscles that covered them.

Finally, Gabe broke away from our embrace. "There," he said, grinning down at me and seeing the desire lurking in my eyes. "Now you can go."

* * *

I stared at the photos on the computer until my eyes were sore and glazed. Some of the images were great. I was happy with them. Others were crap. I sorted through them, selecting the ones I considered worth editing, and deleting the ones that made my skin crawl before climbing into bed, well after midnight. Sleep came quickly and I was up early the next morning to start work on them. I barely noticed the time and worked through lunch, only stopping for the odd cup of coffee, and around four o'clock in the afternoon, I finally emailed them through to Tyler. I didn't include any message, just sent through a few of the images, the ones I thought the investors would be most interested to see, and included the link to the cloud-based software Tyler had requested I use. I waited for a few minutes, clicking on the 'send and receive' button in a desperate attempt for a response to arrive, before admitting to myself that Tyler was probably not waiting at his computer. I had just enough time to flick through the shower, actually get changed out of my pyjamas for the day, and slap on a little makeup before Gabe arrived to take me to the restaurant.

As usual, Peta and Shrek were late. Peta bustled in, face flushed, hair slightly in disarray, Shrek following silently in her wake, and sat down at the table, dumping her handbag on the seat next to her.

"I thought we were never going to make it. First, Henry vomited all over himself, then Charlie decided that he would prefer to eat the cat's biscuits rather than the dinner I made him. Then the babysitter arrived late, and, to top it all off, Nic claimed to have a sore tummy and ran after us just as we were pulling away. I tell you, we're lucky to be here at all."

Shrek removed the bag she had dumped on his chair and placed it on the table.

"Hello," he said, a smile crossing his face at his wife's rambling confession.

"Do I feel like red or white today?" Peta turned to her husband.

"Definitely red," he replied.

"I've never been so pleased for January to end," she said, referring to her sugar-free month. Flicking her hand into the air, Peta signalled for a waiter and ordered two glasses of red. Then she turned to Shrek. "Anything for you?"

It was the first time the four of us had really spent any time together. Gabe was quiet, his hand resting on my thigh under the cover of the table. I knew he wasn't interested in dinner when his hand crept higher and higher, inching the hemline of my skirt up until his fingers moved down to caress the bare skin he had left exposed. A shudder ran over me and I squeezed my thighs shut. But Gabe, still staring intently at Peta as she explained in entirely too much detail about their Christmas dinner at the in-laws, inched them apart again, his thumb moving in gentle circles over the sensitive flesh of my inner thigh.

When our meals arrived, venison for the men and pork belly for Peta and I, the tingling sensation between my legs had intensified to the point where I could barely eat. Gabe didn't even look at me. He engaged Peta and Shrek in conversation, ate his meal and drank his beer as though he had been doing nothing at all. Determined to wipe the calm expression off his face, I placed my knife and fork neatly on my plate as my mother had taught me, and slid my hand across his thigh. Unlike him though, I didn't play around, I moved straight to the bulge that I knew was there and gripped it hard, giving it a gentle squeeze. Gabe choked on a mouthful of venison and coughed, smacking his chest.

"Excuse me," he said, still coughing. "Something must have gone down the wrong hole."

I patted him on the back with my free hand. "Are you okay?" I asked. "You look a little flushed."

Gabe turned to me, his eyes flashing with a mixture of desire and amusement. "I feel great," he said.

"So, how's the course coming along?" Shrek's words were mumbled by a mouthful of food.

I stroked Gabe under the table feeling him grow under my hand.

"Great," Gabe replied, his voice a little higher than normal. He cleared his throat, his eyes closing just a fraction as I toyed with one of the buttons on his jeans. "It's great. Wonderful."

A strange look passed between Peta and Shrek.

I worked the button away from its hole and poked a finger through the opening. Finding the tip of him, I massaged it through the thin fabric of his boxer shorts. He twitched, straining further against the restrictive material of his jeans.

"It's great," Gabe said again. "Really, really good. So good."

My phone started ringing and I released my hold on Gabe to reach into my bag. Tyler's number was displayed on the screen.

"Excuse me," I said getting to my feet. "I've got to take this." And at Peta's enquiring look, I added, "It's about the photoshoot."

Walking out past the bathrooms and into the little courtyard reserved for smokers, I swiped the accept button and brought the phone to my ear. "Speak," I said, mimicking the way Tyler had answered earlier in the day.

There was silence on the other end for a moment before Tyler cleared his throat. "Lauren?"

"Were they okay? Did you like them?" I blurted out, unable to stand pleasantries.

"They were adequate."

My heart sank. "Adequate?" My voice cracked a little.

"They weren't what I was expecting."

"You never told me what you expected," I said, growing a little annoyed.

"I told you to do what you did at the showroom. You didn't. The images were fine, but they were what I would have expected from the original photographer we had organised. There were none of you in there."

"I didn't know I was hired to take selfies."

Tyler let out an exasperated snort of air. "That's not what I meant. I meant, I didn't get to see the site through your eyes. That's what I wanted, not just the regular shots of the construction progress. Yes, I need those, but I wanted more."

I thought of the images I hadn't uploaded. The one of the boot prints in dust. The half-eaten sandwich. "I've got those," I said quietly. "I just didn't send them."

"Could you send them now?"

"I'm out for dinner."

"With Gabe?" His voice stayed in the same gruff tone.

"And friends."

"Well, I will let you finish your dinner. Send through the rest of the photos as soon as you get the chance."

"I will," I promised, a little relief working itself into the tightness of my chest. "I'll send them as soon as I get home tonight."

"Lauren?" Tyler asked.

The door to the restaurant opened and Gabe walked through, looking at me enquiringly.

I pointed to the phone and mouthed "Tyler."

Gabe rolled his eyes.

"Yes," I replied to Tyler.

"I look forward to seeing you again. Does Thursday next week suit?"

I mentally scanned through the café shifts in my mind. I was pretty sure I had a shift that day, but considering I was best friends with the boss, I should be able to swap it for another.

"Thursday will suit fine."

"I will see you then."

"Okay," I said hesitantly.

"Wear decent shoes," Tyler ordered and then hung up.

Gabe grinned. "I would have come out here sooner but I was a little afraid to stand. You left me with a hard-on and an open fly."

15

LAUREN

The first thing Tyler did when he greeted me off the plane was look down at my shoes. I had chosen the sturdiest pair of boots I owned. They were black and plain and boring in every way.

"Those are what you're wearing?" he asked, turning on his heel and striding away before I could respond. Despite being annoyed by his abruptness, a wave of guilt washed over me when my eyes dropped to his backside and the way it looked wrapped so nicely in dark trousers, but I quickly told myself there was no harm in looking. And that was all I was doing. Looking.

I followed him out of the terminal and over to his car. Tyler held the door open for me. There was a package resting on the seat.

"I got something for you."

"For me?" I asked.

"I just said it was for you. Must you question everything?"

"Do I?" I replied, letting a smirk cover my face. Tyler's expression softened, and the smallest of smiles appeared in the corners of his mouth.

"Oh," I said. "You can smile."

"Occasionally my muscles may spasm into what could be considered a smile, but I assure you it's not. Get in and open the package."

"Yes, Mr Thornton," I replied and got into the car, careful to lift the package onto my lap first. It was a simple cardboard box. No marketing packaging surrounded it. There were no words on the side. Curious, I lifted the edge and peered inside. I couldn't see anything but darkness.

"Just open it," Tyler said.

I ripped the tape holding the box together and pulled the sides open.

"Boots?" I said, looking down at the now open box.

"Sturdy boots for walking around a construction site."

"So kind of you," I said dryly, bending down to remove my less-sturdy boots. The new ones were brown and had steel caps over the toes.

"Do you like them?"

I couldn't tell from Tyler's expression whether he was serious or not. "Honestly?" I asked.

"Why would I want you to lie?"

"They are rather ugly."

Tyler snorted. "They aren't supposed to be pretty. They are for safety purposes." He shifted down a gear as he turned off the highway. "What are you doing for dinner tonight?"

"Why?" I asked.

"Because I know your flight doesn't leave until later and you will need to eat."

"I hadn't really thought about it. I'll probably just grab something at the airport," I said, struggling to tug on the new boots.

"I will take you to dinner."

I stopped tugging to look up at him. "To dinner?"

A flicker of amusement crossed over Tyler's face. "Yes. To dinner. You will need to eat at some stage, as will I. You can ask for permission from Gabe, if you wish. Would you like to call him now?"

"I don't need permission," I said, roughly jerking on the final boot with a grunt.

"You don't?" Tyler smirked and lifted a single brow that brought images of Gabe flashing across my mind.

"I don't," I confirmed, reaching down to tuck the cuffs of my jeans into the boots and then frowning at the result.

Tyler's phone rang and Billie's voice filled the car. Hamish and Billie lived in the city most of the time and I hadn't told her I would be here. The thought of being dragged around city shops with Billie terrified me. I hated shopping at the best of times. I still had images of blocking doors and begging to be taken home while my mother and Morgan leisurely strolled from shop to shop.

"Billie," Tyler said, his voice showing no sign of emotion. "How can I help you?"

"You've got to help me," Billie wailed. "I can't go to your father. I just can't."

Tyler didn't hesitate. "What do you need?"

"Well," she began, taking a deep breath. "I thought I'd just pop to the mall and do a little shopping. I found this gorgeous dress. You would love it. It's black but sparkly."

Tyler looked at me, his eyes widening at her continuous chatter.

"Actually," Billie continued on speakerphone, "I'm thinking of using a similar material in my new line. But anyway, I'm getting distracted. The dress turned into two dresses, and then I had to add this gorgeous pantsuit, and a top and a couple of pair of tights. It's all research really. And then I saw these boots. Oh, my goodness. I simply had to have them."

Tyler sighed deeply. "And you called me, why?"

"Well, I got to the counter, and wouldn't you know it? I had left my wallet at home. I can't call Hamish because he'd just go on and on about it, how I ruined his schedule. You know what he's like. And the staff at the store are refusing to let me leave, even though they know I'm good for it. Would you pretty please come and pay for it? I just can't do it to your father. Not again. Not after last time. He got so annoyed and went on about it for days."

"We're on our way," Tyler said, turning off at the next intersection.

"We?" Billie asked.

I looked to Tyler, eyes wide and shook my head. "I'm not here," I mouthed.

"See you soon," Tyler said to Billie and pressed a button on the dash, cutting the call off. "Not a Billie fan?" he asked me.

"Huge fan," I said sarcastically. "Just in very small doses. I've already heard from her three times today and I kind of didn't tell her I'd be in the city."

We pulled up to the construction site and Tyler got out to open my door. "I will be back here at six to collect you for dinner."

"Six?" I repeated as I climbed out.

Tyler's jaw clenched. "Yes, six. I know it is a little early but I will need to get you to your flight on time and I don't want to feel rushed."

He must have noticed the nervous concern cross my face. Gabe didn't like Tyler. I hardly imagined he would be fine with me going to dinner with him.

"It's just dinner," Tyler said. "There is nothing to be afraid of."

"Afraid?" I replied. "Why would I be afraid?"

"You tell me," Tyler said, walking back to the driver's door. "By the way, the boots look good. Very Tomb Raider."

* * *

Jimmy followed me like a puppy around the construction site, constantly chatting as I took shot after shot. I think he enjoyed talking more than he enjoyed working, so accompanying me around the site was more of a break than a chore.

The progress was impressive. Concrete slab walls had appeared on some of the lower levels, and the building was beginning to take shape. Jimmy's eyes lit up as he listed off the restaurants, theatres and stores the development would house. One restaurant would be right at the top, the needle point of the building, and would afford magnificent views of the city, especially at night. Jimmy told me how it would be a revolving restaurant, slowly turning, its walls made only of glass so the diners would get a three hundred and sixty degree view.

When Tyler arrived at exactly six o'clock, Jimmy and I were in the middle of trying to manoeuvre our way through a particularly complex part of steel framework. There was an angle I wanted to get, looking straight up into the sky through the network of steel. When we finally managed to get where we needed to be, Jimmy gave me a high five, but his smile dropped when he turned and saw Tyler leaning against a concrete wall, arms crossed and glaring at us.

"Are you ready?" Tyler asked, his voice dripping with annoyance.

"Sorry." I gathered my gear. "I lost track of the time."

"Obviously." He lifted himself off his leaning post, his left arm and shoulder grey with dust, and walked over to Jimmy. "You were scheduled to finish work two hours ago."

Jimmy's face reddened. "Sorry, Mr Thornton. I was just helping Lauren and we kind of forgot the time."

"So she said. You may go now," Tyler instructed.

Jimmy nodded quickly at me, his eyes showing the slightest hint of fear at Tyler's stern tone and quickly disappeared.

"He was just helping me out," I said, slinging my pack full of equipment over my shoulder.

Tyler took the pack off me, carrying it himself. "I didn't realise you needed help. I would have come back, had I known."

"I can't expect you to do that. I'm sure you have far more important things to do than play my assistant."

"I know how to prioritise. It's something I learned at a very young age."

"And I'm a priority?"

"Yes."

By this stage, we had reached his vehicle. He placed my gear in the back and then held the door open. "Shall we?"

"I'll just make a quick call first," I said, ducking to the side and pulling my cell phone out of my pocket. I had meant to call Gabe earlier while Tyler was away but I got so involved in taking photos it had completely slipped my mind. It took a long time for Gabe to answer. When he finally did, music and laughter filled the background.

"Hey," he said, his voice in a slow drawl. "How's it going up there?"

"What's going on?" I asked. "It sounds like you're at a party."

Gabe laughed. "Nope. Just me and the boys taking some time off. You know, chilling, relaxing." Gabe laughed again.

I stepped further away from Tyler so he couldn't overhear our conversation. "You're stoned," I said.

"Yup," Gabe replied gleefully. "Delightfully so."

I took a deep breath. "I thought you were meeting me at the airport tonight. You dropped me off, remember? I don't have a car."

"Shit," Gabe said. There was a muffled sound and then Gabe's voice came back through the speaker. "Sorry, I dropped the phone. Would you be able to get a taxi home tonight? I'm in no state to drive."

I looked over to where Tyler waited, leaning against the car, glancing down at his watch.

"I'll sort something," I said, trying not to get annoyed. "I'm just heading out to dinner with your brother."

"Jake's there?" Gabe asked.

"No. I'm going with Tyler."

Gabe fell silent. All I could hear was the music in the background and the shouts and laughter of his flatmates.

"You there?" I asked finally.

"What?" Gabe almost shouted.

"I've got to go," I said. "Tyler's waiting."

"Okay." Gabe was distracted. "Rather you than me. Catch you tomorrow." And then he hung up.

"Everything okay?" Tyler lifted himself off the car and held the door open again. "Did you get permission?"

"I never asked for permission and Gabe is fine." I climbed into the car, my eyes falling to the sturdy boots and jeans I was wearing. "I'm hardly dressed to be going out for dinner though."

Tyler walked to the driver's side and hopped in. "We aren't going anywhere fancy."

"And yet you're dressed like that?"

Tyler was still wearing the black suit from earlier in the day. Despite a day's work, he looked impeccable. Not one strand of his slicked-back hair was out of place.

"What's wrong with the way I am dressed?" he asked.

"Nothing. It's just on a whole different level than where I'm at. Mind you," I added, my mouth curving into a smile. "I'm not covered in dust, despite having spent the last few hours at the site. You, on the other hand, were only there minutes."

The restaurant he had chosen was just a small house on the banks of the river. It didn't look like a restaurant. It looked like someone's home. But sure enough, when we walked inside a blackboard was placed at the entrance with 'Today's Menu' written in white chalk across the top. Tyler ushered me down a narrow hallway, his hand resting on the small of my back, and to a quaint outside dining area that held only five tables. None of them were occupied. I tried not to take notice of the heat radiating through my body from Tyler's touch. But when he removed his hand to pull out my chair, the coldness left behind made me shiver. Dust still covered one sleeve of his suit jacket and I ran my hand over his arm, trying to rid it. Tyler's eyes snapped to where my fingers brushed against him, his body stiffening at my touch.

"Sorry," I murmured, unsure of his reaction. "You were still covered in dust."

Our table looked over the river, with people floating in long boats down the lazy water, the courtyard covered in strings of drooping lights and paper lanterns. Soft guitar music played in the background and bowls of citrus fruit sat on each of the small tables.

"It's beautiful here," I said, as another long boat passed below.

"Not many people know about it." Tyler picked up a glass of water and took a sip. "I've been coming here for years. Maria, the woman who lives here, does all the cooking herself and only employs a single server to assist her. There is only ever capacity for five tables of two and Maria serves whatever she feels like on the day. You can't get better food. She is truly talented."

I thought of Mana's, the restaurant back home where I adored the pasta and doubted that Maria would be able to beat it. But I was willing to give her a chance.

The waitress came over and poured some wine into our glasses. Tyler held his up, tipping it slightly in my direction. "Here's to talented people," he said.

I mimicked his action and took a sip of the red. "So? No menu? No choice?" I asked.

"I find it relaxing to have the choice taken away. And I have tried dishes that I might have never tried before if Maria hadn't introduced me."

"But what about personal taste? What if she serves you something you despise?"

"Such as?" Tyler asked.

"Such as…" I paused trying to think of a food I hated. "Such as beetroot. I don't mind the taste of it, but I hate how it stains other foods. What if she serves me beetroot?"

"Then we shall change plates."

"She doesn't make everyone the same dish?"

Tyler shook his head. "Everyone's is unique. Maria has developed quite the reputation. I assure you, you won't be disappointed."

"That confident?"

"That confident," Tyler repeated.

With that, a high wail came from the kitchen and Maria appeared in the doorway, her chubby arms held wide open. "Tyler." She smiled and walked over to embrace him, her floured hands leaving marks on his jacket, joining the faint remnants of dust.

"Maria," Tyler said, stepping back from where he had bent low to return her affection. "I'd like you to meet Lauren Greer. Lauren, this is the wonderful Maria I was telling you about."

Maria took the tea towel off her shoulder and playfully flicked it at Tyler. "You are much too kind, Mr Thornton."

"Please, I've asked you to call me Tyler."

"But Tyler does not suit you," she replied sternly. "You are Mr Thornton."

"Well." Tyler sat back down. "How can I argue with that? What's on the menu tonight?"

Maria laughed heartily. "You know not to ask that, Mr Thornton. You have what you're given." She leaned over to me. "That's how it works here. I don't cook to please others. I cook to please myself."

"And I wouldn't have it any other way," Tyler said.

"You have a beautiful home." I looked over the white walls and faded and cracked blue window shutters.

Maria looked over at Tyler and wiggled her brows. "It is nice to see you with someone. You are always alone." She turned to me. "He is a handsome man, yes?"

I smiled at Tyler. "Yes, very handsome."

Tyler lifted one brow, questioningly. "Lauren is dating my younger brother."

"And not you, Mr Thornton?" Maria looked horrified.

"No, not me. Lauren is the photographer for the casino development."

Maria shook her head and made tutting sounds under her breath. "Mr Thornton is a very handsome man," she said. "You two would make a nice couple."

"Gabe is—"

But Maria cut me off with a swish of her tea towel. "Whoever Mr Gabe is, he is not Mr Thornton."

I had to hold in my laughter at her seriousness. "No, he is not."

Maria took a step back, peering down the hallway as another couple walked through the front door. "I bring you food." And then she was gone.

The meal consisted of six courses, each of them tiny and delicious, completely different from each other and stunningly beautiful in their simplicity. Even though I blanched a little when a plate of char-grilled baby octopus was placed in front of me, I surprised myself by not only eating it but enjoying it. Tyler wasn't a huge conversationalist but he listened to me as I talked of what I hoped to accomplish at the casino, as well as my complaints on how dull I found my job at the café, now that I had a taste of what my life as a photographer could be.

"You just wait until the investor party," Tyler said. "There will be many people who I'm sure will be dying to hire you once they've seen your work. You have a very unique eye. Just stick by me and I'll introduce you to them."

"I will be going?"

"Of course you'll be going," Tyler said. "Your photography will be displayed everywhere."

I took a sip of my wine, the silence between us growing awkward. "So," I said as I broke the toffee top of my lemongrass crème brulee. "What exactly is it you do, Mr Thornton."

"What do you mean?"

"I mean, you work for your father at Thornton Industries, you're overseeing the casino development, but what is it you actually do?"

Tyler leaned back in his chair. "I get people to do things."

"That is your job description?"

"Pretty much. I talk to people and get them to do what I want. I get them to buy things, sell things, build things, go to things, be things, whether it be by control or charm."

"Charm?" I tried to mimic the one eyebrow raise that he and Gabe did so masterfully.

"I can be quite charming when I wish to be."

I laughed. "I look forward to seeing it."

Once I had spooned the last mouthful of crème brulee into my mouth, we called into the kitchen to wish Maria goodbye and tell her how delicious her meals were. She brushed our praise aside and I was surprised when she moved to embrace me.

"You look after him, yes?" she said, nodding to Tyler.

There was no point in correcting her yet again, so I simply assured her I would.

The night had cooled somewhat, and without the warmth of the courtyard fire, I wrapped my arms tightly around my chest for the short walk back to the car. People still floated on the long boats down the river, the eerie glow of the paper lanterns lighting their way. I moved ahead of Tyler, drawing in a deep breath as I walked to the grass bank, the lights of the city twinkling in the background.

"I've never really thought of the city as beautiful," I said.

Tyler came to stand beside me, his hand dangling next to mine, only a breath of night air between us. I looked up to the sky but the pale glow of the street lights blocked my view of any stars.

"I would miss the stars though," I said.

Tyler's fingers brushed against mine. I froze, my body electrified by the slight touch. My heart beat in my chest as I felt Tyler turn, his body tilting to face mine. He drew in a breath as though he was going to say something, and I was torn between wanting to know the words about to come out of his lips and wanting to leave. I chose to leave, turning back to head towards the car.

"Lauren." Tyler's hand caught my wrist, and again I froze, the skin under his fingers burning. Why did his touch do this to me? Why did my heart beat so rapidly? I was with Gabe, not Tyler. I wanted to be with Gabe, not Tyler, and yet I couldn't help the way my body responded to his.

"Lauren," he said again. Gently, he pulled my wrist towards him and, as if an invisible thread stretched between us, my body turned.

I looked up to meet his eyes. They were burning with an intensity I hadn't seen before. The steel-grey bore into me and I quivered inwardly under his stare.

Tyler stepped forward, my wrist still trapped by his hand, my heart still racing in my chest. He was only inches from me. I could feel the heat radiating off his body and, for once, I was thankful that his touch froze me. I was scared of what I might have done otherwise.

"I want you," Tyler said, his voice deep and dark. "I've wanted you from the moment you ran into me."

"Ran into you?" My voice almost came out squeaky.

"At the charity boxing match when Gabe fought Derek. I was there. You ran into me, and spilt beer all over me."

"I did?" I asked, nervously laughing. He was too close, his scent too overwhelming.

"I asked your name but you ran away. I wish I had chased after you. Things might have been different. You might have been mine instead of his."

"Tyler." My voice came out breathless in the night. "You can't say that."

"I believe I just did." His eyes pierced into mine and I wanted to melt under their burn.

"You hardly even know me."

"That's my point," he said. "I want to. I very much want to. I want to know all of you."

"Gabe is your brother," I whispered, stepping away a fraction.

Tyler took another step forward, reducing the space I had just created. He didn't let go of my wrist. Instead, he brought it to his mouth, tenderly brushing his lips over the soft skin. "You think I should do the honourable thing and step aside?" Tyler said.

Part of me wanted to say yes. Part of me wanted to rip my hand from his grasp. But a bigger part of me didn't. And it was that part that had me scared.

"Why?" he asked. "Why should I step aside?"

"Gabe is your brother," I repeated.

"I believe it is more honourable to tell the truth than to hide it."

Tyler pulled me forward and I stumbled, falling into him. I looked up into those steel-grey eyes, my heart beating in my chest as he reached down and tucked my hair behind my ear. He looked at me with hunger and I was scared by the intensity with which I wanted to quench it. I looked down, trying to escape from his mesmerising eyes.

"If you feel nothing in return then I have not lost a thing," he said. "But, if I say nothing and miss out on the chance to be with you, I would regret that for the rest of my life. I will not be silent out of some twisted sense of honour to a brother who despises me. I want you. It is that simple."

Tyler bowed his head, his mouth coming dangerously close to mine before I mustered the strength to push him away.

"I can't," I said.

Tyler took a step back, dropping my hand. "You can't, or you won't?"

"I won't," I said firmly. "I won't do that to Gabe. I won't hurt him like that."

A slow smile spread over Tyler's face. "You never said you don't have feelings for me."

"I never said I did, either," I replied, looking back at him with more determination than I felt.

"I will wait."

"For what?" I asked. "I'm with Gabe."

"And you'll be with him forever?" Tyler raised that single brow again, the one that made him and Gabe blur into a sexy mess of light and dark.

I walked over to the car, wrapping my arms around my chest, suddenly feeling the cold again.

"Can you take me to the airport, please?"

"As you wish," Tyler said. But he couldn't help the smirk covering his face.

He had got under my skin. And he knew it.

16

LAUREN

I did everything I could think of on the flight home for my thoughts not to dwell on Tyler. I listened to music. I crushed some candy. I tried to read. But with every second of distraction, my mind would quickly turn back to him every chance it got.

Those words.

I want you.

The way he said them sent tingles all over my skin. The way he looked at me. The way his touch on my wrist sent my hormones into overdrive only hinted at what he could do to my body.

I was grateful Gabe wasn't there to greet me. He would have seen the shame in my eyes. I loved Gabe. In a way, I loved him very much. He had been so good to me, so sweet, so why was I tempted by his brother?

My night was spent tossing and turning, the sheets twisting around my body as a suffocating cocoon. I checked my phone repeatedly, telling myself that it was to see if Gabe had reached out during the night, but I knew I was lying to myself.

When my phone did finally ring the next day, it was when I had my hands in a pile of soapy water at the café. Peta raised her eyebrows as it vibrated in my pocket. We weren't supposed to have our phones on us. Without checking who it was, I quickly offered an excuse and walked into the storeroom.

"Hello?" I answered breathlessly. There was only sobbing on the other end. "Hello?" I said again, this time briefly pulling the phone away to check the caller ID. "Billie?" I asked when the crying continued.

"My life is over," she wailed.

I shushed her as the sobs continued. "Take a deep breath."

Peta popped her head around the corner. "Everything okay?"

I mouthed, "Billie," and pointed to the phone before miming tears dotting my cheeks. Peta tapped her finger to her wrist, indicating that I really should be back in the café. I held a single finger up, promising to only be a minute.

"Billie, tell me what's happened. Are you okay? Are you hurt?"

Billie half laughed, half snorted. "Okay? Am I okay? No," she almost screamed. "I'm not fucking okay!"

I was taken back by her anger. "Just calm down and tell me what happened," I said, letting the tiniest hint of annoyance colour my tone.

"Hamish happened. That's what happened."

"You're going to have to give me a little more information than that."

Billie took a deep, but shaky breath. "I told him that we shouldn't. I told him it was dangerous that night, but would he listen? No," she said sarcastically.

"Billie, you aren't making any sense."

"Don't you get it?" she wailed. "I'm fucking pregnant!"

My world stopped. My skin turned cold. No, not cold. It was though it disappeared altogether and every nerve was left exposed.

"Did you hear me?" Billie asked. "I'm pregnant. Hamish is going to be so annoyed. Shit," she cursed. "I'm so annoyed. I'm not ready for this. I don't want this. Lauren, would you please say something?"

Ever since I lost my own child, the announcement of a pregnancy brought back that fresh wave of fear, of guilt, of sadness that swelled within like nothing else could. But I always managed to fake a smile and murmur my congratulations. Somehow, though, hearing it from Billie was worse.

"Would you fucking say something?" Billie yelled down the line. "I'm freaking out here. I don't want to be a mother. I don't know how."

I cleared my throat, hoping it would dislodge some of the pain that was stabbing my chest. "How far along are you?" I managed to stammer out.

"Too fucking far to do anything," Billie replied. "What am I going to do?" she wailed. "I told Hamish I never wanted children and he was happy about that. He's had four already so why would he want another? What should I do? How should I tell him?"

My brain was thick with fog. I couldn't think of a single word to say.

"Lauren!" Billie screamed. "I've come to you for help. I'm stuck up here with no one to talk to, no idea of what to do and I'm completely freaking out. I feel trapped. I feel as though someone has locked me in a room with no door or windows and even though I'm perfectly safe, I'm completely freaking out. Did I say I was freaking out, Lauren? Because I am!"

"You need to tell him," I said finally.

"I know that," she hissed. "I need to know what to tell him. How to tell him. I need your help."

I squeezed my eyes shut at the tears that were threatening. My mind went back to the time I discovered I was pregnant. My first call had been to Peta. She sat on the other end of the line, laughing as I completely panicked. Similar to Billie, I hadn't wanted children at that stage of my life. Derek, on the other hand, had been so happy, so pleased. Peta laughed and comforted me at the same time. She already had two of her own. The thought of me freaking out over one when I was in a safe and serious relationship mystified her. And then the baby was gone along with my chance to ever have children again.

"Look," I said down the phone. "I'm sorry, Billie, but I just can't talk at the moment. I've got to go. Talk to Hamish." I hung up on her protest.

The door to the storeroom swung open again and Peta walked in, hands on hips, ready to rip into me for taking so long on the phone when the café was filled with waiting customers. She stopped in her tracks.

"Ren?" she asked, her eyes widening with concern at my ashen face. "Is everything okay?"

I sunk to the floor. "Billie's pregnant."

Peta walked out the door again and returned seconds later. She bent down and helped me to my feet. "Right," she said. "Mark is taking over, he's calling someone in to cover your shift and I am taking you back to your place where we will spend the night getting deliriously drunk, okay?"

I nodded numbly and let her guide me from the café. Mark looked over, his eyes softening with concern, but Peta shook her head. She knew I couldn't possibly explain how I was feeling to Mark. How could I tell someone of the guilt I felt at the loss of a child I never wanted? How could I explain the loss I felt over something I claimed to never desire?

Peta drove me home, chatting about everything and nothing as I stared out the window at the streets of my small town flashing by in a blur. She ran into the liquor store and grabbed bottles of something. I didn't know what and I didn't care. As well as being devastated, I was confused as to why Billie's announcement had upset me so much. I had survived other pregnancy announcements with much less drama. In the end, I put it down to the freshness of reopening the wound at Christmas.

We walked inside, Peta bending down to scoop Smudge into her arm, expertly balancing him in one arm as she poured the wine into glasses and handed one to me.

"You haven't said much." She joined me on the couch.

I shrugged, the pain I felt earlier dissolving to numbness. "What is there to say? Billie is pregnant. I never will be."

Peta gently rubbed my arm.

"I know." I sighed. "I never wanted children."

"But," Peta said, finishing my thoughts. "You wanted the choice."

We'd had this conversation many times over the past couple of years. Peta knew how I felt. She knew the confusion of the battling thoughts in my mind. She knew the devastation, the pain, the guilt and the anger.

"You know," Peta said, lying back on the couch and adjusting the cushion under her head. "I often wonder what my life would be like if I hadn't had children. Would I still be married to Shrek? We only got married because I was pregnant. Despite all the advancements in birth control, accidents still happen. Would I still own the café? I love the kids. I love them more than life itself, they mean the world to me, but sometimes I wonder what happened to the parts of me that existed before I had children." Peta swung her legs off the couch, sitting back up to face me. "Before I had children I had an iron gut. I could literally eat anything, go on anything, and now, I can barely sit on a swing without feeling nauseated. Sometimes I wished I had the chance to go back to that life again. Having children was kind of thrust on me. I never made the conscious decision to have children, I just got pregnant."

"Is that supposed to make me feel better?" By this stage, I had drained two glasses of wine, as had Peta, but although her cheeks were flushed in a warm glow, I felt nothing but cold.

Peta screwed up her face. "Of course it's not supposed to make you feel better. I can honestly say I have no idea what it feels like to be you, but I can understand Billie freaking out."

"I also got pregnant without intentional thought, remember?"

"But you can't now," Peta said quietly.

"You are crap at cheering me up."

"I'm not trying to cheer you up, I'm just pointing out some facts. When you want to have children, if you want to have children, it can only ever be your choice, Lauren. Sure, you'll have to use less traditional methods than say, I have, but I know if you want to be a mother, you'll find a way. And you'll be a wonderful mother."

Peta had never been one to beat around the bush. It was part of what made me love her. She never said something merely to make me feel better, she never sugar-coated her thoughts, she just blurted them out.

One bottle of wine later and the warm glow that flushed Peta's cheeks had begun to spread to mine. Instead of making me forget though, all the thoughts that had niggled away at the back of my mind, began to shout. By the time we finished the second bottle, I was a mess.

"I'm dating someone nine years younger than me," I said to Peta, my words slurred by either alcohol or my mental state. I wasn't sure which. "Nine years! What am I doing?"

"You're having fun, that's what you're doing." Peta stroked Smudge sitting on her lap.

"But what sort of a future have we got? Why is he with me? What if he wakes up one day and wants children I can't give him? What if I want children and he doesn't? What if I never want children?"

It felt good to blurt it all out. I wasn't even sure if Peta was listening but it didn't matter. Just saying the words out loud brought a sense of relief.

Peta stopped patting Smudge and pushed him to the ground. He looked back at her with disdain.

"First of all," she said. "You are beautiful. And I'm not just talking on the outside, pretty and all that, I'm talking on the inside. You are a beautiful, smart, kind-hearted woman. Any man would be lucky to have you and Gabe knows that. The reason he's with you is because you are you. Heck, I'd be with you if I was into that." She took a sip of wine but ended up laughing and spitting some of it onto the couch. "And secondly—" she pressed down the second finger on her left hand. "We are at secondly, aren't we?" I nodded. "Okay, and secondly, if you want to have children one day, either of you, you will need to talk about it. But you're not there yet. You're bringing tomorrow's troubles into today. Heck— have you noticed my fondness for the word, heck, tonight?— you're bringing years into the future's troubles into today. You've got to stop, okay? Stop listening to those voices in your head and just enjoy your life. You've got a beautiful boy to fuck, sorry, man to fuck. You've just started a job you actually want to be in, and you've got a wonderful boss at your other job. Life is good. Why are you trying to stuff it up? So what if Billie is pregnant?"

I chewed on my bottom lip.

"What?" Peta asked.

"There's something else," I said quietly.

"Another worry to borrow?"

"This one is a little more in the present."

"Well, spit it out then."

I took a deep breath, trying to quieten the screaming voices that told me not to open this particular topic. But Peta was my girl. I told her everything. Well, most things. "A tiny bit of me, just a little, tiny, minuscule part might like Tyler."

"One of Gabe's brothers?" Peta laughed. "Even without knowing which brother you are referring to, I can assure you that's perfectly natural. In fact, if you weren't attracted to at least one of them, I would think there was something wrong with you. I've seen the photos. So is he the dark and intense one, or the wild one with the hair?" She shuddered. "Both of them are fine specimens of the human race."

I swallowed as she laughed. "The thing is though, he's told me that he wants me. He's made it perfectly clear."

Peta looked over to me slowly, a smile crossing her face. "Really? So maybe you need to tell me a little more."

And so I did. I told her about Tyler and the dinner we had. I told her of the way he looked at me, the way he made me feel, ending with, "So what do I do?"

"You realise this isn't helping with my yearning for my single days, don't you?" She drained the last of the wine, pouting when she realised there was none left. "You do nothing, that's what you do. If it turns out you do have feelings for Tyler, then you break it off with Gabe. But at the moment, you have no idea how you feel, so to throw everything you have with Gabe away for guilt over some feelings for Tyler would be stupid. He may turn out to be nothing more than a pretty face."

"See, this is why I have you." I offered her my glass of wine, just a drab sitting in the base. Peta drunk it hungrily. "You talk sense into me."

"It's what I'm here for." Peta lazily saluted. "To be the voice of reason."

17

LAUREN

We had started early so it wasn't that late when Peta called Shrek to come and pick her up. I waved goodbye, assuring her that I was fine and that the shouting voices of my worries had gone back to their usual niggling state.

Billie called early the next morning. I was tempted to ignore her call, but she would have no idea as to why I reacted the way I did and I felt a little bad for hanging up on her. I took a deep breath and plastered on my best smile, hoping it would seep into my voice.

"Hi," I answered chirpily.

There was no preamble. "So I told him," she said, her voice deadpan.

"And?" I prompted.

"He's thrilled."

"Thrilled?

"Thrilled."

"And you're still not?"

Billie sighed. "I don't know."

I wasn't sure what to say. Surely she had other friends or family she could talk to about this.

"We're coming down tonight for that boxing match," she said. "I've got tickets for you and Gabe. You've remembered, haven't you?"

My mind rapidly started going through excuses, but Billie didn't give me the chance to use any of them. "I need you there, Lauren. I don't know how I even feel about this and even though my voice is calm, I'm still completely freaking out. Don't say anything to Gabe or any of them. Hamish wants to have some family dinner and make an official announcement."

"But how do you feel?"

"Does it matter?" she asked dejectedly.

"Look," I started. "I'm not sure if Gabe—"

"Don't worry about Gabe. Hamish is on the phone to him as we speak. I've bought the tickets and it's for charity so there is no way you can say no. Besides, you know how the Thornton men are about their boxing. You probably won't be able to drag Gabe away once he's there. Look, got to go. See you tonight." And with that, she hung up.

* * *

Half an hour before Gabe was due to pick me up, I stood at my wardrobe and flicked through the dresses on the hanger. There weren't many to choose from. The nicest dress I owned I had already worn to a Thornton family function, the black one with the silver zipper, so I was in desperate need of getting new clothes if I was to keep going to these sorts of functions. In the end, I pulled a greyish dress out of the back. I hadn't worn it in years and it firmly belonged in the era when my hemlines were a little shorter and my dresses clung a little tighter. I pulled it over my head and stood dejectedly in front of the mirror.

A low whistle sounded behind me and I turned to find Gabe leaning against the doorway to my room.

"You look beautiful," he said, walking over and standing behind me.

"I look stupid."

Gabe laughed and wrapped his arms around my waist. "You always say that and yet you never do." He kissed the curve of my neck, peering up at my reflection in the mirror. "Are you okay? You've been rather quiet lately."

A thick lump lodged itself in the back of my throat. I wanted to tell him, but I also didn't want to bring up that aspect of my life again. I put on a smile and twisted around in his arms, lifting my face to his. "I'm fine. I've just missed you."

Gabe moaned his delightful moan that sent shivers down my spine and lifted butterflies to their wings in my stomach. "It's been a while," he mumbled, his words getting drowned by the pressure of my lips against his. I was filled with the need to have his hands on me, to feel his mouth against my skin, for him to be inside me and wash away all thoughts of Tyler and of Billie.

Gabe returned my kiss passionately. Twisting his hands in my hair, he tipped my head back and trailed kisses down my neck and onto the soft fullness of my breasts. My need turned to urgency. I fumbled with the buttons on his jeans as he eased my breasts from the constraints of my dress.

"Have we got time?" he asked breathlessly.

"I don't care," I said, tugging his jeans down as he awkwardly stumbled out of them.

With his mouth still pressed to my skin, we fell onto the bed. Gabe rose over the top of me, his mouth on my nipple, his hands lifting the hem of my dress. I reached down and pulled my underwear off, just before he sank into me, letting out a deep sigh of contentment. Resting on his elbows, his eyes stared down as his hardness filled me. He didn't move and I ground my hips against him.

"I need you," I pleaded.

Gabe shook his head. "I want to taste you."

"Not now," I urged. "Please?" I moved my hips in a slow circle, making sure he felt every movement. Gabe pushed against me, trying to get me to remain still.

"What's the hurry?" he asked, brushing a strand of hair away from my face.

I threaded my hands under the material of his shirt, running them over his shoulders and digging them into the flesh of his back. "Fuck me," I pleaded.

Gabe's eyes darkened and he brought his mouth down to mine as he moved in and out. With each thrust, the fog began to lift from my brain and the tightness in my chest began to loosen. I moved in time with him, forcing his body onto mine with a hard slap each time we met.

"Lauren, I'm going to come if you keep that up."

I pushed harder against him. I didn't want to come. I didn't need to come. I needed him to fill me. I needed him to claim me as his own. Maybe then, thoughts of his brother would flee my mind.

Gabe's movements got faster and faster as the need for release grew inside him. He cried out when he came and fell against me. I held him close, relishing in the pressure of his body, slack and content against mine, and traced swirls over the skin under his shirt with my fingertips.

"We better get going," I said finally when he made no attempt to move.

"Seriously?" he asked. "You're going to make me go after that?" Gabe lifted himself from the bed, grinned, and pulled his pants on, smoothing out the wrinkles from his shirt.

I got up. "I'll just quickly jump through the shower." But Gabe stopped me.

"No," he said. "Go as you are. You've got that freshly fucked look on your face and it will drive me insane all night." He tugged the hemline of my dress down and tossed my underwear away. "No one will ever know," he said and added a, "Please?" and a pout when I objected.

I quickly freshened myself without a shower and joined Gabe in the car.

"I can't believe I'm even going to this," Gabe said, as we pulled up to the venue. "Don't get me wrong, tickets to this boxing match are something I could have never afforded on my own, but I'm not sure if the cost of sitting with my family is worth it. You've got me spending a lot more time with my family than I ever wished, Lauren Greer."

We parked beside Hamish's black four-wheel drive and I quickly looked around to see if Tyler's car was parked nearby. Thankfully, it wasn't. Hopefully, he wasn't even coming.

It was a bigger event than the one Gabe had fought Derek in last year, a professional fight, rather than an amateur one. The large gymnasium had been draped in black and silver, and the clamour of voices mixed with the metallic sound of live music could be heard before we even walked in the doors. Billie waved enthusiastically from a table covered in black, a low chandelier hanging overhead, and we wove our way through the maze of tables. Billie sat with Hamish, Jake sat beside a girl I had never met before, and Tyler sat beside him. My heart sunk and soared at the same time. His eyes roamed over my body, narrowing slightly when he caught my eye. I thought I saw a hint of disappointment or sadness hovering in them, but I blocked it from my mind.

Tyler Thornton was not going to get the better of me, no matter what those steel-grey eyes did to my insides.

Gabe pulled out a chair beside Billie and sat down, leaving only the seat beside Tyler, or the seat beside Jake's date spare. I walked around the table and sat beside the unknown woman, earning myself a confused look from Gabe. As it turned out, the seat beside Tyler was occupied anyway. A long-legged girl glided over to the table and sat down, planting a kiss on Tyler's cheek. My heart stopped beating. Or maybe it beat faster and louder. I couldn't tell anymore.

"Gabe, Lauren," Tyler said with control. "This is my date for the evening, Molly." We murmured hellos and then Tyler introduced the girl beside Jake as Amelia, saying she was Molly's sister and Jake's date for the night. Jake rolled his eyes at the introduction.

Amelia turned to me, wine glass at her mouth, and stuck out her hand. "Amelia," she said. She was a pretty girl but nothing like what I thought Jake would go for. Her dark hair was cut in a blunt bob style with a thick fringe that hung over her eyes and she wore a bright red dress with white polka dots.

I shook her hand politely. "Lauren."

Amelia drained the last of her wine and reached for the bottle on the table to refill it. "Have you been dragged along as an uncomfortable side-piece too?" she asked.

I looked over to Jake. He was staring at the bottle of beer on the table in front of him, head held in his hands and elbows resting on the table. His expression was one of complete boredom.

I smiled a little. "Jake's not so bad."

Amelia's eyebrows lifted sky high and she downed her glass in one go, placing it back on the table to refill it, the outline of her lips in red left on the rim. "At least the booze is free." She filled her glass to the top and plonked the bottle back at the centre of the table. "There, that should help a little," she said, resting back in her chair. "So you're with the pretty blond?" She nodded to Gabe.

There was something about the bluntness of this woman that I liked. There was no pretence, no adoration over any of the Thornton men, just honesty.

"I'm with Gabe, yes."

"Is he more talkative than this one?" She jerked her finger at Jake.

Jake's eyes flicked over to mine in a plea of help, but his exaggerated look just made me laugh. "I would say, yes, along with just about all the other men in this room."

The musicians in the centre of the ring finished their song, announcing it was the final serenade until after the boxing had finished, and began to clear away their instruments.

Hamish smacked his hands together. "Right, boys," he said, looking around the table. "Who's your money on for the main event?"

"Rosewood," Gabe said without hesitation at the same time Tyler and Jake said, "Parker."

Hamish looked over his sons. "I see we have a split in the family." Reaching into his pocket, he placed a crisp hundred dollar bill under the water carafe in the centre of the table. "Anyone care to join?"

Tyler immediately reached into his pocket and produced two hundred dollar notes telling Jake, "I've got you covered."

Hamish turned to Gabe, waiting expectantly. Without a word, Tyler reached back into his pocket and produced another hundred.

The girl beside him, Molly, smiled and looped her arms through his, latching onto him like a limpet. I smiled at the display, but my teeth hurt from how they were clenched.

Beside me, Amelia reached into her purse and pulled out a note. "Rosewood," she said dryly.

Tyler detached himself from his date and leaned with elbows resting on the table. "So, Lauren," he asked, staring directly at me, his gaze not wavering as Molly attempted to wrap her arm around him again. "What do you think of the development so far?"

"Yes," Hamish said. "I would love to hear your thoughts."

"I really know nothing about construction," I said, carefully avoiding Tyler's eye, and instead, turning to Hamish.

"But you've got an eye, a talented eye from the photos I've seen so far," Hamish said. "I've had some wonderful feedback from the investors on the website and Tyler has been singing your praises."

"I have," Tyler said. "I'm really quite taken."

Gabe, previously pouting from his inability to produce the money to join in the bet, looked up at Tyler's comment, his eyes narrowing.

"Well, it's a pleasure to be able to work for you, Mr Thornton." I directed my words to Hamish. "And from what I can tell, the construction is coming along nicely. I would love to see the vision for it."

"Has Tyler not shown you the concept the architect produced for us? It's a virtual walkthrough of most of the floors, something I imagine you will be learning about in your classes, Gabe?"

"Yes," Tyler agreed. "How is school going?"

Amelia leaned close and whispered in my ear. "Just how young is this man of yours?" I clenched my teeth a little tighter and Amelia held up her hand, claiming innocence. "Hey, no judgement here," she said. "At least he talks."

"He's twenty-five," I lied, though I tried to justify it in my mind by reasoning that he was close to twenty-five. Close enough.

"School is fine," Gabe said, his voice deadpan. "Thrilling, in fact."

Jake snorted. "Thrilling?"

Amelia drew in a sharp breath of air. "It speaks!"

Jake gave her a look of contempt and I wondered just how on earth this delightfully incompatible couple came to be. Jake sure didn't seem impressed that she was his date for the night.

Dramatic music filled the venue and the low-hanging chandelier above our table dimmed and lifted to the ceiling. Spotlights shone randomly over the tables as the announcer began the usual theatrical introduction. The table quietened as the first two boxers made their way down the carpeted walkway.

Billie kept quiet for most of the night, nursing a single glass of what I suspected was sparkling apple juice. She barely ate and kept her eyes trained on her lap. When Hamish left the table, I moved to take his place. Billie jumped when I placed a hand on her shoulder.

"Are you okay?" I asked under my breath, careful not to alert the others to our conversation.

Billie looked up at me, eyes wide and glazed with tears. "I actually think I am. I was dreading tonight, dreading not being able to have a wine, of not being able to relax and have a good time, but all I can think about is this life growing inside me and the fact that I will be its mother."

"So those aren't tears of sadness?"

Billie shook her head. "Don't get me wrong, I'm still completely freaking out, but there's this part of me that's excited too. I never really thought about having children, but now that I am, something's changed."

I patted her shoulder. "I'm very pleased for you."

Billie smiled brilliantly. "You'll feel the same way too one day."

And there it was. The pain was back. I swallowed the lump in my throat and moved back to my chair just as Hamish sat back down. He looked over at Billie, reaching out to take her hand in his, and he smiled at her in a knowing way, a loving way, and tears sprung to my eyes. I plastered on a smile for no one but myself in an effort to rid the tears. Gabe was watching me when I looked up, a questioning glint to his expression. I stretched my smile further.

The rest of the night was spent in a rowdy debate between the Thornton men. Tyler and Gabe opposed each other in almost every fight. Tyler's date hung off him in a way that made me want to slap her and Amelia drank every available drop of red wine. The meals that were served in between matches were divine and by the end of the night, my dress felt a lot tighter.

I tried not to stare at Tyler and Molly, but my eyes drifted to them unconsciously. An ethereal mixture of flesh and limbs, Molly looked nothing like her sister. She was almost a twin to the date Tyler had brought to Billie's fashion show. I briefly wondered if he had a catalogue and flicked through it, choosing the best fit for each event.

I had at least three glasses of wine under my belt when Tyler excused himself just before the final match. I hastily followed him out of the gymnasium, my heels clicking over the floor. But, instead of walking to the restroom as I assumed he would, Tyler turned and leaned against the wall, waiting for my approach, a wicked smirk on his face.

"How are you enjoying your evening?"

I held my head high, determined to stride by him even though he was the sole reason I left the table in the first place.

"It is fine, thank you, Mr Thornton." I walked past him but he reached out and grabbed my wrist, causing my heart to pound in my chest again. He didn't hold it though. He let it fall back to my side and I crossed my arms, looking at him expectantly.

"Don't be like this," he said quietly.

"And yours?" I asked, ignoring his comment. "You seem to be enjoying yourself."

"You're jealous," he said.

"Who have I got to be jealous of?"

"You're jealous I'm here with Molly."

"I'm not," I said firmly.

Tyler took a step closer. "Why are you being so rude then?"

"I'm not."

"Yes, you are." He took another step forward, close enough so I could see the streaks of colour in his grey eyes. "You want me as much as I want you."

"I'm not sure where you are getting your information from, but there is no doubt it's stemming from your inflated sense of ego. I am not jealous and I do not want you. I have been nothing but polite all night."

"Apart from when you refuse to acknowledge I've spoken, or how you won't look me in the eye, or how you've been shooting daggers at my date. Even she's commented on it. And why did you follow me out here?"

"I didn't follow you."

Tyler laughed. "Yes, you did. You waited until I left the table and then you followed."

"Maybe it has something to do with what you said the other night and the fact that you still turned up with a date."

"So you are jealous." Tyler reduced the space between us again. "That's why you're acting so cold. But what about me?"

"What about you?" I asked, trying not to let my voice break from the feelings rushing over me at the closeness of his body to mine.

"I told you I wanted you, and the very next time I see you, you turn up freshly fucked by my brother."

Colour flooded my cheeks and I stumbled back, pressing to the wall for support. "I—I—" I stammered.

"You what?" Tyler stepped forward again, framing my body with his and caging me with his arms either side of where I was pressed against the wall. "Do you know how that makes me feel? The feeling of extreme jealousy and desire it arouses? It makes my blood boil to know his hands have been on you, his mouth—"

Tyler stopped abruptly, his eyes closing and his Adam's apple bobbing up and down. He leaned even closer, so his mouth brushed my hair as he spoke. "I want to fuck away every memory of him."

Tyler turned and walked away, leaving me a quivering mess as he returned to the table without a backwards glance. I stood pressed against the wall for a few moments longer, my heart racing and skin tingling before entering the restrooms. Amelia was inside, leaning over the sink, looking into the mirror as she applied a thick layer of red lipstick. She tilted her head to the side as she caught my eye in the reflection.

"You're an interesting one," she said.

I flashed her what I hoped was an innocent smile. "As are you," I said and attempted to slip into one of the stalls.

Quicker than I thought possible, Amelia crossed the floor and blocked my entrance. "Oh, no you don't." She grinned. "I can't witness what I just witnessed with the intense one and not get an explanation. He was virtually humping you out there."

"There is nothing going on between us."

"And that's what I'll tell Molly, though I'm dying to say otherwise. My stuck-up bitch of a sister has an entirely too big opinion of herself sometimes and I would love to bring her down a peg or two, but I won't, as long as you tell me the truth. A girl cannot live on assumptions alone." Amelia crossed her arms, amusement playing on her lips.

"Fine," I said, letting my shoulders fall.

"So you've fucked him? He looks like he'd be great in bed, not that the blond one doesn't, but the intense one, what's his name? Tyler? He looks like he'd know how to treat a woman, well, in bed anyway. Or so my sister tells me. I was a little disappointed when I got the wild one, though I'm willing to give him a chance."

"Do you always talk this openly with everyone you've just met?" I asked.

"Nope. Just the ones who look like they have good stories to tell."

"Well, there honestly isn't anything happening between Tyler and me. I have never fucked him, as you so eloquently put it. I simply work for him."

"But he wants more," she said, more of a statement than a question.

"Apparently so."

"And you're not tempted?"

"No." Lies were the theme of my night.

Amelia moved away from the entrance so I could enter the stall I never needed to enter in the first place. "You're lying," she said as I closed the door in her face.

The main fight had already started as I picked my way back through the maze of tables. All the men were on their feet, shouting at the ring, Amelia standing beside Jake and swearing louder than any of the men. She didn't look as I slipped into place beside Gabe, threading my arms around his waist and holding on as though it would stop my emotions from wavering. Tyler's date stood beside him, eagerly jumping up and down, clinging to his arm as Parker's fists flailed into Rosewood. Tyler detached himself from the girl, his steel eyes sliding over to mine which, despite sternly telling myself not to, were already fixed at him.

"Just one punch," Gabe whispered in my ear. "Wait until he gets a punch in, and it will be lights out for Parker. Just wait and see."

As soon as the words fell out of Gabe's mouth, Rosewood's fist connected with Parker's jaw and the large man collapsed to the ground. The crowds roared as the countdown began. Hamish reached into the centre of the pile and changed the notes so he could divide it between Gabe, Amelia and himself. Gabe pocketed the money, flashing an antagonising grin at Tyler and then clamped his mouth onto mine, kissing me deeply in celebration.

"Should you at least pay Tyler back his money?" I asked. Even with returning the hundred dollar bill, Gabe still had money left over.

Gabe shook his head, his eyes gleaming. "He can afford it."

Tyler reached across and held out his hand to his younger brother. "Well done," he said. "Though I may have to look at taking something different of yours as payment."

18

LAUREN

Almost a full week passed before I had to travel to the city again. A week spent telling myself not to let my thoughts drift to Tyler. A week spent pleasing Gabe in all the ways I could think of as a penance for the thoughts I couldn't block. Jimmy greeted me off the plane, his usual goofy grin spread over his face.

"You're stuck with me again today," he said as he tossed my bag into the back seat. I winced as it bounced, and Jimmy reached back and patted it nicely, apologising for tossing it yet again.

"I'm sending you the bill if any of it breaks," I teased.

The traffic leaving the airport was moving at a snail's pace and Jimmy cursed under his breath. "Sorry," he said. "I don't mean to swear all the time, it's just that this traffic is ridiculous. There are all these events going on in the city. Some garden show or horse racing or something. All the accommodation is booked solid and getting around the city has turned into a nightmare. Even the bus drivers are pulling out their hair. Mr Thornton is thrilled though. They own half the hotels here. I'm pretty sure Mr Thornton senior will be rubbing his hands together with glee."

There had been a lot of progress on the site. The building now extended high into the air, still covered in scaffolding.

I followed the line of the construction up high, shielding my eyes from the glare of the sun. "Am I allowed to go up?"

"Up there?" Jimmy asked, his hard hat wobbling on his head as he followed my line of sight. "On the scaffolding?"

I nodded. "I could get some amazing photos from up that high."

Jimmy frowned. "I'm not sure Mr Thornton would approve."

"Who says we have to tell him?"

"Well there are all these rules regarding safety and I'm not sure if you're authorised to—"

I cut him off by holding a hand over his mouth. "Enough. Go get your boss."

Once I was fully equipped with a harness, a bright vest, and everything else deemed necessary for the climb to the top, I cautiously followed Jimmy's lead. It wasn't long before the wind whipped through my hair as I looked out over the city.

"And this isn't even as high as it's going to go," Jimmy said.

The view was magnificent. The sun was beginning to set over the hills, the hazy spray of the ocean could just be made out, and the buildings surrounding us looked small in comparison.

I had never been afraid of heights, but I could tell from Jimmy's expression that he was not a fan. "I'll be fine if you want to head back down," I said, laughing at his pale face.

Jimmy refused to look directly down and kept his eyes fixed on the horizon. "I'm under instructions to wait. Mr Thornton has just come onto the site and if he knew I left you unaccompanied up here, I would lose my job."

Once I had finished taking the shots I needed, I followed Jimmy back down, his steps shaky, but they grew firmer the closer we got to the ground. When he finally rested his feet on the concrete, he turned and wrapped his arms around me tightly.

"I think that was the scariest thing I've ever done," he said when he released me.

My phone buzzed in my pocket and I reached to retrieve it. "Are you sure you're in the right profession?"

Jimmy laughed. "I'm going to make sure all the work sites I get assigned to from now on have two storeys tops."

The text was from the airline. My flight had been cancelled due to fog on the runway. "Shit," I said, then grinned at Jimmy. "You must be rubbing off on me."

"Was there a reason for the embrace?" Tyler's deep voice startled me and I jumped a little.

Jimmy turned beet-red.

"I generally do not approve of my contractors embracing on the job." Tyler's eyes were cold. He wasn't serious, was he?

"I'm sorry Mr Thornton—" Jimmy began but I interrupted him.

"You have nothing to be sorry for, Jimmy." I removed the strap from around my neck and placed my camera securely in my pack. "We were just getting some shots from above," I said. "I was a little shaky from the height and Jimmy comforted me. Is that okay with you, Mr Thornton?"

"You weren't the one who looked shaky."

"You appear to have taken a lot of notice. Is there a reason for that?"

"The reason is I need to make sure my contractors are doing their job while I'm paying them."

"I'll be sure to reduce my bill by one embrace," I replied.

Tyler nodded dismissively to Jimmy who gave me a quick wave before leaving.

"You will be staying at my apartment tonight," Tyler said.

"Excuse me?"

"Sadie just informed me that your flight has been cancelled."

"Sadie?"

"My assistant. You will stay at my apartment tonight."

"I will not," I stated.

"No? Well, where do you intend on staying? All the accommodation in the city is booked, even the backpackers. Do you have friends you could crash with?"

"I am not staying with you, Tyler." I reached down and started to place the various pieces of equipment I had used on the shoot into my pack.

"Are you afraid I'll try something?" The corner of Tyler's mouth lifted a little.

"Honestly?"

"I've told you I don't like it when people lie."

"Yes. I'm afraid you'll try something."

Tyler leaned against the wall, not caring that his suit jacket rubbed against the dust again, and held up one hand like a boy scout. "I solemnly swear that I will not try anything. I will not touch you. I will not attempt to kiss you. I will not engage with you in any way that could be perceived as romantic or sexual in any manner. Even if you beg me to."

"My answer is still no."

"I have given you my word, Lauren." The way he said my name sent shivers down my spine and I turned away from him, not wanting him see the effect he had over me. "I do not go back on my word. Unless..." Tyler paused. "Unless it's not me you're worried about. Unless you're worried about what you'll do."

"That's not—"

"You don't need to explain yourself, Lauren. Obviously, I'm so tempting that you can't even trust yourself to spend one evening in my company. It's quite the compliment, really."

"It's not like that at all."

"Then you'll stay? Jake will also be at the apartment so it won't be just the two of us."

"Fine," I said, feeling slightly relieved. I didn't know where else I was going to stay, other than with Billie and Hamish, and the fact that Jake was also staying at Tyler's helped. "I'll stay."

A wide smile crossed over Tyler's face. "Great. But I do have one final question before I'm on my best behaviour."

I rolled my eyes and crossed my arms. "What?"

Tyler pulled himself off the wall and walked over to me, a wicked glint in his steel-grey eyes. "What were you scared you might do? Were you worried you were going to kiss me?"

Inadvertently my eyes dropped to his lips.

Tyler smirked. "You were," he said.

I slung my bag over my shoulder, ready to leave him standing there with that stupid smirk on his face and take my chances sleeping at the airport.

"You weren't thinking anything dirtier, were you?" Tyler called after me.

"Goodbye, Tyler," I said.

Chuckling, he ran ahead of me and opened the passenger door to his car. "Okay, I'm done now. I'm officially on my best behaviour." He bowed low as I climbed into the front seat.

I thought Tyler's apartment would be close to the city centre, but we pulled back onto the highway. "Where are we going?" I asked.

"I have a standing appointment that I need to keep."

"And I'm expected to wait in the car?"

Tyler shook his head. "You can attend it with me. I assure you it's highly unromantic."

We drove through the city until the houses were less tightly packed together and fields of green grass dotted the background. We pulled into a long tree-lined driveway and stopped outside the entrance to a nursing home. Without a word, Tyler got out of the car, expecting me to follow. I ran to catch up with him. The woman behind the counter in the entrance smiled widely when she spotted Tyler.

"Mr Thornton," she greeted. "They are eagerly awaiting your visit. I believe they are in the lounge."

Tyler walked over and signed the register on the counter, pushing it towards me once he was done and indicating I should do the same. The guests he had listed to visit were Barrett and Annie Thornton. I quickly scribbled my signature and followed Tyler who seemed to know exactly where he was heading. We walked through a room filled with elderly people on cushioned reclining chairs, and over to a couple playing chess at a circular table next to the window overlooking the garden. They didn't look up as we approached, and Tyler cleared his throat.

"Tyler!" the old woman exclaimed when she saw him. Tyler leaned down to embrace the woman and then did the same with the elderly man.

"Grandmother, Grandfather, I would like to introduce you to Lauren. She is Gabe's girlfriend." Tyler spoke slowly and clearly, and somewhat loudly.

"Who?" Tyler's grandmother asked.

"Lauren," Tyler stated even louder.

"She's very pretty," the lady said. "Come sit, dear. We can have some tea." She held her hand high in the air, and a young girl came over and nodded when informed to bring over a pot of tea. Earl Grey and hot.

Tyler and I pulled chairs up to the table. Grandmother Thornton patted my knee affectionately. "It's a pleasure to meet you, dear," she said, loud enough for the entire room to hear.

"You too," I replied. "It's great to meet Gabe's grandparents." I would have added that I had heard a lot about them from Gabe, but he had never mentioned them. I guess when he made the move away from his family, it included his grandparents too.

"Who?" she asked.

"Gabe," I repeated. "It's great to meet Gabe's grandparents, Mrs Thornton."

Confusion crossed over her face, but she must have caught the last part. "Call me Annie," she said, patting my hand with her wrinkled one. "Isn't Tyler a sweet boy?"

Tyler leaned over from where he was chatting with his grandfather about the casino. "She's dating Gable, Grandmother, not me."

"Nonsense," Annie said and flashed a toothless smile my way. 'Tyler's a wonderful man," she said to me. "Every second Friday are the highlights of our lives. He visits every fortnight. Did you know that? He's such a sweet boy, our Tyler. Sometimes he even comes over more frequently. Like last week, he came to fix the television in our room, didn't you Tyler? He's so good like that. So handy around the house. And he can cook too, can't you, Tyler?"

"I'm pretty sure Lauren is not interested in hearing about my more redeemable qualities, Grandmother." Tyler smiled gently at her. Not a smirk, not a smile laced with amusement, but a smile that showed how much he cared.

"She needs to know these things if she is to marry you, Tyler."

Tyler rolled his eyes. "She's with Gable, Grandmother, not me."

"Of course she's with you. If she was with Gable he would have been the one to bring her here. Why would you bring her, if she is with Gable?" Annie attempted to whisper her next words. "And isn't she a little old for Gable? He's just a boy. Not that we've seen him recently. When was the last time we saw Gable, dear?" Annie turned to her husband, but he was intent on working out his next chess move and didn't hear her.

"It was the funeral," Tyler said quietly.

Annie sighed. "Clark." Her eyes misted over with tears. "He was such a kind-hearted boy. You and he were the most similar." She nodded to Tyler.

Tyler took her hand in his. It was dwarfed by Tyler's large hand. "I'm not sure the rest of the family would agree there, Grandmother."

Annie patted his cheek with her other hand, her wrinkled face creasing into a wide smile. "You've always been such a sweet child."

The conversation continued, loudly, as Tyler updated his grandparents on the casino development and the various members of the family. Part of me was dying to tell them about Billie's pregnancy, if only to see their eyes shimmering with happiness at having another grandchild, but it was not my secret to tell. When the time came for us to leave, Annie shakily stood and embraced Tyler, him bending down low to meet her. She whispered in his ear, but it was still loud enough for us all to hear. "She's a lovely girl, Tyler. You've done well picking her."

Tyler looked over the shoulder of his grandmother to where I stood patiently waiting and smiled. "I know."

19

LAUREN

Tyler's apartment building was not what I was expecting. I expected stylish pomp and modern comfort. Instead, the building it was housed in looked old and run down and more like an abandoned warehouse than a house, something Gabe would have loved.

The elevator with a metal cage whined loudly as we rose to the top level. Tyler slid the rusted metal door aside and his apartment stood open and exposed. The walls were brick, painted a faded white. Bare piping ran along the brick and clung to the ceiling. One wall was covered with a large window that looked out over the city. Shelves stuffed with books and records lined another. Everything was decorated in white, black and shades of grey. Jake was slumped on a white couch, watching a large screen TV, crumbs of potato chips resting on his chest.

"Lauren," he said, getting to his feet and brushing the crumbs away to fall on the plush mat covering the floor of the living area. "I didn't know you were in the city." His steps sounded loudly over the polished concrete floor.

"My flight was cancelled." I looked around the large room wide-eyed. It covered almost the entire level of the building, open and exposed, only two doors on the opposite wall. There was a bed in one corner beside an open fireplace, logs of wood stacked appealingly beside it. Black and white images hung over the painted brickwork in between the black pipes. "Tyler said it would be fine if I stayed here the night."

Jake lifted one bushy eyebrow in Tyler's direction, then turned back to me. "Of course." He extended his hand and then thought the better of it and gave me an awkward embrace.

"Give her the tour, would you?" Tyler removed his tie and walked from the room.

"Ah..." Jake spun on his heel. "Kitchen and dining." He pointed left. "My bedroom." He pointed to the bed in the corner. "Tyler's room and bathroom," he finished, pointing at the two doors opposite us.

Tyler returned moments later, his hair damp and messy and dressed in jeans and a tight fitting t-shirt. His feet were bare. "A tour usually involves moving from one spot, Jake."

Jake grinned and spun on one heel, fanning his arm out to rotate around the room. "This is pretty much it."

The ceiling of the building rose high above, skylights letting in the last few hints of the sun. I studied the pictures that dotted the walls, some hanging, others merely leaning against the brickwork, all in black and white. The only hint of family or friends came from a single photograph of the four brothers. Tyler stood to the side as Jake, Gabe and Clark stood with their arms flung over each other's shoulders. They were dressed in matching black tuxedos, sunglasses covered their eyes, and a classic car, bumper in polished silver, glinting with the sun's reflection was blurred in the background. I guessed it was from Hamish and Billie's wedding.

The image of footprints in dust I had taken on the first day of the job was clearly displayed near the entrance.

"I'm cooking." Tyler walked across the floor, a glass of wine and an opened bottle of beer in his hands, offering the wine to me and the beer to Jake. "Any preferences?"

"Pizza," Jake said.

Tyler shook his head, returning to the beautiful kitchen and pulling pans out of the cupboard. I walked over and took a seat on the stool on the opposite side of the marble island bench. "What are you cooking?" I asked, running my hands over the smooth surface. True to his word, Tyler had not even given me a sideways glance since his promise of good behaviour.

"I'm thinking a green curry," he said, opening the fridge. I was surprised by the amount of produce inside.

"So your grandmother wasn't exaggerating? You really can cook?"

"My grandmother does tend to embellish my qualities, but yes, I can cook. I like to cook, actually. It relaxes me. Spice level?" he asked.

"I don't mind a bit of spice," I replied, waiting for the smart comment to tumble out of his mouth.

But Tyler simply nodded and continued to pull ingredients out of the fridge. The end result was mouth-watering. Even Jake grunted in appreciation. After dinner, Tyler flopped down onto the couch, beer in hand. "TV boring enough for you, or would you like to go out?" He flicked the cap off his beer.

"I'm fine just here." I placed myself in the gap between the two men. My thigh pressed against Tyler's and he moved a fraction. We started watching a movie, something light and filled with slapstick comedy that Jake laughed heartily at but Tyler watched without a single twitch of amusement. But before the movie could end, the TV crackled and the room fell into darkness.

"What happened?" I asked, surprised by the blackness of the night.

Tyler got up from the couch and walked over to the large window. "Looks like the whole block is down." He pulled out his phone and the glow of the screen illuminated his face. I traced the lines of his features with my eyes, drinking in the way his chin was dusted in stubble and the way his hair flopped over his eyes, still damp from his shower earlier. "Yep, car crashed into a power box. Shouldn't be long before it's back on.

The couch jostled as Jake got to his feet. A door creaked open and Jake called back into the room, "I'm going to the pub," before I heard the door shut and his footsteps thudded down the stairs.

"Well," Tyler said, coming to sit back beside me on the couch. "I guess the movie is over. Any ideas? Want to head to the pub with Jake?"

I shook my head and then realising he couldn't see in the darkness, cleared my throat. "I'm good."

"But you're alone with me."

"And?" I replied. "You promised to behave and you always keep to your word."

"That I did," Tyler said.

"Is Jake okay though? He seems rather quiet."

Tyler cleared his throat. "He's got things to sort through. He'll get there though. We always do." He got to his feet. "I'll be back in a minute."

As soon as I was alone, I pulled out my phone, checking for messages from Gabe. I had tried to call him a number of times but my calls went straight to voicemail. I had left a message as well as texting him, but he hadn't replied.

A gentle glow started behind me and I turned to see Tyler lighting a candle, a flat box held in one hand. He walked around the apartment, lighting several candles and then came to sit on the ground near the coffee table at my feet.

"Monopoly?" he asked, setting the box down. "It's about the most unromantic thing I can think to do on a candlelit night." He began to take the pieces from the box and spread them out over the table. "Dog, boot, iron, hat or thimble? I think the others have been lost along the line somewhere."

I reached over and took the boot, placing it at the start of the board. "I have to warn you that I'm rather good at this game," I said. Growing up under the strictness of my mother, Morgan and I were well versed in the techniques of board games.

"Get ready to eat your words." He handed me the dice. "You start."

As it turned out, my monopoly skills had sadly diminished in the years since I had played it, and luck wasn't on my side. But it was only when Tyler had completely bankrupted me that I admitted defeat.

Tyler just sat there with a huge smirk on his face after we had finished. "What was it you were saying before the game started?"

"Hmm," I said, feigning memory loss. "I can't seem to remember."

"Funny that." Tyler moved to clear away the game pieces. "I seem to remember it was something along the lines of being good at the game."

I poked my tongue out, a childish thing to do, but Tyler merely smirked back at me. "I will show you to your room for the night."

"I thought I'd be sleeping here?" I patted the couch.

Tyler shook his head. "I'll take the couch and you can have my room."

"I can't do that."

"So you'd prefer to sleep out here with Jake's snoring? Besides, I don't really sleep all that much anyway. I guess you could say I'm somewhat of an insomniac." Tyler boxed the game up and stood. "Follow me."

Guiding me through one of the doors, we entered his bedroom. Decorated in the same black, white and grey theme, his room was approximately quarter the size of the rest of the apartment. Another large window looked out over the city, only the lights in the distance shining as the repairmen still worked on restoring power. Tyler's large bed rested against the wall, the dark leather bedhead climbing up the brick behind it.

"Did you purchase it like this?" I asked.

"I bought the building a few years back and decided to convert the loft. I'm not sure what I'll do with the other levels just yet. They've sort of been forgotten in the wake of the casino build."

"It's really quite amazing."

Tyler pressed a button on the wall. Sheer curtains fell over the window. "I hope you'll be comfortable here. The bathroom is right next door. I've left a clean towel and things you may need on the bed, but call out if there is anything more you need. Goodnight, Lauren."

"Goodnight," I echoed as the door closed behind him.

I stood and looked around at the room in wonder. It was classy and industrial and everything I would choose, given the choice.

And it smelled of Tyler. Crisp and clean.

True to his word, Tyler had left clean towels and some clothing on the edge of the bed, my pack resting on the floor beside them. I lifted the clothing to find a white t-shirt and black satin boxers and proceeded to get changed into them. I slipped through the doorway and into the bathroom. As deep as the bedroom was long, the wall adjoining the bedroom was engulfed by a narrow strip of mirror overhanging two basins. On the other side, a shower behind a single glass panel was large enough for at least four people to comfortably stand within. Another window looked out over a different angle of the city, and I hoped it was made of one-way glass. At the end of the bathroom stood a large square bath made of the same polished concrete as the floors. Tyler's taste in interior decorating was certainly impressive.

The room smelled of Tyler. The bed smelled of Tyler. The t-shirt I was dressed in smelled of Tyler. His scent was everywhere and because of that, I couldn't sleep. I lay in the enormous bed, tossing and turning and trying not to think of him. But it was like trying not to think of Christmas when all you could smell was pine needles and cinnamon.

My phone told me it was two o'clock in the morning when I crept out of the room, hoping a glass of water would help me sleep. Opening the door just a fraction, I was surprised to find Tyler still awake, lying on the couch wearing nothing but grey sweatpants and black-framed reading glasses. A laptop rested on his thighs. He didn't notice as I opened the door, his concentration firmly on the screen, a slight frown on his face, and the headphones covering his ears and blocking out all sound. His hair, instead of being in its usual slicked back style, sat messily around his head. The glasses gave him a more academic, almost nerdish appearance that was divinely sexy and I cursed under my breath as my heart tumbled a little. The light of the laptop reflected in his glasses and there was nothing but numbers and figures covering the screen. I contemplated making him aware of my presence, but in the end, I just tiptoed over to the kitchen and silently looked through the cupboard until I came across a glass. He didn't stir when I filled it, or when I stood behind the island bench and studied him. It was only when I tried to slip back into the bedroom that he noticed me. Startled, Tyler took the headphones off and hurriedly put his laptop aside, getting to his feet.

"Is everything okay?" he asked. His eyes slipped down to the outline of my breasts under the white t-shirt before quickly snapping back to my face.

I held up the glass of water. "Can't sleep."

Tyler walked over to the kitchen, opening the fridge door and studying the contents. "Are you hungry?"

"Not really."

Closing the door, he looked over at me, eyes firmly locked on mine. "Do you want to eat something anyway?"

Jake's bed was still empty and so I shrugged and took a seat on one of the stools. "Why not. Tell me, what does Mr Thornton like as a midnight snack?"

He opened the fridge door again and pulled out a block of cheese. "Grilled cheese sandwich?"

"Perfect. You got any onions?"

Tyler opened the pantry door and disappeared into the large space, coming back out holding two options. "Red or green?"

"Red," I replied, getting up from the stool. "Here, let me cut the onions while you slice the cheese." I walked around the edge of the counter and took the onion from Tyler. "Knife?"

Tyler pointed to a drawer and I bent down to open it. Behind me, he let out a tight exhale of air. "Can I ask you something?"

Having selected a knife I stood back up. "Of course."

"Please don't take offence at this, but would you mind putting some pants on?"

I looked down at my bare legs under the hem of the t-shirt. Tyler's top was long on me, with him being a lot taller, and it hung well below the cheeks of my backside, leaving me, what I considered, reasonably modest.

"And if I do mind?" I asked.

Tyler smiled ever so slightly. "The choice is entirely yours and it will make no difference to my behaviour, I just might require a little assistance to keep to my word. You can't possibly prance around my kitchen dressed in only a t-shirt, my t-shirt, and not expect me to notice."

"I'm prancing?"

Tyler lifted a chopping board onto the bench and then leaned against it, crossing his arms over his bare chest. His eyes slowly moved down my body. I felt my nipples harden as he lingered on my chest and I resisted the urge to cover myself. It would only bring more attention.

"If you insist on remaining dressed like that, I respectfully ask that it is me who gets anything from the lower cupboards." Tyler's head tilted to the side. "Or the higher ones."

"Well," I placed the onion on the board, "since you asked so nicely, I will."

He nodded once and I could feel his eyes on me as I walked across the floor to the bedroom to pull on the boxers he had left out. When I returned, a black t-shirt covered his chest.

"I don't seem to remember asking you to cover up," I said.

"I thought it would be better than watching you drool."

I laughed. "I was in no way drooling."

"Your eyes tell a different story, and besides, personally, I find frying pans and bare skin don't go well together."

I sliced the onions as Tyler constructed the sandwiches and turned on the frying pan by lighting the gas hood with a match. He heated butter and produced two golden and crispy cheese sandwiches. Once finished, Tyler hoisted himself onto the bench, legs dangling lazily over the edge as he lifted his plate. "Bon appétit."

I copied him, sitting on the bench on the other side of the sink. The sandwich was delicious and gooey, and even though I wasn't hungry to begin with, I devoured it easily. Once Tyler was finished, he hopped down and took my plate, pulling out the dish drawer directly under me. I moved my legs wider to accommodate the drawer and when Tyler closed it, he took a step forward, standing in the space left.

He placed his hands on the bench, either side of my thighs, and looked up at me hesitantly. His expression held a dark longing, and his chest rose and fell as his eyes dropped down to my breasts before falling to my legs which framed him. Cautiously his hands moved so just the tips of his fingers brushed against my skin through the thin satin material. My breath caught and goose bumps dotted my skin as he lifted his eyes to mine, a question of permission hovering in the grey depths. I knew I needed to back away before I did something I would regret, but as Tyler's hands feathered my thighs and his body leaned closer to mine, I found myself trapped in his gaze. Then, without warning, the power came back on and the moment was lost to the blaring light.

Tyler tore himself away, turning his back to me just as the whir of the elevator announced Jake's return.

Jake stopped when he walked in, his eyes flicking between us, an accusing glare firmly directed Tyler's way. "The power is back on," he said.

"So it is. You want a coffee?" he asked, turning back to me.

"A coffee? At this time of night?"

"I'm a night drinker," Tyler said.

Jake walked across to his bed and pulled the covers aside. "I'm going to sleep." He ripped off his shirt, revealing a muscled body dotted in scars, pushed his boots off and slid under the covers, tossing them back over his head.

"I guess I should get back to bed too," I said.

Tyler looked at me, his eyes still burning with desire. "Night, Lauren."

I swallowed the lump in the back of my throat. "Night, Tyler."

20

LAUREN

The rest of the night was divided between being intoxicated by Tyler's scent and feeling guilty. Tyler was Gabe's brother. Half-brother. I was with Gabe. Not Tyler. I shouldn't be having the thoughts I was.

I must have fallen asleep at some stage as I was woken the next morning by gentle tapping on the door.

"Come in," I said croakily.

"Hey." Tyler walked in holding a cup of coffee and a paper bag. "Here. I figured you were more of the morning coffee sort of person judging from your reaction last night." He placed the coffee and the bag on the bedside cabinet. "I got you a croissant too."

Tyler's chest was drenched in sweat. He must have just returned from the gym and I wondered if he had slept at all.

"Look," he said as I sat up, wrapping the sheets close to my chest. "I'm sorry about last night. I gave you my word and I very nearly broke it. It won't happen again. I apologise."

I took a sip of the coffee. "It wasn't all your fault."

"It was." He crossed, then uncrossed his arms, nervous hesitation shadowing his movements. "Do I have your permission to discuss something with you?"

I took another sip and nodded, my heart thudding in my chest.

Tyler shifted uneasily before perching at the base of the bed leaving a large space between us. "Do I have a chance?"

"What do you mean?"

"What can I do to let you know I'm serious, to get you to choose me?"

I wanted to burrow down into the sheets. Conflicting thoughts battled in my head. I was attracted to Tyler. Majorly attracted to Tyler in a way I had never been to Gabe, but I was with Gabe. Beautiful, sweet Gabe. "There is no choice, Tyler. There is no competition. I'm with Gabe."

"But if you weren't?" he asked, shifting a little closer.

"I am," I said firmly.

"But if you were free, if you weren't with him, which of us would you choose?"

"Tyler," I warned.

He stood and shook his head. "Sorry," he apologised, running his hands through his hair. "I shouldn't have said anything. I know you are with Gabe but I also know the way you look at me. It's not just in my head, Lauren. You want me as much as I want you."

"Don't say things like that," I said breathlessly.

"But you want it to be true. Why won't you just admit it?"

"Because there's no point. I could never hurt Gabe like that. I've had someone do it to me and believe me, it rips your heart out. I won't be that person." I took a deep breath. "Besides, you only want me because you can't have me."

"That's not true."

I laughed, tossing my mind back to all the things Gabe had told me about Tyler, and all the times he had annoyed me. I needed to concentrate on those and not the way he smelled, or the way his shirt clung to his chest, the way his pants hung from his hips. "It is, Tyler. It was just last week that you brought a date to the boxing match. Clearly your attention is elsewhere."

"I always take a date to events like that. It doesn't mean anything." He crossed his arms, looking at me intently.

"I'm sure the women you date would be thrilled to hear that."

"I never promise them more than I can deliver. They know what they are getting into. Besides, they are just friends."

My mind went back to when Gabe said something along the same lines. "Is that a Thornton code of honour or something? It's okay to treat women like rubbish as long as they agree to it?"

"When have I ever treated you like rubbish? And the fact that it annoys you so much tells me something."

"It doesn't tell you anything," I said, tugging the sheets tighter. "But it does tell me something. It tells me that I am nothing but a game to you. If you were serious about me, you wouldn't have brought her."

Tyler lifted one brow. "If I don't bring a date to the investor's party, that will say to you that I'm serious?"

"I'm ending this conversation." I threw the sheets off the bed and got to my feet. "None of this matters. I'm with Gabe." I stood before him, arms crossed and glaring. I didn't want to be in this position. I didn't want him to bring to light all the doubts I was already facing.

Tyler glared back at me, his eyes burning into mine. "What can I do to make you love me?"

"You want my love now?"

"I've always wanted your love." Tyler smirked and my irritation at his arrogance rose.

"I thought your intentions were more of the flesh."

"Of the flesh? How biblical of you." Tyler quickly crossed the distance between us, all promise of staying away from me vanishing. Stopping a hairsbreadth away, his eyes trailed down to my lips, my neck, my chest. "Fleshly desires. Sins of the flesh," he growled. "Why can't my intentions be both?"

My heart pounded, but I took a step back. "Please, Tyler." My voice broke on his name. "Don't do this."

"Why?" he asked. "If you really have no feelings for me, what does it matter?"

I looked to the ground, not trusting myself. "Because I'm scared of what I'll do."

With my eyes still trained on the polished concrete floor, I felt, rather than heard, Tyler's laboured breathing. He was so close to me. Just a slight adjustment of his body position and he would be pressed against me. I waited as part of me begged for him to leave and part of me begged for his lips on mine, his hands to roam my body. With a final sigh, Tyler walked away, leaving me lost in the large room, my heart pounding with exhilaration, fear, and guilt.

* * *

I felt defeated on the flight home. Tyler had called Jimmy to collect me and take me to the airport. I was pleased for the space away from him, hoping my thoughts would clear before returning to my life. The one where I dated his brother. As I pulled up outside my house, I noticed all the curtains were pulled and Gabe's jeep sat parked on the road outside. After pulling into the driveway, I grabbed my pack and inserted the key into the lock. The house was dark, but it vibrated with the sound of machine gun fire.

"Hello?" I called out gingerly.

"Welcome home," Gabe called.

Gabe and Stefan were lying on the floor of my lounge, backs propped against the couch, eyes glued to the TV screen. Gabe paused the game when I walked in and got to his feet.

"Hey," he said, pressing a kiss to my cheek.

"What are you doing here?" I asked.

"You have far better food in the fridge," was Gabe's cheeky reply.

"Aren't you supposed to be in class?"

Wrapping his arms around my waist, he pulled me close, his lips brushing against the skin of my neck.

"Gabe," I said, pushing back from him. "Why aren't you in class?"

"It's boring."

"It's boring?" I repeated.

Gabe shrugged and sat back beside Stefan who was sighing impatiently at being made to wait. "It's just one day," He took the game off pause.

After my encounter with Tyler, the last thing I needed was to come home to find Gabe slacking off and playing games. All the frustration I felt earlier in the day came flooding back.

"Well, make yourselves at home," I said angrily and stormed from the room.

The sound of gunfire stopped abruptly and I heard Gabe tell Stefan to leave. "Just take my car," he said.

Stefan snorted. "Good luck." And then the outside door slammed shut.

Once I knew he was gone, I stormed down to the bedroom and slammed the door shut behind me, letting Gabe know just how pissed off I was. I sat on the bed, staring at my reflection in the mirror when the door creaked open.

"You okay?" He peered around the corner.

Anger seethed under my skin, but I knew it wasn't really directed at Gabe. It was directed at myself. "Why didn't you return my calls?"

The bed dipped as Gabe sat beside me, reaching out and taking my hand in his. "Sorry, the boys and I had a big night last night. I got your messages. At first, I was a little annoyed that you were staying with Tyler. What was I supposed to think? But then Jake called and I knew you were safe, but by that time I was rather drunk. I'm sorry. I didn't mean to upset you."

"I had no choice. The city was all booked out."

"Jake said." Gabe squeezed my hand. "I missed you."

"It doesn't sound like it."

He brushed his lips across my fingers. "Did you miss me?"

"Of course I missed you," I said gruffly.

Leaning over, he pressed a kiss to my cheek. "How much did you miss me?"

I tugged my hand away from him and stood. "I'm annoyed, Gabe. I'm annoyed you didn't call me. I'm annoyed that I had to spend the night with your brothers with no idea how you felt about it. I'm annoyed that you got drunk and ignored me. I'm annoyed that you skipped class."

Gabe grinned. "I'm getting the impression you might be annoyed."

I groaned and rolled my eyes. "I'm serious here, Gabe. What are we doing? Where are we heading?"

Gabe held out his hands. "Whoa. Where's all this coming from?" He poked his bottom lip out, pouting delightfully.

A small smile tugged at the corners of my mouth.

"I'm sorry," he pleaded, taking my hand in his again. "I didn't mean to annoy you. I just really couldn't stand another day sitting in that stupid class as the tutor droned on and on about things that don't even matter. I promise I'll go back tomorrow. It's only one day." He pulled me into him, placing an arm around my shoulder. "And as for all that other stuff, does it really matter what we are doing, where we are going? I'm happy, you're happy, isn't that enough?" He pressed a kiss to my scalp and tightened his embrace. "You're happy, aren't you?"

I nodded against his chest and Gabe reached down and placed a finger under my chin, tilting my head upwards until I was looking at him. His warm blue eyes shone as he slowly lowered his lips to mine. A shot of electricity tingled through me when our lips touched and with an urgency I didn't know I felt, I reached up and threaded my fingers into his hair, pulling him closer, wanting him to soak into my skin and make everything right again. Gabe moaned as I reached down and stroked his crotch, his hardness growing under my hand. Fumbling with the buttons of his jeans, I struggled to release him, surprised by my need to feel him inside me. With lips still locked on mine, Gabe stood and dropped his jeans and underwear to the floor, only releasing from our lip-lock as he lowered me onto the bed. I fumbled with my own pants as he hovered above me, his eyes set where my flesh was exposed to him. Pushing my thighs apart, he moaned again when he saw the wetness gleaming at the apex of my thighs.

"God, Lauren," he said. "Maybe we should fight more often."

I reached up and pulled his head to mine, silencing him with my mouth. Gabe entered me quickly and hungrily, grunting in pleasure as my wetness engulfed him. He tried to rise above me, but I held him close, murmuring words in his ears which I knew would be his undoing. I didn't want him to pleasure me. All I wanted was for him to wipe the memory of my attraction to Tyler away. I kept my eyes trained on his face as he moved in and out, his eyes rolling back in his head as I gripped his shoulders.

"I want to taste you," he said.

I shook my head. "I just want you."

Gabe stilled inside me, looking at me questioningly as his faintly copper-stained hair fell into his eyes. "Why won't you let me?"

I pushed him off and climbed on top, sinking down onto his hardness. "I just want you," I repeated, slowly rising and then falling as my hand pressed on his chest. Still crouching, I got to my feet so I could move easily, lowering myself up and down. Gabe became transfixed with where our bodies met, his eyes dark with passion and desire as I rode him until he couldn't stand it anymore, and he lifted me off and tossed me onto the bed. Driving into me, he fucked me hard until he cried out in pleasure, pulsating before slumping over me. I kissed his cheek, his nose, his shoulder. He shuddered as I took the lobe of his ear in my mouth, biting it just a little.

"What are you doing to me, Lauren Greer?" he asked.

"Nothing," I replied as he rolled off, flopping his arms out wide, one falling across my chest.

"Believe me," he drew in a deep breath, "that was not nothing." Turning to his side, he faced me. "Billie called."

"She did?" I swallowed the tight constriction in my throat at the mention of Billie's name. "What for?"

I waited for the news. I waited for Gabe to tell me what I already knew, but he didn't.

"She's insisting on us going to some family dinner next weekend. I tried getting us out of it but she was quite insistent and she said you'd be fine with it. Do you know what it's all about?"

I shook my head, then changed my mind. "She has some news but she's asked me not to tell you."

Gabe flopped back onto the bed. "Please don't let it be another fashion show."

Running fingers over the black inked letters that marked his side I studied the words. Don't die wondering.

"It's not," I said.

21

GABE

I tried prying the news out of Lauren but she was tight-lipped. If I was honest, I would have done anything to get out of the dinner with my family. Things never went well when I spent time with them.

Lauren was quiet on the drive up to the holiday house. I tried talking to her, engaging her in conversation, but most of the time she directed her gaze out the window and watched the blurs of green pass by. In the end, I simply let her. There was too much I didn't want to say. I didn't want to tell her, or anyone else for that matter, how much I despised the course I was taking. I didn't want to tell her that thoughts of Isabel had crossed my mind ever since I saw her at the fashion show. Only they weren't just thoughts of her, they were of her and Clark. How her smile brought back memories of my heart pounding in my chest but also of the guilt. I thought it wouldn't get to me. So much time had passed, but yet, I still couldn't block her or Clark from my mind. It wasn't that I wanted to be with Isabel. Far from it. I wanted to be with Lauren, but I don't think she could ever understand my loss the same way

Isabel had. Although my family never knew, we clung to each other in the days after Clark's death, only finding solace in each other's arms. But it nearly killed me. The guilt of what I had done, for the hand I played in his death, coupled with the guilt I felt each time I returned to her embrace drowned me. It was why I had to leave. It's why I hated to be around my family. But here I was again, travelling along the road that would bring me back to them again.

I had no idea why they had called a family dinner. And it annoyed me a little that Lauren wouldn't tell me. It was as though she was choosing Billie over me, but then I would look over at her, at the wistful glaze in her eyes, at her soft lips and slightly flushed skin and it would all fade away.

God, I loved her. I couldn't even put into words why. She was everything I never knew I wanted.

Billie welcomed us with the usual sickening display of affection, hugging Lauren tightly and whispering in her ear. Dad nodded and shook my hand, inquiring how my classes were going. I lied and told him they were brilliant. I didn't need him glaring at me all night.

We had arrived a little late so Tyler and Jake were already at the table when we walked in. Jake engulfed me in a bear hug while Tyler nodded and shook my hand in a way that was so similar to Dad it was spooky. Lauren smiled tightly at them both and took her seat, not noticing the way Tyler's eyes followed her. I didn't know how he felt about my girlfriend, but I certainly didn't appreciate the way he looked at her.

It was the same way I did.

Billie chatted to Lauren throughout the dinner while the rest of us sat around wondering why we had all been called there. Was Dad about to announce some business deal? Was he going to retire, leaving Tyler at the helm of his empire?

It wasn't until dinner was finished and the conversation had lapsed into an awkward silence that Dad finally cleared his throat.

"Billie and I have an announcement," he said, looking across at Billie who gazed lovingly back at him. It made me feel a little sick. "Although unplanned, Billie and I are thrilled to announce that we are expecting a child."

No one said a thing. We all just sat around the table in stunned silence. I looked over at Lauren. She had a tight smile plastered across her face. No wonder she had been acting so strange. Reaching under the table, I squeezed her hand. She briefly glanced at me, before smiling wider.

"Congratulations," she said to Hamish. "I'm sure you will be thrilled."

Dad lifted Billie's hand to his lips, much in the same manner as I had done many times to Lauren. "We are, thank you, Lauren. Boys?" he asked, casting his gaze over each of us.

I picked up my water glass and drank deeply, avoiding his eye. Did he seriously expect us to be happy about this? By the time this kid came into the world there was going to be a twenty-two year age gap between us.

"You're fucking kidding, right?" Jake asked.

I choked on the water I had just swallowed.

"No, we are not fucking kidding," Dad replied sternly. "Say congratulations to your step-mother."

Tyler was the first to speak. "Congratulations Billie," he said simply, offering no other words.

Lauren leaned close. "Say congratulations," she urged under her breath.

I looked at her quizzically before muttering congratulations in Billie's direction.

"Do you know when you're due?" Lauren's voice was quiet and polite but I could hear the tightness in it.

Billie smiled widely. "October."

Lauren's hand tightened around mine.

Jake pushed his chair back from the table. "I need a drink," he said.

"A toast!" Billie exclaimed, clapping her hands. I wondered if she simply didn't pick up on the tension in the room or if she was deliberately choosing to ignore it.

We followed Jake into the lounge where he tossed a whiskey down his throat before filling his glass again.

"To my sons who are here, to the one we loved and lost, and to the one to come," Hamish said once we all had a glass in our hands.

"It's a boy?" Lauren asked when no one else did.

"Did I not tell you?" Billie asked, surprised.

"You knew?" Tyler directed his question to Lauren. "Why wouldn't you warn us?"

Lauren looked down at her glass, tossing her long hair over her shoulder. "It wasn't my place."

Hamish's cell phone rang and he excused himself, Billie following dutifully as he left the room.

"They aren't fucking serious, are they?" Jake blurted out.

"Why didn't you warn us?" Tyler demanded of Lauren.

She took a step closer to me, choosing to ignore his question.

"Are you okay?" I asked as she tucked herself into my side.

She nodded but didn't lift her eyes to meet mine.

"Why didn't you warn us?" Tyler demanded again.

Lauren tensed by my side. I couldn't imagine how she must be feeling, standing here in a room filled with my family while they discussed yet another child my father was about to bring into the world when she never could.

"Enough," I said to Tyler. "It's got nothing to do with Lauren."

"I was talking to Lauren, not you," Tyler shot back, though he wasn't looking at me, his gaze was firmly on Lauren. "Lauren?" he asked. "Are you not even going to look at me?"

"For god's sake Tyler, leave her alone," I said, frustrated. "Billie probably wanted it to be a surprise and asked her not to tell us."

"Did she?" Tyler asked, his eyes still locked on where Lauren was tucked into my side. I held her tightly. Somehow she seemed smaller than usual, and all I wanted to do was protect her from Tyler's onslaught. I didn't know why he was attacking her when it had nothing to do with her. There was no reason other than Tyler was an arsehole. If Billie had asked her not to tell anyone, what other choice did she have?

"And why would she tell you, Tyler?"

Tyler ignored me. "Lauren?" he asked, but his voice was a little softer this time. "Lauren, would you at least acknowledge me?"

Lauren took a step away and looked up at Tyler defiantly. "She asked me not to tell. What was I supposed to do?"

Relief flooded Tyler's expression at her words. Why did it matter to him whether Lauren told us or not?

"Nothing," Tyler said. "You were supposed to do nothing. I just wanted to know if you heard me."

I shook my head, confused by the conversation, and walked over to the bar, pulling a bottle of vodka from the shelf. "Do you want one?" I asked Lauren.

She shook her head. "I'll drive home."

"We can stay the night if you'd prefer to have a drink," I offered.

She shook her head again. "I just want to go home."

Shrugging, I poured some of the vodka into a glass with a few ice cubes. I didn't need any mixer.

Lauren sat quietly on the couch as Jake and I laughed over the thought of our father changing nappies. Tyler sat opposite us and stared into his drink, only occasionally bringing it to his lips. Every now and again, I reached out to stroke Lauren's cheek, bringing her fingers to my lips, but she was lost in a world of her own, her eyes hooded with sadness. Dad and Billie returned, and after about half an hour of Billie retelling the details of her first scan over and over, and listening about her excitement when she heard the heartbeat for the first time, Lauren excused herself and walked outside onto the deck.

Minutes later, Tyler followed.

22

LAUREN

"So you're just going to ignore me now?" Tyler's deep voice sounded behind me.

I didn't turn to look at him. I was confused and it sickened me. "Just go away, Tyler."

"I haven't done anything wrong," he said. He came to lean on the railing beside me, looking out over the lake. The lights of the town quivered on the water.

"You're putting me in an impossible position."

"It's not impossible. You can break it off with him."

I laughed. "And what would that look like? Breaking up with one brother to date the other? Besides, I barely know you. I don't know what you want from me."

"I don't want anything from you. I just want you." He moved a fraction closer and my heart fluttered in response. Damn heart. "What do you want to know? I'll tell you anything. All you have to do is ask."

I pushed away from the railing. "I can't do this tonight."

"Then when?" he said, watching me intently.

"I'm with Gabe," I said firmly. "I want Gabe."

"No, you don't. I can tell from the way you won't meet my eye, from the way you're ignoring me. If you wanted Gabe, I wouldn't be in your head. You wouldn't need to ignore me."

Tyler took a step back as the door swung open and Jake and Gabe joined us on the balcony. "Billie's turning in for the night," Jake said.

Gabe looked across to me, one eyebrow raised. "You want to stay here the night or go?"

I stepped beside him and wrapped my arm around his waist. "Let's go," I said, looking into his blue eyes and reminding myself of how he made me feel. But it wasn't the same anymore. My heart didn't beat like it used to. My body didn't respond in the same way.

"Looks like we're off," Gabe said to his brothers. Stepping away from my embrace, he clapped Jake on the back and nodded in Tyler's direction.

I left without saying anything, but I could feel Tyler's eyes burning into my back as I walked away.

* * *

As much as I tried, I could not distract myself from Tyler. Each time I pulled my mind away, each time I banished him from my thoughts, he returned with a burning intensity that left me quivering. Even Peta noticed my distraction at work.

"Is everything okay?" she asked for what seemed like the millionth time.

I nodded and turned back to wiping down the bench. Mark, having appeared from the kitchen, leaned against the doorframe, tea towel flung over his shoulder and exchanged curious looks with Peta.

"Is it the brother?" he asked finally.

"Peta!" I exclaimed. "You told him?"

"I didn't exactly tell him, it was more that he overheard."

"Overheard what exactly?"

"Overheard her discussing with Shrek the dirty details of your little dalliance with the dark side."

"There has been no dallying," I shot back at Mark, while still glaring at Peta.

She shrugged and offered an apologetic smile. "Sorry, but it's not as though I told him intentionally."

"And what if she did? I wouldn't spill your little secret." Mark smirked. "Well, not intentionally anyway." He shot an amused look Peta's way and she rolled her eyes. "I must say, Lauren, you have certainly surprised me. I didn't think you had it in you."

"I haven't done anything," I said firmly.

Mark smiled again, a slow smile that started at one corner of his mouth and spread across his face like a deadly disease. "Maybe not. But you want to." Taking the tea towel from his shoulder, he crushed it into a ball and threw it at me. "Don't tell me you're not tempted."

"Enough," Peta said, hands on hips, frowning at Mark. "Get back in the kitchen."

Mark held his hands up in surrender but the smirking smile was still plastered on his face.

"Things haven't got any easier then?"

I shook my head. "I'm just so confused. I love Gabe, I really do. I'd never want to hurt him."

"So this thing with Tyler is more than just attraction?"

"That's the problem." I leaned against the counter, lowering my voice so the one customer sitting in the café had no chance of overhearing. "I don't know what it is. All I know is that I can't get him out of my mind. I scold myself. I think of Gabe. I remind myself of how it felt when Derek left me for the lying-man-stealing-bitch. But still, he's there, looking at me the way he does. I just don't know what to do."

"Maybe you need to talk to him."

"And say what? I don't even know how I feel so how is talking to him going to make things better?" I turned back to wipe the already clean counter. "I'm just going to avoid him."

"Won't that be a little hard? I mean, you still have to photograph the casino development, don't you?"

"I won't have to see him again until the investor party." I groaned. "Even that annoys me. I should be excited. Tyler promised to introduce me to some people who might want to hire me, and instead of concentrating on that, all I can think about is how it would feel for him to kiss me. I'm pathetic. I'm a shame to women worldwide."

Peta laughed, but flung her arms wide and engulfed me in a hug. "Stop being so hard on yourself."

"And this Billie thing isn't helping," I mumbled into her shoulder.

"Just stop it," Peta said as she stroked my hair, like she would to soothe one of her children. "You don't have to do anything. You don't have to make any decisions. You don't owe anyone a thing."

I pulled away from her and sighed. "This was supposed to be easy."

"What was?"

"Gabe."

"I think we always knew Gabe was easy," Peta said with amusement.

"That's not what I meant."

"I know." Peta leaned over and tried to smooth the frown lines that marked my forehead. "Speak of the devil."

The door swung open and Gabe walked in. He was so young. So happy and carefree. So unsuspecting of the torment that was going on within me. Why couldn't I just be happy with him? Why did Tyler have to come along and ruin everything?

"Hey," he said, walking over and wrapping his arms around my waist, his lips brushing against the skin of my neck. "Good day?"

"It's been slow," I replied, removing his hands and stepping away.

"I've been meaning to ask about Saturday night," Gabe said, walking into the storeroom to retrieve his apron. He tied it securely around his waist but let the bib hang unattached.

"What about it?"

"It's Stefan's twenty-first. I said we would go. That alright with you?"

"You've remembered we've got the investor party in the city the night before?"

"Shit," Gabe said. "Do we have to go?"

"A lot of my photographs will be on display. I kind of have to."

"I still blame you for all this," Gabe said, smiling.

"All of what?"

"This time I have to spend with my family."

"It's not that bad, is it?"

Gabe rolled his eyes. "Well, we can still do Stefan's twenty-first on the Saturday night, can't we?"

By this stage, the clock showed it was the end of my shift and I pulled the apron strings over my head. "Don't see why not."

* * *

The days before the investor party flew by quickly. Peta and I went shopping and I bought a new dress for the occasion. It was a floor length, blush coloured dress that sparkled in the light. It cost more than any item of clothing I had ever worn before, but the event was black tie and I was determined to look like I belonged. The function was going to be held in one of the hotels that Thornton Industries owned, and Gabe and I booked a room for the night. The arrival of our flight meant we only had about an hour to get ready before we had to be there to greet the investors alongside the other members of the Thornton family.

I quickly jumped through the shower, pulled my hair into a messy bun that had trails of hair still framing my face, applied some makeup and stepped into the nude coloured shoes I had bought to match the dress. They had taken Peta and me hours to find, as most of the shoes that would have suited the dress had really high heels, and I didn't want to tower above Gabe.

When I finally emerged from the bathroom, Gabe was sitting on the bed, dressed in a dark tuxedo. The lengthy strip of faded copper-blond that stretched along his scalp was pulled back into a ponytail at the base of his neck, the rest of his hair was slick with gel. He was gorgeous.

"Wow," he said, getting up from the bed. "You look…" He paused, tilting his head to the side. "You look amazing."

"Thank you." I curtsied, and Gabe's eyes darkened. "No," I warned as he stepped towards me. "Now is not the time."

While biting his lip, Gabe grinned, holding one hand behind his back. "Well, I will just have to keep my thoughts until later." He brushed a chaste kiss on my cheek and then held out a single lily which bloomed from deep pink to white. "Here," he said. "This one's not all white. I learned my lesson."

I laughed nervously and took the flower, thinking back to when Mother scolded him for bringing me a white lily on my birthday, a flower she thought was strictly for funerals.

Gabe held his arm out, I looped mine through his and we walked out the door.

23

LAUREN

My photographs had been enlarged and stood on display throughout the room. Some showed the construction workers laughing while on break, their faces covered in dust, their hands smeared with dirt. Some were only of the building itself. All of them clearly displayed my name in bold print at the bottom.

Billie and Hamish spotted us as soon as we walked in and floated across the nearly empty room. Billie's shoes sounded loudly on the wooden flooring. She embraced me tightly. "Don't they just look fantastic?" she said, nodding to the displayed photographs. "Tyler said you were talented but I don't think I knew just how much until I came here. You must be so proud, Lauren."

"I am," I said, stepping back to admire my work as if I had never seen it before. "Thanks."

"Surely you must be considering giving up your job at the coffee shop and working for yourself full time?"

"I agree," Hamish said. "I'm sure Tyler would be more than willing to help you in any way he can. He's got a good head for business, not to mention countless contacts."

"I hadn't actually thought about it," I replied, my eyes sliding over to where Gabe stood stiffly at my side.

"Well, you need to start," Hamish said.

The first of the guests appeared in the doorway and Hamish and Billie excused themselves to greet them.

"And so it begins," Gabe said dryly.

"What?" I asked, wondering if he was against the idea of me starting a business. But Gabe wasn't even looking at me. He was looking over to where his father and Billie were shaking the hands of distinguished looking gentlemen and glamorous women.

"The arse licking," Gabe replied.

Tyler chose that moment to enter the room. His eyes immediately locked onto mine, although he didn't walk my way. He turned towards the incoming guests, a professional smile on his face. A shudder ran through me as I looked him over. His tuxedo was tailored perfectly to suit his frame. It sat beautifully across his wide shoulders and tapered down to his waist. He made Gabe look like a little boy playing dress up.

"I'm going to get us something to drink," Gabe whispered in my ear.

As soon as he left, Tyler strode across the room, his eyes direct and steps confident. "Lauren," he said. My name sounded different on his lips than it did on anyone else's. It was both a command and a question.

"Tyler," I replied, and raised my chin just a fraction. His eyes roamed over me. I wanted to ignore the sensation that his gaze brought, but the tingles that spread over my body left me little choice but to acknowledge them.

"Tyler." This time it was said by Gabe.

"Gable," Tyler replied. "If you don't mind, I'd like to steal your girlfriend for a while."

Gabe simply lifted that one brow, something I had come to realise was a Thornton trait.

"A few of the investors have expressed an interest in obtaining her skills for themselves."

Gabe took a sip of the drink he was holding and held a wine glass out to me. "Knock yourself out."

Tyler looked over and held out his arm. "Shall we?"

Without saying a word, I looped my arm through his and smiled apologetically at Gabe. Tyler gushed about my talent with each introduction and at the end of a whirlwind tour around the room, I was left with many business cards in my bag, and the promise to call them each. The possibility of starting my own business didn't sound so far-fetched anymore. Tyler was entirely professional and promptly guided me back to Gabe once all the introductions were complete.

Jake was sitting beside Gabe, glaring at the bottom of his glass. He looked up when we approached, eyes narrowing. "Where's your date?" he asked Tyler.

"I didn't bring one," Tyler replied. His eyes flicked quickly over to mine, reminding me of our conversation a couple of weeks back.

"No date?" Jake asked, barely able to contain his amusement.

"Tyler Thornton going stag," Gabe joined in. "I never thought I'd see the day. Those girls finally click to what sort of a man you are?"

"There's a point I wish to make," Tyler said, ignoring the jibes of his brothers and staring directly at me.

"Being what?" Gabe laughed. "That you can't keep to one girl? That they finally grew some brains and dumped your arse?"

"I was never dating any of them," Tyler replied, his mouth in a hard line.

"So you keep saying, though I wonder if they knew that," Gabe replied.

"Enough, you two," Hamish interrupted. "Tyler," he said, turning to his eldest son. "It's time for your speech."

Tyler nodded and left our group, heading to the small stage at the front of the room.

As the night dragged on, the clinking sound of glasses grew more frequent, the volume of the voices increased and laughter echoed through the room. Gabe and I sat in the corner with Jake, both the men sulkily glaring at where Hamish and Tyler made the rounds, clasping hands and talking animatedly. When the music started, I tried to get Gabe to dance, but he wasn't in the mood. He just sat in the chair beside Jake, drinking glass after glass of whiskey until his eyes glazed over and a lopsided grin spread across his face.

So when Tyler asked me to dance I had little choice other than to accept. It was a slow song, and Tyler's hand slid around my waist and rested on the small of my back, holding me firmly against him.

"Do you realise you've stared at me the entire night?" he asked.

I flicked a look up, but quickly lowered my gaze when his steel coloured eyes met mine, causing my heart to jump.

"I haven't," I replied.

Tyler bent his head so his lips brushed against my ear. "Your eyes don't lie, Lauren, even if your mouth does."

I straightened in his arms, trying to put some distance between his body and mine, but he merely held me tighter, pressing firmly against me as we danced across the floor.

"Enough of this nonsense, Lauren," he said, his voice like gravel. "Stop denying this. Stop denying me. There is no point in lying. I can see it in your eyes."

I pressed my eyes closed and took a deep breath.

"Closing them won't help," he said.

"Tyler, please," I begged, and looked up. His eyes were burning with both intensity and amusement.

"You told me not to bring a date and I didn't."

"That doesn't mean anything."

"But it does. You told me what I'd have to do to prove I was serious, and I've done it. You cannot deny me that."

"I don't know what you want from me," I said, my heart pounding in my chest. From across the room, Gabe watched intently as I danced with his brother. I smiled and waved, trying to relieve some of the anxiety in his expression. He didn't wave back.

"I want you to admit you feel the same way I do. I want you to admit you want my hands on your body just as much as I want to put them there." His fingers spread over the small of my back, the thinness of the material doing little to shield me from the heat of his touch.

"I can't," I said, attempting to pull away. But he held me tight, pulling me closer.

"The moment I saw you, I wanted you," he said, head bowed low and whispering in my ear. "When you ran into me at the boxing match, and again, when you walked down those stairs with Gabe, I was both entranced and filled with rage when I realised you were with him. I've never had that response to a woman before. I've never felt that way about anyone and it all happened within a moment." He forcefully pulled me closer, the breath leaving my chest as he held me against him. "The way your cheeks were flushed, the way you looked at me, the exposed flesh of your back, my body responded to everything about you in such a violent way it was all I could do not to attack Gabe there and then for having your hand in his. Do you know what it feels like to watch you with him? Do you know what torture it is?" Tyler's breath was laboured as we swayed across the floor. "Do you know how hard it is for me not to press my lips to yours?"

Before he had a chance to tighten his grip on me once again, I broke away and walked across the floor, ignoring Gabe's questioning glare and going outside.

I needed fresh air. I needed to breathe.

But I wasn't given the chance.

Tyler was quick to follow. I could feel him standing behind me as I looked out over the lights of the city.

"Tell me what to do and I'll do it, Lauren. Whatever it takes. I want you." His words danced through the night air and floated around my mind, confusing my thoughts and scrambling my common sense. "I need you," he added hoarsely.

I flicked my eyes to his as he stood there, a devilish temptation dressed in a tuxedo. Stepping forward, his hand reached out to take my wrist between his fingers, twisting me until I faced him. My eyes fell down to where I was trapped and he released me, letting my hand fall limply back to my side.

"It's just you and me. Block everything and everyone else out. Do you want me, Lauren? Look me in the eye, tell me you don't and I will walk away right now. Just tell me you don't want me and I will leave."

I kept my eyes trained to the ground, not trusting myself to look at him. I was afraid if I did, I would throw my arms around his neck and kiss him like there was no tomorrow. Like there was no one else who existed apart from him and me. Like there was no Gabe.

"Look at me," he said softly and tipped my chin upwards.

My eyes met his and I knew in that moment that I wanted him more than I had ever wanted anyone else. Derek and Gabe faded to nothing. Every inch of me ached to be held by him, ached to know what his body would feel like, how his lips would feel on my skin.

"Do you want me?" His voice was low, almost begging.

There was only a fraction of space between us. I took a step forward, my heart pounding, my legs shaking, and before I could register what I was doing, I pressed my lips to his for the briefest of moments.

It was all the invitation Tyler needed. His hands cupped my face and he brought his lips back to mine, kissing me passionately as desire and pleasure swirled inside. He tasted of mint and smelled of musk. Crushing himself against me, his mouth devoured mine. All other thoughts fled. All I could think about was Tyler. How big and rough his hands felt as they cupped my cheeks. How, even though the rest of our bodies weren't touching, I could still sense every inch of him as though we were pressed against each other. How his mouth felt like heaven.

It was only as someone cleared their throat behind us, that the waves of panic and shame rippled through me. Tyler pulled away, his hands still clasping my face, my eyes searching his even as my mind flew to Gabe.

"Dad's looking for you," Jake said.

"Give me a minute," Tyler said, his voice rough and broken.

"I think it best you come now."

Tyler's breath came out in short pants over my face. His eyes searched mine as the panic began to rise. "Don't," he whispered. "Don't regret this."

"I—" But Tyler pressed his lips to mine again, silencing the words that never came.

"Wait," he said. And then he was gone.

"So?" Jake asked, leaning against the wall and crossing his arms. "Are you going to tell him or am I?"

The tears came immediately. "I never meant—"

Jake cut me off angrily. "You or me?"

I hung my head. "I will," I said.

"When?"

"Now?" I asked.

Jake shook his head. "Not tonight. Not here. Not while Tyler and Gabe are in the same area code. But you will tell him."

I nodded as the tears fell down my cheeks. "I never meant—"

"No one ever does," Jake replied. "But it doesn't change the fact that you did. Is this thing between you and Tyler serious?"

I shook my head and shrugged. "I don't know what it is."

"Well, I suggest you figure it out before you tell Gabe."

I nodded again and wrapped my arms around my chest, suddenly feeling cold.

"We all make mistakes, Lauren, there is no shame in that. But there is in lying. Don't put Gabe through that. He loves you."

A sob escaped and I covered my face with my hands. "I know," I said. "I never meant for this to happen. I know what it's like to be on the other side of this equation and I never thought I would be the one to—" The words fell away as another sob escaped me. "I never meant—" I hiccupped and Jake's expression softened.

"Tyler can be very persuasive when he wants something," he said. "And if he's the one you want to be with, then you need to own up to that. I warned him not to go near you, but you turned out to be too much of a temptation for him."

"You knew?"

"I'm one of the few people he actually confides in."

"So is it all about the chase for him? Am I just caught in some sick game he's playing with Gabe?"

Jake shook his head. "Only he can answer that. All I know is I've never seen him pursue someone as relentlessly as he's pursued you, even when he didn't want to. In fact, I've never seen him pursue someone at all. You've certainly got under his skin."

24

LAUREN

Music poured through the open doors and windows of the house, spilling onto the street and greeting us long before the shadows passing over the open spaces became people.

I gripped Gabe's hand tightly. I still hadn't told him. I didn't know how to tell him. What to tell him. And tonight wasn't the night. Tonight was a night for Gabe to enjoy himself, for Stefan to celebrate his twenty-first, for them to have some fun together.

Gabe released my hand long enough to wipe a sweaty palm down his jeans. "You okay? Your hands are all clammy."

I looked down at my hand as though it wasn't a part of me, instead, a stranger, and wiped it down my jeans, mimicking Gabe. "Sorry." I swallowed the tightness at the back of my throat. "I guess I'm just a little nervous."

"Of this lot?" Gabe jerked his thumb in the direction of the house. Two girls moved to sit in the open window, placing cigarettes between their lips and lighting the ends. It was Elise and Haleigh, the girls that came to the beach with Gabe and me not long after we had first met. I groaned and Gabe laughed, taking my hand in his again and tugging me closer, before releasing my hand and slinging his arm around my shoulder instead. He placed a sloppy kiss on my cheek.

A wolf whistle sounded. "Well, well, well. If it isn't Ashton himself." Haleigh leaned out the window, cigarette dangling from her mouth, breasts bulging from her top.

"Ashton?" I asked Gabe, but he just shook his head.

"Haleigh, Elise, you remember Lauren, right?" We stopped in front of the window and Haleigh and Elise looked over me slowly before tilting their heads to the side and taking a long drag on their cigarettes. They did it perfectly in unison as if they had been practising before our arrival. I had met Haleigh a number of times, but she still looked as though she were struggling to place me.

Finally, she smiled. "Of course," she replied. "You work at the café with Gabe, right?"

"Actually," Gabe said. I could see him preparing himself to tell them we were together and I didn't want to stand there and see the smirks on their faces so I interrupted him.

"Was good to see you again, Haleigh, Elise." I nodded to each of them and snaked my arm behind Gabe's back, hooking my fingers into the waistband of his jeans. I tugged him towards the door, letting my actions speak the words I wouldn't let Gabe use.

The lounge of Gabe's flat pulsated with music, people and light. Someone had strung a disco ball in the centre of the room and particles of light danced across faces and walls. Stefan spotted Gabe across the room and raised his beer bottle, leaning back and yelling a greeting into the room. Threading his way through the heaving mass of bodies, shoving them aside when they wouldn't move, he hugged Gabe, sweat glistening from his forehead and dampening his shirt. "You're just in time," Stefan said, releasing Gabe from his grasp.

"For what?" Gabe yelled, even though Stefan was standing right next to him.

Stefan cupped his hands around his mouth, funnelling the words, "Make way! Make the path clear."

Bodies jostled and moved until a path to the coffee table appeared. Twenty-one shot glasses filled with clear liquid lay in perfect lines across the table.

"Tradition," Stefan yelled. "You have to do them with me."

Gabe laughed. "I think I'll give it a miss tonight."

Stefan shook his head, little droplets of sweat flew from the ends of his hair and splattered across my face. I wiped them away, taking a step back, but bumping into another body when I did so.

Stefan poked a finger into Gabe's chest. "It's my birthday and the birthday boy gets to nominate who does the shots with him. I choose you!" Stefan threw his arms around Gabe's neck and held him in a head brace. "You can't say no," Stefan yelled. He leaned closer. "I'm in no state to do all twenty-one," he hissed. "You need to help a fella out."

Gabe grinned and stumbled backwards when Stefan leaned heavily on him. "Do you mind?" he asked me.

I looked around the throng of people crushed into the lounge. It felt like all eyes were on me. "Mind?" I said, laughing, though it sounded strange even to my own ears. "Why would I mind?"

Gabe planted another sloppy kiss on my cheek. "Thanks." Then he followed Stefan to the table, the clear path disappearing behind him.

I found myself on the outskirts of the crowd, pressed next to Haleigh, watching Gabe and Stefan down the shots one by one, the crowd chanting the countdown. Gabe shook his head after the fifth shot and wiped his mouth with the back of his hand. His eyes widened and he let a whoop into the air. Stefan wiped his hand across his forehead, dripping with sweat. His t-shirt clung to his body in large wet patches.

"Take it off!" someone yelled. Stefan raised a thumb into the air and fell into the wall as he twisted himself into knots while trying to remove his shirt. The chants of numbers turned into the chant of 'take it off'. Hands appeared out of the crowd to help remove the shirt, and then I lost sight of them as cat calls and whistles filled the room. When shirtless bodies rose high into the air, standing on the table and downing the remaining shots, Gabe's toned body flashed back at me, his t-shirt now slung around his neck.

Haleigh put her fingers into the air and whistled loudly, almost deafening me. When the last shots were done, the glasses were thrown against the wall but since they were only plastic, they ricocheted off and bounced into the crowd. The shirts were next. Stefan threw his into the crowd, then grabbed Gabe's and did the same, tossing it further, close enough for Haleigh to grab it and bring it to her nose, inhaling Gabe's scent while winking at me.

I walked away. Well, I tried to walk away but every part of the house was crammed full of people. Even the bathroom had a couple making out in one corner while a girl sat on the toilet relieving herself. I finally found space outside on the steps but the repetitive thud of the music still pounded in my ear.

Drew was already there, his head jerking up in greeting. "Too many people," he said.

I sunk to the concrete beside him. Drew took a sip of beer and then let the bottle hang loosely in his fingers, dangling it between his legs. When he saw me looking, he tilted it my way. "Want some?"

I shook my head. "I'm pretty sure Gabe has drunk enough for both of us tonight."

Drew laughed. "So Stefan convinced him, huh?"

"Didn't take much."

Laughter spilled out the door behind us. We twisted around in unison to see Gabe in the middle of the dance floor, Haleigh seductively writhing up and down his body as the people cheered them on.

I waited for the pang of jealousy. It didn't come.

Gabe looked up, caught me watching and blew me a kiss. Somehow, the misshapen shagginess of his hair made him look even younger than he did before the haircut.

"He loves you, you know," Drew said quietly.

As I watched Gabe move, I noted the way that even as another girl had her body plastered against him, he only had eyes for me. It was the moment that I knew I had to tell him before I hurt him any further.

Detangling himself from Haleigh, Gabe pushed through the crowd, lowering himself to the step behind me and placing his legs either side of my waist, cocooning my body in his. His chin was heavy on my shoulder.

"You want to go home?" he asked.

I pressed my cheek against his and shook my head. "I'm good. You look like you're having a good time in there. It's just a little too crowded for my liking. Besides, Drew's keeping me company out here."

"You sure?" Gabe got to his feet. He moved across to Drew and wrapped his arms around him, crushing him into a bear-hug.

"Get off." Drew laughed, pretending to struggle away from the embrace.

"I love you, man," Gabe said, squishing him hard.

"Put a shirt on," Drew said, finally breaking free.

Gabe merely laughed and blew me a kiss before disappearing back into the house.

It turned into a struggle when it was finally time to get Gabe home. He was drunk, but happy drunk, flirty drunk, affectionate drunk. He kept trying to kiss me as we drove, and he made a fumbling attempt at convincing me to have sex with him when he fell into bed. But soon he was quietly snoring beside me with his jeans half unbuckled and his shoes still on.

* * *

By the time morning rolled around I felt like I had barely got a wink of sleep. The guilt that ate at me as I lay beside Gabe was unbearable. I couldn't live like this any longer. I couldn't go on knowing that I had hurt him, betrayed him the way I did.

"Hey, beautiful," Gabe said as he woke, rolling over to his side and grinning at me. His hair was scrunched awkwardly, parts sticking upwards, other parts plastered against his scalp.

My heart ached. My throat was raw and my chest tightened with anxiety. I couldn't drag it out any longer.

"Gabe, I'm so ashamed."

He sat up, shuffling himself closer as my tears began to fall. "Hey," he said, brushing one of my tears aside while blinking rapidly to get the sleep out of his eyes. "Hey, it's okay." He attempted to put his arm around me but I reeled away, knowing I didn't deserve his kindness.

"Gabe," I said. "I'm so sorry."

He shifted uncomfortably, running a hand through his hair and attempting to smooth it back. "It's okay, it's okay," he whispered, his eyes wide as he looked at the space between us. "Whatever it is, it's okay."

A sob escaped and I covered my face.

Gabe peeled one hand away and peered at me through the remaining fingers. "You're beginning to worry me a little here, Lauren. Whatever it is, just tell me."

"I want to," I said. "But I can't."

Gabe scooted closer. "Yes you can. You can tell me anything. I hate seeing you upset like this. Just tell me."

I drew in a shaky breath, trying to regain my composure, but as I looked back over at Gabe's eyes, ones filled with such compassion, another sob racked my body.

"Hey," Gabe said and pulled me close.

This time I was unable to resist and melted into his body.

"It's okay, it's okay," he repeated into my hair.

Taking another deep breath, I pulled away so I could look at him as I blurted my confession. "I kissed Tyler."

Confusion crossed over Gabe's face and he sat back a little. "Tyler?" he repeated.

I nodded, a nervous knot of guilt and fear twisting in my gut.

"My brother?" he asked.

It was almost as though I could see the thoughts racing through his mind as he processed the information. I expected him to be angry. I expected him to yell and to curse, but he merely sat back from me a little more, and that fraction of distance hurt more than any words, even though I knew I deserved it.

"How did it happen?" he asked finally. "Did he come onto you?"

"No," I whispered, my voice nearly failing.

"What sort of a kiss? Did he kiss you, or did you kiss him?"

"Does it matter?"

The anger began to rise. "Of course it fucking matters," he said. "If we talk about it, if I understand, I might be able to move past this. But I sure as hell won't be able to if I don't understand. When did it happen? Where did it happen?" His voice rose in volume. "Tell me, Lauren, tell me or I won't be able to move on from this."

"But that's the thing, Gabe," I said quietly, scared to look up at him. "I don't want you to move on from it."

Gabe looked as though someone had just knocked the wind from him. And when he realised what I was saying, all the colour fell from his face. "Fuck," he cursed. "This is about last night, isn't it? This is payback for dancing with Haleigh. You want me to feel the same pain as you did, right? You were scared I would cheat on you? You know I'd never do that." He moved closer again, hesitantly looking over at me, his expression begging for me to tell him this was all made up as a payback over jealousy.

I shook my head. "It has nothing to do with last night."

"You know she means nothing to me, right?"

I shook my head again, too scared to say the words I needed to make him understand.

"What then? What is this all about? You haven't—" Gabe swallowed deeply, his Adam's apple bobbing up and down as he worked to get the words out. "Did you sleep with him?"

"No!" I said quickly, reaching out to take his hands in mine, but he jerked away. "There was a kiss. Nothing else."

"Nothing else, but the kiss was enough for you to decide you didn't want to be with me anymore?"

"You would still want me after what I did?"

"If you're saying it was only a kiss and nothing more, then yes." He reached across and hesitantly took my hands in his, the ones that had jerked away so violently only seconds before. "Yes, I want you. I will always want you." The words caught in his throat as tears sprung to his eyes. "Don't do this to me, Lauren. Don't do this to us."

"I have to," I said, gently removing my hands from where they were trapped under his. "I—I don't know what to say."

"You've fallen for him, haven't you?" Gabe half snorted, half laughed. "He's taken you from me. I guess now I know how Clark felt. I deserve this. It's karma."

"No," I said. "You don't deserve any of this. You deserve a girl who wants you just as much as you want her. You deserve someone better than me."

"But what about what I want, Lauren? Does that not matter?"

"Of course it matters."

"Just not to you."

"Yes, it matters to me. That's why I'm doing this. You deserve so much more than what I've given you, Gabe."

He looked up at me with pleading eyes brimming with tears that were threatening to spill. "But it's you I want," he said.

I didn't know what more to say. My eyes were fixed on the sheet wrapped around his waist and the trail of soft blond hair that covered the space between his belly button and boxers. I was torn between wanting to climb on top of him and comfort him, take away my words with action, but I couldn't do that. Not when I was this confused inside.

Silently, Gabe rose from the bed, reaching down to gather his clothes from the floor. He walked into the bathroom and moments later appeared fully dressed.

There were no tears in his eyes. There was no anger in his expression. There was only hurt.

And, as a sob rose from my chest, he walked over and pressed a kiss to the top of my head.

"Bye, Lauren."

25

LAUREN

Gabe didn't turn up for work on Monday. He didn't text. He didn't call. For days, he simply disappeared. No one heard from him.

There were moments I regretted my decision. I would lie on the bed, reaching out to the cold space he left behind. At work, tears would suddenly spring to my eyes and I would have to blink them back. Part of me wanted to hear from him, but I knew it would be best if I didn't. I imagined him on a drinking binge. I imagined him getting in a fight. I imagined him finding comfort in Haleigh's arms. Then I stopped imagining.

* * *

It was the third night after we broke up before I woke to banging. Pulling the door open, I found Gabe leaning against the door frame, beanie pulled down over his hair, eyes glazed, and the corners of his mouth pulled into a lazy smile.

"Hey," he said. His eyes slipped down to where my dressing gown hung loosely around my shoulders and I pulled it tighter and tied the cord. Gabe pouted. "Please don't," he said.

I stayed standing in the doorway, blocking his entrance. "What do you want, Gabe?"

He reached out to stroke my cheek. I closed my eyes at the touch, willing myself not to melt. Not to look into his eyes too deeply. Not to respond to his plea. "I want you," he said. "I only want you."

"Gabe—"

He pressed a finger to my mouth. "Shhhh," he said, pushing past me and into the lounge. "Don't say anything."

"Gabe," I started again, but he shushed me again and took my hand, leading me to the couch, trying not to stumble as he walked backwards.

"Don't say anything," he said again. We sat side by side on the couch and Gabe reached out to tuck a strand of hair behind my ear. "I've missed you."

"Gabe I—" His lips pressed to mine. He tasted of beer and whiskey. I pushed against his chest, creating distance between us. "Gabe don't."

Reaching out, he placed his hand on the flesh of my leg exposed by the opening of my gown. His thumb rubbed in circles on my skin. "I don't care," he said. "I don't care what happened. I just want you."

He tried to kiss me again, but I pulled away, moving down the couch until he couldn't reach me. Gabe looked at the space between us as though it were a cavern.

He swallowed. "Can I stay?" he asked. I shook my head and he inched closer. "Let me stay." I shook my head again. "Fuck," he cursed. "Don't I mean anything to you? Am I nothing?"

"Of course not," I said.

"Why won't you have me back then? Why don't you love me?"

The sadness in his voice almost broke me. I wanted to hold him in my arms, comfort him, love him, but I knew that if I did I would end up in the same sticky mess that I did before. And I couldn't do that to him.

Gabe let out an anguished noise and jerked himself up from the couch. He stumbled as he walked, knocking into the wall as he fumbled for the keys trapped in his pocket.

"You're not driving, are you?"

"What the fuck do you care?" was his sharp reply.

"Gabe, please, don't be like this."

He whirled around, losing his balance again and clinging to the wall for support. "Like what? Like you've fucking broken my heart? Because that's what you've done, Lauren. You've fucking broke my heart." He walked over to me, pointing his finger at his chest. "It hurts, Lauren. It fucking hurts."

"I know," I whispered as he glared at me, only inches away from my face. Gabe swayed and then finally sunk to the couch, twisting himself tightly into a ball and covering his face with his hands.

Leaving him there, I grabbed a blanket from the hallway cupboard. "You shouldn't drive." I draped the cover over him. "You can stay here tonight. On the couch." He didn't answer. I didn't know if it was because he had fallen asleep, or if it was simply because he was done talking to me. But as I walked to the hall, flicking off the light switch, his broken voice floated across the darkness.

"Why did you have to do this?"

I walked silently back to the bedroom, his words sounding in my head. Why did I do this? Why did I let him get so close? Why did I kiss his brother? Why did I manage to ruin the good things in my life?

* * *

I kept checking on him through the night, scared that he would wake, still drunk, and attempt to drive home. But when morning finally dawned, he was still there on my couch, legs hanging off the edge, blanket thrown to the ground, and his hand draped over his face as he slept. He was beautiful.

"Morning," I said, swallowing the emotion stuck at the base of my throat and gently shaking him.

The first thing he did when he opened his eyes was smile. He forgot. For that brief moment, he was happy again, and then the darkness returned. Sitting up, he looked around the house, rubbing his eyes, and then looking again as though he couldn't quite figure out how he got there.

"You turned up about two o'clock," I said, watching as his eyes scanned my lounge.

When they finally fell back on me, his smile was long gone. He picked his beanie up from where it lay discarded on the ground and shoved it over his hair.

"I've got to go to work," I told him.

Gabe stretched into the air, then felt his pockets for the keys, pulling them out and getting to his feet.

"Sorry," was all he said as he passed. His eyes barely met mine. Just a quick flash, one of anger and pain, and then they were directed back down at the ground. "I won't do this again."

"Gabe, I—"

He shook his head. "You've said all you need to."

"But I just want to explain—"

"Don't," he said, somewhat gruffly, and sighed deeply. "I don't want to hear it." Gabe walked outside before turning to face me again. He adjusted his beanie and shoved his hands into the pockets of his jeans. "Are you with him?" He looked up and down, as though he was unsure if he really wanted to hear the answer.

"No," I said. "I haven't talked to him since."

Chewing on his bottom lip, his glance flicked up to mine again. He opened his mouth as though he was going to say something, then closed it again before turning and walking down the driveway to his car.

* * *

Gabe disappeared from my life just as quickly as he had appeared, never returning to his job at the café. Six months of him being in my life boiled down to a single t-shirt left in my top drawer. I missed him, but at the same time, I was surprised with how easily life continued. I went to work and eventually laughed at Mark's jokes again. I ignored the times Gabe's friends came into the café and whispered remarks under their breath. And I continued to travel to the city to document the construction on the casino, although Tyler was hardly there anymore. And when he was, he kept his distance. I wasn't sure if it was Jake who had told him to stay away, or whether it was because I had left with Gabe the night we had kissed. I had missed calls from him after the investor's party, but I never returned them and he never left a message.

In a way, my life became mundane, but I didn't mind. I was content being single. Guilt didn't eat at my insides. Indecision didn't plague my thoughts. I had no one to think of other than myself. Despite the invitations to Peta's for dinner, the calls from my parents and my sister, I mainly kept to myself. Of course, everyone at work knew what had transpired between Gabe and me. The gossip mill worked its magic before my first shift after the breakup. But my parents didn't know. My sister didn't know. I couldn't tell them and hear the glee in my mother's voice.

But after the one month break-up mark passed, the familiar feeling of worry began to gnaw at me again. There was to be an unveiling of the first stage of construction at the casino. I was expected to be there. I was expected to take photographs. Gabe would be there. Tyler would be there. The entire Thornton family would be there. I still received frequent phone calls from Billie and, even though the conversation topics mainly revolved around her, I got the distinct impression that she was unaware that Gabe and I had broken up.

* * *

Jimmy greeted me off the plane as he had done every week over the past month and a half. He chatted easily, completely unaware of the tension that existed between me and Tyler. As well as being for the investors, this unveiling was also a celebration for all the construction workers on the site. Jimmy was dressed tidier than I had ever seen him, although his shirt could have definitely done with being pressed.

The room was already crowded when Jimmy and I walked in. With my camera hanging around my neck, I wandered through the crowd, taking candid shots as well as getting groups of people to pose for the typical images. Wine glasses in hand. Fake smiles plastered across their faces. But when Billie spotted me, she pulled me over to where she, Tyler and Jake were standing in a tight corner.

"We were just talking about you," she said, her hands resting on the small round of her tummy. At seventeen weeks, she was beginning to show.

I smiled, feeling uncomfortable as Jake looked at me hesitantly and Tyler avoided my gaze.

Billie leaned in close. "Where's Gabe?" she asked. "Hamish has been asking where he is and I have no answer to give to him."

Billie stared at me openly and I struggled to know how to reply. "I'm not sure," I said, taking a sip of wine and scanning the room for any sign of Gabe with my heart thudding in my chest. "Did he say he was coming?"

A look of confusion passed over Billie's face. "What do you mean? Is he not with you?"

I coughed. "Me?"

Billie patted my back gently. "Yes, you. Gabe assured his father he would be here, yet here you are with no sign of Gabe."

It dawned on me that Gabe hadn't told his family of our breakup, just as I hadn't told mine. I cleared my throat nervously. "He hasn't spoken to you about us?"

Tyler's eyes snapped to mine.

"No," Billie exclaimed. "Don't tell me you two broke up? That's just awful. I'm so sorry." Billie hugged me. "I will have a talk with that boy. He doesn't know what he tossed aside."

"You broke up?" Tyler asked sharply.

I ignored him and turned back to Billie. "It was more of a mutual decision."

"Well, that explains why he won't return my calls," Jake said.

"When?" Tyler demanded, pushing past Jake to stand in front of me.

"A few weeks ago," I said quietly.

"How many exactly?" he asked, his teeth clenched.

"Tyler!" Billie scolded. "There is no need to be rude. The poor girl is probably going through enough without having you rub her face in it." She pulled me close again and squeezed my shoulder. I wanted to push her away.

"How many?" Tyler repeated.

"Six weeks," I said quietly.

"Six weeks?" Tyler's gaze held mine in an intense, scorching glare. He opened his mouth as if to say something only to turn and leave.

Jake looked at me expectantly. "You told him?"

I hung my head.

"Told who what?" Billie asked. "And what's Tyler's problem?"

Jake muttered, "Never mind," just as I excused myself and followed Tyler outside to where rain had just begun to splatter onto the concrete. He stood with his back to me, arms crossed over his chest and shoulders rising and falling with each deep breath.

"Tyler?" I said quietly.

He didn't turn around but he still spoke. "You broke up with him?"

"Yes."

This time he turned. Rain dusted his hair and lay like glitter across his shoulders. "Why didn't you tell me?" he asked, his voice breaking a fraction.

"It's not that simple."

Tyler took a step forward. "It can be." He reached out and took the tips of my fingers in his. They lay like a thread between us. "Do you like me?"

I almost smiled at his simplicity. "Of course I like you. I just don't know if I like who I am around you," I said as he toyed with our brushing fingers. "I kissed you while I was with Gabe. I've had someone hurt me like that and I didn't think myself capable of doing it to someone else. It's not who I am. It's not who I want to be."

"We need to talk," he stated simply.

"We are talking."

"Not here. Come back to the loft."

I shook my head. "Tyler, imagine what everyone would say?"

"Who?" he asked. "Who would say anything and why would you care?"

I shook my head again, confusion and attraction to this man clouding my thoughts. Tyler grasped my hand and walked back into the building, pulling me behind him. Weaving through the crowd, Tyler didn't even glance when people spoke his name. He guided me over to his car and opened the door expectantly.

"Get in," he said.

I crossed my arms and glared at him, fighting the urge to obey his command.

"Damn it, Lauren. I just want to talk to you somewhere away from all this. Get in," he demanded again, then added a soft, "please," though it was still a demand rather than a question.

This time, despite telling myself not to, I sighed and got into the passenger's seat. Tyler didn't speak as we travelled the short distance to his apartment, he kept his gaze fixed on the road, his hands wrapped around the steering wheel, knuckles white. The elevator groaned as it rose to the top level, but still, he didn't speak. It was only once we were inside the building, once he had removed his jacket, once he had tossed his tie aside and leaned against the kitchen counter with arms crossed that he spoke.

"Why didn't you tell me?" he asked.

I stood awkwardly in the middle of the room, not sure if I wanted to sit or stand, but certain that I needed to keep distance between us. "What would be the point?" I said finally.

Tyler ran a frustrated hand through his hair. "You can't tell me there is nothing between us."

"I'm not saying that."

"Then why didn't you tell me?"

246

"What would this something between us look like, Tyler? Last time I checked, you were still Gabe's brother. I can't see how anything can happen."

"Despite the fact that you are attracted to me."

"Yes," I said without thinking. "Despite that."

Tyler smiled and walked towards me. "So you admit it then? You admit that you're attracted to me?"

I rolled my eyes, stepping backwards as he stepped forward. "Of course I admit it. You are..." My words faded as he stepped closer. I stood frozen to the spot, trapped by his steel-grey eyes.

"I'm what?" he asked, stopping only a fraction from me. I could feel the heat radiating from his body, the intensity of his gaze as he undressed me with his eyes. He was so devilishly handsome. All I wanted to do was crush my mouth to his. I wanted him to take me. Claim me. Do everything he ever wanted to me. Looking up into his eyes, I tried not to inhale and let the scent of him get to me. He made me feel small and insignificant at the same time as making me feel like the only person that existed in this world.

"I want you," he said. "But I want you to want me too." He bent his head so there was only a hairsbreadth between our lips. "Do you want me, Lauren?"

26

LAUREN

My heart pounded in my chest. My body longed to melt under his. I wanted to fall into him. I wanted to run from him. But all I could do was stand there, frozen with indecision, torn between desire and my sense of morality.

"Fuck it," Tyler said just before he crushed his lips to mine.

All my hesitation fled the moment our mouths met. Tyler's hands wound behind me, one twisting into my hair, pulling me closer as he kissed me more passionately, and the other pressed against the small of my back, tugging me closer. My breasts crushed against his chest as we kissed fervently, my desire for this man overwhelming in its intensity. Tyler's hands found their way down to cup the cheeks of my backside, our mouths still devouring each other as he pulled me to him. He lifted me as I wrapped my legs around his waist, raising my mouth for air as he carried me to the bedroom, his lips trailing down my neck and nuzzling into the soft curve.

"You have no idea how many times I've thought about this, about you," he said breathlessly. He lay me on the bed before pulling his shirt over his head.

The sight of him took my breath away.

He was perfect.

Everything about this man ignited the desire within. Lowering himself to the bed, he pressed his body against the length of mine, propping himself on his elbows as he smoothed the hair back from my face.

"The things I want to do to you," he said, bending to kiss me again. "The things I will do to you."

Wrapping my arms around his waist, I ran my fingers over the smooth flesh of his back as he claimed my mouth. His hardness surged, straining against the constraint of our intertwined bodies. My head rolled back into the pillow as his mouth eagerly explored my skin, leaving moist trails in its wake. Rising up, he moved down my body until he reached the hem of my dress, sliding his hands under it and up my thighs. He watched hungrily as the dress lifted higher and higher until he eventually tugged it over my head, leaving me bare and exposed in nothing but my underwear. His eyes darkened as he explored my body. But instead of wanting to cover myself, the opposite was true. I longed to open myself to this man. I wanted him on top of me, under me, inside me.

Tyler placed his hands over the scar that crossed my lower abdomen and ran them over my skin, around my back, flicking the clasps that held my bra together and tossing it to the floor. Then he just stared. His eyes grew wide and dark, his breathing increasing as he watched me. Gently, he encased each breast with his hands, the excess spilling between his fingers. He lowered his mouth towards my chest but did not touch. His breath was hot against my skin. I wanted to arch my back and force my breast into his mouth.

Squirming beneath him, ever so slowly, he ran his tongue over my nipple, lapping until I moaned with pleasure.

"I plan on making this last," he whispered in my ear. "As much as I want to plunge into you right now and fuck you senseless, I also want to savour every moment."

Then he bent his head again and assaulted my breasts, so slowly, so gently, I felt as though my chest would explode underneath his mouth. He sucked and licked and massaged, and just when I thought I couldn't stand it any longer, he moved to the other breast and started the process all over again.

I quivered with desire. The wetness between my legs was no longer just a burning sensation, it throbbed with longing. But Tyler was intent on taking his time. He moved down my body and started from the bottom, taking my toe in his mouth and running his teeth across the underside of the flesh. I gasped, shocked at how such a small—and what I had previously thought of as a nonsexual part of my body—created ripples of pleasure that tingled through every inch. He moved so he could kiss his way up my body. Lifting my leg, he bended it at the knee so he could kiss the tender flesh underneath. My breath came out in pants as he kissed his way up the inside of my thigh, running his hands over the outer sides, leaving me a trembling mess. My entire body tensed as his mouth came closer and closer to the apex of my thighs, but he stopped before he got there, sighing contentedly as he lay between my legs, the warmth of each breath hitting me where I wanted his mouth to be. Reaching out, he ever so gently ran his fingers over my underwear, inhaling as he did so. He brought his head closer so his lips pressed to the material and the sound of his voice vibrated against my sensitive flesh.

"I can't wait to taste you," he said, the gentle movement of his lips through the thin and damp material driving me insane. I squirmed again and he reached up to trap me by pressing my hips firmly against the bed.

"Patience," he demanded and the command of his voice froze my body even though my heart beat erratically. My whole body throbbed as Tyler's lips met the inside of the thigh previously left unattended, and then he travelled back down my body, running his mouth over every exposed inch of flesh until his teeth ran over the toe of my other foot.

I sat up, reaching for him, but Tyler shook his head, forcing me back onto the bed. "I'm not done. Roll over."

Without thought, I rolled over willingly even though all I wanted was to feel him inside me. Tyler began at the top this time, sucking on the tender flesh in the crook of my neck, working his way down until his hands ran their way up my sides, holding my arms above my head with one hand, while his mouth kissed every inch of skin he could reach, causing me to twist and turn, tormented by the sensations.

"Be still," he said softly between kisses.

Releasing the grip around my wrists, he pulled my underwear down and threw them to the ground beside my discarded bra. I was now completely naked and exposed as he sat on top of me, only his chest bare. His hands moved to my backside, his legs either side of mine, the material of his dress pants pressed against the back of my thighs. I tilted my head so I could see his reflection in the large mirror on the side wall. His hands massaged my backside, his eyes dark and stuck on the sight of my pale flesh caught between his fingers. I felt his body tremble, quivering with need. Pressing a single finger against me, he moaned when he brushed the wet flesh, ready and eager for him.

Getting up from the bed, Tyler stood with his eyes fixed on me as he undid the zipper of his pants and let them drop to the floor along with his boxers. He stood before me completely exposed, and I rolled over so my eyes could roam his body freely, locking in on his cock, hard and ready. Tyler walked to the end of the bed, completely comfortable with being naked and having me watch him. There was a confidence to his movements that both excited and relaxed me. Everything about him was sure and controlled. Like he was exactly where he was supposed to be. Like he knew I was exactly where I was supposed to be. Naked on his bed.

"Are you on birth control?" he asked. "I don't want to use a condom. I want to feel you. All of you. And I want you to feel me."

I nodded, ignoring the words of truth that I knew I should utter. Now was not the time. And right now, I didn't care.

"Open," he said.

When I didn't respond, too distracted by the sight of his beautiful body towering over me, he grabbed my legs and tugged me down the bed, pulling them open and leaving me exposed. Sinking to his knees between my legs, he pushed them even further apart to gain better access. Rubbing his finger over my clit, he brought it to his mouth. His eyes closed, as though savouring the sensation, and then, lowering his head, his tongue finally pressed against me. It felt like velvet and fire. Like ice and silk.

I gripped onto the cover of the bed, twisting the material between my fingers as his mouth delivered wave after wave of pleasure. When I finally gained some control, I propped myself up on my elbows, wanting to see him between my legs, his mouth pressed to my sex. He latched onto me, sucking as his grey eyes lifted upwards and met mine over the mounds of my breasts.

The sight of him was almost too much for me and my breathing quickened, my head fell back against the bed as the desire to come rose within. As if he sensed the intensity of my need, Tyler removed himself and stood. Feeling a little dazed, I sat up, my legs still dangling over the edge of the bed and was greeted by the glorious sight of his enlarged cock dangerously close to my mouth. Tyler grasped his hardness in his hand, stroking it a few times as he stood in front of me. Stepping forward, he ran his hand down the side of my face. I grabbed it and brought it to my mouth, placing my lips over one of his fingers, sucking it in until I reached his knuckle.

"Careful," he growled. "You don't know what I want to do to you."

I withdrew his finger only to take in two at a time, sucking them into my mouth as far as they would go. Tyler looked down, mesmerised as he pulled his fingers in and out of my mouth, his chest rising and falling and his cock twitching as I gently ran my teeth over his fingers.

He sucked in a sharp breath of air. "I told you to be careful," he warned. "I want to be gentle, but if you keep up this sort of thing I may not be able to keep that promise."

Again I drew his fingers into my mouth, gagging slightly as they hit the back of my throat. Tyler cursed quietly and pulled them out, placing his hand around my neck, rubbing the flesh, before twisting his fingers into my hair.

Gazing up the length of his body, I met his eyes. I wanted to taste him. I wanted to feel the fullness of him inside my mouth, but Tyler's hands came to rest under my armpits, gently pulling me to my feet. Then he simply kissed me. His hands cupped my face, his cock pressed against the base of my stomach, and he kissed me. His lips were soft and full and I had never been kissed so sensually. He used lips and teeth. His tongue was gentle and soft. Moans of pleasure trembled up my throat and the more that escaped the more intense his kiss became. I lifted my hands and ran them over the toned muscles of his chest. He pressed closer, inviting me to touch him further. Inviting me to explore his body as he had mine. His skin was smooth and soft and hard. My hand ran over the dips of his biceps, the ripples of his stomach, the wide expanse of his shoulders.

Stepping forward, Tyler pushed against me until I felt the edge of the bed against the back of my knees. Placing his hand on the small of my back, he lowered me to the covers of his bed, once again.

My hand snaked between us. I wanted to feel him.

He was hard like steel and he froze and closed his eyes when my hand wrapped around him. Before lowering his mouth to mine again, he took a few deep breaths as my hands worked him up and down, my mind imagining what it would feel like to have him inside me. A slick sheen of sweat covered our bodies. Our breathing was heavy and feverish and when he finally guided himself to my entrance, I held my breath. He moved slowly, pushing his hard length inside me one inch at a time, his eyes locked on mine, the faintest of smiles playing at the corners of his mouth.

I couldn't help but cry out when he entered me fully. With his hardness pressed against my insides, we were still locked together, him kissing my mouth, my neck, my breasts, as I adjusted to the feel of him. Pressing a little deeper, he groaned into my shoulder and began to rock back and forth. With his arms wrapped around my body, my arms wrapped around his, and our mouths locked together in a feverish and lazy blend of kissing and panting, his movements began to become more forceful. He plunged deeper and harder, each time pulling me closer to him, wrapping his arms around me as though he couldn't bear for any parts of our bodies not to be connected.

We were wound together like that as the desire mounted inside me, trembled through my every cell and finally erupted as his hardness surged and he came inside me.

He didn't withdraw. He lay on top of me, his body warm and heavy and content as he ran his lips over my collarbone, gently placing kiss after kiss until our breathing returned to a steady and even pace. Then he rolled off, lying on his back and staring up at the ceiling.

When he turned his head, a smile danced on his lips. "That was worth the wait." He held his arm out, inviting me to roll closer. I shuffled closer to him, placing my head on his chest, listening to the steady thud of his heart beat, and watching the gentle rise and fall of his stomach as he breathed.

I was happy. I was content. Until I started to think. About Gabe. About the rest of his family no doubt still back at the unveiling, no doubt wondering why we had disappeared.

I lifted my head. "What are we—"

"Shhhh," he said quietly, laying my head back against his chest. "Don't ruin this with thinking."

I closed my eyes and listened to the gentle thud of his heart. It seemed to beat in time with mine. Thud. Thud. Thud. Gentle and steady.

Until the creaking of the elevator sounded.

We both sat up.

"Fuck," Tyler said. "I'm supposed to introduce Dad before his speech." He reached over the side of the bed and grabbed his pants, fishing his cell phone out of the pocket to glance at the time. "I'm sorry," he began. "But we've really got to get back. I'm on in thirty minutes. I got carried away. I didn't want things to end like this." Tyler pulled his shirt over his head and placed a hurried kiss on my lips before someone pounded on the bedroom door.

"Tyler!" Jake yelled. "Dad is getting more pissed every second you make him wait."

Tyler ran a hand through his hair, fumbling with the buttons on his shirt at the same time as scanning the bedroom floor for items of my clothing.

"Give me a minute," he yelled back.

"Is she in there?" Jake said, quieter this time.

Tyler looked at me, one eyebrow cocked, before bending down and holding my underwear out so I could slip my legs into them. Sliding them up the sides of my thighs, he pressed another kiss to the soft flesh of my stomach, before standing, a question held in his expression. I leaned forward, rising to the tips of my toes, and kissed him hungrily. Tyler's hands wound behind my back as mine threaded through his hair, deepening the kiss.

"Well?" Jake asked through the door.

Tyler broke away. "Yes," he said. "She's here."

27

LAUREN

Tyler took the bra hanging over his arm and turned me so he could loop it under my breasts and attach the clasps behind my back. Lastly, he held the dress over my head so I could shimmy back into it. I ran my fingers over my hair cautiously, certain that I must look exactly how I felt. Freshly fucked.

"You look stunning." His eyes darkened and he took a step towards me.

"Tyler!" Jake shouted, somewhat impatiently. "I'm not standing here while you two finish fucking. Gabe turned up. And he's drunk. Dad sent me to get you. We need to go."

Tyler froze with his hands on my shoulders. As we stared at each other, dread settled in the base of my stomach.

"Don't regret this," Tyler growled. "Don't," he said more softly. "Don't regret this."

Jake's slightly muffled voice continued through the door as Tyler pulled me to his chest. "Dad's fucking fuming, Ty. I've never seen him this pissed at you before. What the hell were you thinking?"

"This will all work out," Tyler whispered, his lips pressed to my hair. "You'll see."

But I couldn't help the sickness that had welled in the base of my stomach. I never meant for this to happen, but now that it had, I knew there would be no turning back. I knew I was drawn to this man in ways I couldn't resist. But that still didn't mean I wanted to face Gabe.

Jake was in the middle of a tirade when Tyler threw the door open and stormed past him. "It is an introduction, for fuck's sake. Anyone could do it."

Jake's eyes slid over me but he didn't say anything, just nodded briefly as though I were little more than a random girl he had stumbled across in Tyler's bedroom.

"You know Dad," Jake said, directing his gaze back to Tyler who was busy knotting his tie.

"We'll meet you there." Tyler dismissed his brother.

"I think it would be better if she came with me," Jake said.

"Is Gabe going to be there waiting when we pull up?" Tyler snorted. "I will drive her back."

Jake shrugged. "It's your funeral."

"You okay?" Tyler asked as soon as we were on our way.

"We shouldn't have done this."

Taking my hand from my lap and pulling it to his mouth, Tyler shook his head. His lips brushed over my fingertips, sending shivers of pleasure into the base of my stomach. They mixed together with the butterflies of dread, dancing and floating until they reached my chest. I pulled my hand away.

"You can't say anything," I begged.

"I'm not hiding you," Tyler replied.

"Please," I insisted. "Not yet. Just give it a little time."

"You said you two broke up weeks ago."

"We did. But this is the first time I've seen him in a long time. The first time he has seen any of his family. Telling him now would only make things worse."

Tyler sighed. "Fine," he agreed. "But just this once. I don't want to hide. And if he places even one finger on you, all bets are off."

Jake was waiting at the elevator door when we arrived. He held me back when Tyler entered, shaking his head. "I think it would go down better if he arrived without you."

Jake stepped into the elevator with his brother, leaving me alone in the foyer as the metal doors closed on them. I decided to take the stairs instead, allowing enough time for them to enter before I did. Tyler was already on the stage at the front of the room, slightly bent forward, speaking into the microphone, calm and controlled, and looking nothing like he had only minutes before, tousled hair and gloriously naked. The crowd broke into thunderous applause when he introduced his father and Tyler stepped to the side, allowing Hamish the limelight.

He caught my eye across the crowd and started walking towards me, only to stop when Gabe broke the line between us.

Gabe's hair had grown out fully since I had seen him. It was no longer kept in the scruffy, grown-out mohawk style left over from when Billie had insisted on it for the fashion show. The reddish tinge had all but disappeared, but his boyish smile was still firmly in place.

"Lauren." Gabe engulfed me in an embrace, Tyler staring daggers at his back. "It's good to see you." His words were slightly slurred. "I was hoping I would run into you here." He leaned close, so his lips brushed against my ear when he spoke. "I had to have a little Dutch courage before I made an appearance. I might be the littlest bit drunk." He held the pads of his fingers together and squinted at the distance to emphasise his point. "You look good." His eyes travelled over my outfit, resting on the swell of my breasts just visible over the neckline of my dress. "You look amazing."

"Gabe," I said, my voice softening as he drew his gaze up to my eyes. "How have you been?"

"Good." He nodded emphatically. "Great. Couldn't be better." He lifted one eyebrow. "You?"

"Good," I replied quietly, my eyes flicking between Gabe and where Tyler leaned against the wall, arms crossed and eyes like steel, behind him.

Gabe noticed and twisted around. "Ah," he said. "Just who I wanted to see."

"Gabe don't."

His gaze dropped to where I wrapped my fingers around his arm and I loosened my grip.

"Am I too late?" he asked. "Have you fucked him already?"

"Gabe, please," I pleaded with him, attempting to pull him away from where he was advancing on Tyler.

Tyler pulled himself from the wall, standing up straight, his arms dropping to his sides in clenched fists. Gabe stopped. The brothers stared at each other across the room, oblivious to the people milling about them.

Jake crossed the floor and spoke to Tyler. I wasn't sure what he said, but Tyler backed down, turning away from Gabe and walking back with Jake to talk to some important-looking people dressed in suits.

"So?" Gabe crossed his arms. "Have you?"

"I'm not talking about him, Gabe."

He let out a low breath of air. "I'm not sure I can do this, Lauren. I'm not sure I can see you here with him."

"I'm not here with him. I promise." It was true. Mostly.

Gabe took a step closer. "I'm going to win you back."

"I'm not yours to win, Gabe. We broke up, remember? I did it because I didn't want to hurt you."

"You didn't want to hurt me? Do you know how much you've messed with my head? You're all I can think about. I've slept with, I don't know how many girls over the past few weeks, trying to rid you from my mind, but it's like you're burned in there." He took my hand, peering up at me through a fringe of blond. "The way you feel. Your laugh. Your smile. The way you taste. Everything. I miss everything about you, Lauren. Please don't do this to me."

My heart pounded in my chest. Gabe was so familiar. So beautiful. So tempting. But it was Tyler I wanted. Tyler who made my heart beat erratically just from a single look.

As though sensing my thoughts, Tyler broke away from the crowd and began walking towards us. I took a step back from Gabe. Billie caught my eye. The look on her face told me it had dawned on her what was happening.

"I can't," was all I said before I turned and walked out the door.

* * *

I didn't bother to change before I boarded the airplane. I sat, squashed in the small seat, breaking off pieces of a cookie and shovelling them into my mouth. The air stewards performed their pre-flight checks and soon I was sailing through the air, looking down at the patchwork of paddocks.

* * *

It was raining when I walked across the pavement, looking for the spot I had parked my car. When I finally found it, I was drenched. I caught my reflection in the window of the car, mascara streaked down my cheeks, hair slicked to my face and dress plastered to my skin. I pulled on the door but it wouldn't open. I pulled again and again, but it wouldn't budge. Kicking the side of the car, I let out a wail of frustration. Finally, when all else failed, I pulled out my cell and dialled Peta.

"I need you," I said into the phone.

When Peta pulled up, I was slumped against the side of my car, not caring that the rain was falling, or that my phone was dead. She wound down the window. "Come on," she said, looking me over. "Let's get you home."

I told her everything during the short trip back to my house. I let it all out in one long breath and when I was finally done, we were sitting in my driveway, the car idling, the radio playing softly in the background and watching the tears of rain slip down the windscreen.

"Well." Peta sighed.

"Well?" I repeated. "That's all you have to say?"

"I'm not sure what you want me to say. It's clear you're attracted to this Tyler, but it's also clear you don't want to hurt Gabe."

"That part I know." I groaned in frustration. "Tell me what to do about it." Peta sighed again, exaggeratedly, and I whacked her arm. "You're not helping."

"Well, part of me wants to tell you to get back together with Gabe simply because I will get my best barista back. No offence, but your coffee-making skills don't even come close to rivalling his."

"Peta," I wailed and let my head fall to the headrest.

"And part of me wants to point out the absurdity of asking my advice on this matter when I literally left to pick you up after having a quickie with my husband in the pantry because every other room in the house was occupied by little people. While you—" She glared at me. "You are having a hard time with the fact that two gorgeous men are laying themselves at your feet."

I opened the door, letting the rain fall in. Peta reached across and pulled it shut.

"Okay," she said. "I get it. You're all upset because you almost got caught having mind blowing sex with the brother of the man you just dumped."

I opened the door again.

"Okay, okay," Peta said, laughing and pulling the door shut once more. "The boy you just dumped."

"Seriously, Peta."

Peta was still laughing. "Okay." She wiped the smile from her face. Or, at least attempted to. "Okay. Look, Ren, you know I can't tell you what to do. You know only you can make that decision. But my suggestion would be to get rottenly drunk, fall asleep and worry about it in the morning."

"Will you get rottenly drunk with me?"

Peta shook her head. "Not this time, sorry. Remember? Little people everywhere. That includes the one currently, hopefully, asleep in my bed with an extremely annoying cough which will ensure I get very little sleep. As tempting as staying here would be, I promised Shrek I wouldn't."

I sighed and leaned forward to cover my face with my hands, not caring that I was smudging the already terrible stains of makeup across my face. "Solitary drinking it is."

Peta leaned into the backseat of the car. "Here," she said, passing me a bottle of wine. "Shrek sent this."

I half laughed, half cried and took the bottle.

"I'll call over tomorrow and take you to your car once you've found your keys," she said and I climbed out.

Grabbing my carry-on luggage from the boot, I stood under the shelter of the doorframe. Thankfully, I had a spare key hidden under a pot plant and I was able to let myself in. Peta wound down the window and yelled through the rain as she reversed out the drive. "Remember. Drinking only tonight. Leave the thinking and worrying for tomorrow. And don't talk to them. Either of them!"

* * *

I took Peta's advice and got rottenly drunk. I don't know what time I finally passed out, but I was still dressed when I woke. I also had a pounding headache. Reaching across the bed, I fumbled until I came across my phone laying on the bedside cabinet. At some stage during the night, I had the foresight to plug it into a charger. The screen glowed too brightly when it turned on. The notifications started vibrating through immediately. Messages from Tyler, Gabe and Peta filled the screen.

I switched it off. I needed a shower before I could deal with any of it.

The warm water felt good on my skin, like it could wash away all my worries, but when I stepped back out of the shower, wrapped a towel around my head and another around my chest, the reflection staring glumly back at me did nothing but remind me of the night before.

I would be better off forgetting I had ever met the Thornton Brothers. But I knew that would be impossible. They were forever burned into my brain. Both of them.

It was still raining outside, so I dressed in the oldest pair of track pants I could find, pulled a stained t-shirt over my head, piled my hair into a messy bun and determined to spend my day eating junk food and watching TV. I was only one episode into a reality cooking show that Peta had been following religiously when there was a knock at the door.

History told me it would be Gabe. I adjusted the messy knot of hair on top of my head and pulled the door open. Tyler stood in the rain, hair hanging in wet threads over his eyes, black t-shirt clinging to his chest.

"You left," he said.

I didn't say anything. I was not expecting Tyler Thornton to turn up at my door.

"I tried calling but your phone was off."

He took a step forward and I took one back. Pain flashed through Tyler's eyes with that one backwards step.

"Can I come in?"

About the Author

Sabre Rose writes about love and lust. Flawed people in messy relationships. Happiness and heartbreak. Loyalty and betrayal.

With stories as unpredictable as they are steamy and intense, Sabre draws you into the lives of her characters and their complicated families.

The ideas floating around her head range from delightful to dark, so sign up to her newsletter at

www.subscribepage.com/sabrerose

to keep up to date with her latest news and releases.

Social Media:

www.facebook.com/sabreroseauthor

www.twitter.com/sabreroseauthor

Website:

www.sabreroseauthor.com

Email:

sabreroseauthor@gmail.com

Other books in the Series

Touched (Thornton Brothers 1)

Taken (Thornton Brothers 3)

Torn (Thornton Brothers 4)

Printed in Great Britain
by Amazon